ROSWELL REDEMPTION

To honor those who came before us...

Cindi Crane

CINDI CRANE

Outskirts Press, Inc.
Denver, Colorado

Roswell Redemption
All Rights Reserved.
Copyright © 2012 Cindi Crane
v3.0 r1.2

Cover Photo © 2012 JupiterImages Corporation. All rights reserved - used with permission.

Outskirts Press, Inc.
http://www.outskirtspress.com

ISBN: 978-1-4327-8090-6

Library of Congress Control Number: 2011915220

Outskirts Press and the "OP" logo are trademarks belonging to Outskirts Press, Inc.

PRINTED IN THE UNITED STATES OF AMERICA

Acknowledgements

It was a thrill to bring Jade and Carolyn's stories to life. Writing this novel gave me the opportunity to say "out loud" how the Cherokee impacted all of our lives here in the great state of Georgia. Everywhere we look we see the beautiful land that they walked, cultivated and loved. I often meet people who proudly say they are part Cherokee. The beautiful town of Roswell is part of the original Cherokee Nation and a perfect setting in which to weave the historical and current day facts with my fictional story of two courageous women.

To my wonderful husband, Steve. I dedicate Roswell Redemption to you. Thank you for inspiring and encouraging me every day. It's because of you that this story came to be. Your patience and witty suggestions made a special impact to our book. I love you.

To my parents, Don and Carolyn Varner for always supporting me in ways that helped me to grow and follow my dreams. And thanks Mom for loving my book as much as I do.

To my little brother Don Varner (Donnie to me), his wife Lizette and my super cool, smart, athletic and creative nephew and niece, Noah and Hannah for being such avid readers and teaching me what book clubs are really all about. Thank you Lizette for editing my book; you are next and I will gladly return the favor.

To my BFFs whom I crafted my characters around, Suzi and

Mark Halliburton, Julie Porter, Sarah Embro, Monica Turnblacer, Tracy Bowers, Kathy Noland, Gloria Minick and Michelle Volgenau; beautiful, amazing, lifelong friends. You are all so full of spirit, ambition and love. You'll have fun figuring out which parts of which characters I modeled after you. I'll never tell.

To my book club for taking me seriously and reading and editing Roswell Redemption in its infancy. Your feedback was priceless and helped make it what it is today. Thank you Erin Doyle, Kathi Myers, Suzi Halliburton, Julie Porter, Sarah Embro, Susan Braker, April Weldon, Molly McLeod, Karen Welch, Laurie Herron, Gwynne Baker and Adriana Curry.

I am so very grateful to you all.

Chapter 1
April 20, 1838

The Hawkins family walked quickly but with trepidation toward the rickety wagon and her father gently placed her mother inside it. It was dusk and the air was beginning to chill. Jade gently covered her mother with the worn quilt she had brought from their parlor. Her mother looked frail as she curled up in the wagon trembling from the gunshot wound. Joe and George each put a hand on their mother's back as if they could protect her from the vicious gang of men that had come to take their home.

One of the men grabbed Jade from behind and ran back a few steps. She screamed, kicking her legs, trying to release his hands, scratching at him. He was thin and dirty and his whiskers scratched her face. He smelled of whisky and grime.

"We're keeping her," he said, then looking at the other four men, "this squaw's a fighter!" The men laughed.

Her mother shouted with all the strength she could muster, "No, you cannot have her! Please! Please let us take her with us!"

As her mother yelled, her father ran hard at the man to take him off guard. Unfortunately, he was shot in the chest before he reached Jade. He fell backward hard due to the force of the shotgun blast. George ran to their father and kneeled down to him trying to put pressure on his father's wound. His Cherokee brothers had taught him to do this during their battle training. As her father lay on the ground, blood trickling down his coat onto the red clay, he looked at Jade. His breathing became labored. Her father reached his hand out to her and then he stopped breathing altogether.

There was another gunshot. Jade screamed, "Mother!" Joe, who had stayed by his mother's side, jumped back at the sound of the shot. He quickly returned to the wagon, his face showing the horror of what he saw. Her arm dangled over the side, her chin was on her chest and her eyes were closed. The blood began to seep through her flowered dress; she was already gone.

"Boys we have lightened your load. Your parents have gone to their god, so I suggest you get down the road before I change my mind." The man in charge had considerable height and girth, sand colored hair and intense green eyes. He glared at her brothers then pointed. "Go west!" he snarled.

Joe, with a trembling voice yelled, "We won't leave our sister, give her to us!" Feeling he had nothing left to lose, he ran to the skinny man holding her. He hit the man several times with balled fists and the men all laughed. The man easily pushed Joe to the ground.

"Almost as tough as your little brother; if you don't want to end up like Michael, you had better get going."

Joe scrambled to his feet. Joe and George stood staring at Jade, unsure of what to do. There was silence amongst them all, waiting for the next move. Then the boys backed down the path to the road slowly, never taking their eyes from Jade.

Jade cried and screamed reaching her arms toward them as the man held her around the waist. "Don't leave me! Joe! George! Don't leave me!"

"We will come back for you, Jade." And they turned and ran.

The large man with the green eyes laughed as he watched the boys run down the gravel path out of the plantation. Then he turned and looked at Jade, inspecting and appreciating his prize, as the

other man held her. Jade spat in his eye. He raised his thick cal-
lused hand, struck her across the face, grabbed her long dark braid
then pulled her face within inches of his. She could taste the blood.
He was so close she could smell his disgusting breath. "My name is
David Greyson." He lifted his chin defiantly at her, glaring at her
then smiled. To the men he said, "Take her into my new home. I
will be there shortly. I want to walk around my new plantation and
survey this land that belongs to me now; all because I had the lucky
draw in the lottery."

Chapter 2
April 21, 1838

J ade woke from a deep sleep and slowly opened her eyes. At first she didn't recognize her surroundings. The pillow was soft and comfortable but she was groggy so it was difficult to focus. She raised her head and pushed her long black hair away from her face. As she looked around the room she realized that she was in her parent's bedroom. The window was open and she could hear the finches chirping outside in the oak tree that towered above their home. The white sheer curtains were slowly blowing in the morning breeze. The sun was coming up and its rays pierced the early morning darkness of the room. Her mother's comb and brush were on the dresser and her shawl hung over the back of the chair near the door. Her father's worn suede moccasins were next to the chair. Why am I here? She put her hand on her forehead, trying to concentrate then rubbed her brown eyes. Focus. Then it all came rushing back. She buried her face in the pillow. "No, no. Please god, let it be a dream."

Jade threw the blanket back and quickly slung her thin dark legs off the side of the bed nearest the door. She stood up and looked down at the gown she was wearing. It was her mother's pink night-gown. Her hand went to her mouth to attempt to hold in the deep sob that was forcing its way out. As she touched her mouth, she felt the sting again. She went to the mirror and saw the cut on her lip, the dried blood and the bruise on her cheek. Her hand still on her mouth, she looked around the room for her clothes. She walked slowly around the end of the bed toward the open window and discovered her clothes in a pile on the floor next to the dresser. She looked back at the door and noticed the lock was not bolted. She ran to the door to secure the lock and just as she reached for the bolt, the door opened.

He walked in looking at her with those intense green eyes; a look that told her he was in charge. She remembered that look from when she first saw him yesterday. She backed toward the window and kneeled down, picked up her clothes and held them to her chest. He continued to stare. His blond hair looked dirty, as did the rest of him. He reeked of sweat. She gathered that he hadn't slept last night; probably celebrating his conquest.

He took his time looking at her from head to toe. "There will be plenty of time for us to get to know each other better, and we will, I promise you. Put your clothes on and come downstairs," he said, his hand on the pistol at his waist. He took a step back into the hall and shut the door.

Again Jade ran to the door and this time locked it. She heard it click and she backed toward the bed. She slowly sat down on the bed realizing it was not a dream. He was really here. Her parents and her brother Michael were dead. Joe and George had left her. Tears streamed down her face. The salt burned her lip. She pulled her mother's nightgown off over her head then buried her face in it and let the tears and racking sobs flow. Jade lay back on the bed, staring at the ceiling and thought about yesterday; all the while clinging to her mother's gown.

From the foyer she had been able to see her father standing on the porch, smoking his pipe, looking at the cotton fields their family had cultivated for many years. Just beyond the fields, the Georgia mountains gradually rose majestically. It had been raining on and off for weeks. The leaves on the trees that covered the hills and valleys were already coming out and the vivid green covered the mountains like a blanket. Her father had seemed worried. She could hear him grumbling. She could see him lower his head, shake it, then take a deep breath and hold his head up high. He had a strong profile with a defined jaw line and a slightly crooked nose. He had earned that crooked nose a few years back in a fight with a drunken white man he found digging for gold on their land. Although he was a strong man, she knew he carried the weight of the Cherokee turmoil on his shoulders. They all did. It was a warm April afternoon and she remembered seeing him remove his coat and drape it over his arm. She knew he was thinking about the events of the last few months. John Ross, one of the younger Cherokee leaders, had pleaded with John Ridge, one of the more elder leaders to stand their ground; to wait until a new president was elected. President Andrew Jackson refused to uphold the Supreme Court ruling confirming the land belonged to the Cherokee. John Ross was sure a new president would abide by the ruling. But John Ridge was not convinced and had led several thousand of their brothers on the trail westward with the promise of new Cherokee land.

Jade remembered she walked out onto the porch at the front of their plantation home and took her father's hand. At thirteen, she was still small and the warmth of his hand gave her comfort. She followed his gaze as he looked out over the plantation and the mountains beyond. He told her he could feel the spirits of his ancestors surrounding them. He pointed at the children playing stickball in the fields and they both smiled. Her father explained that he was glad he and fifteen thousand of their tribe stood with John Ross to wait it out.

He then said it was time to gather the family to discuss the upcoming planting season. He knew they would do their best to continue life as usual and hope the whites in Georgia would not make good on their threats to take the land by force. May 26th was the deadline for the voluntary removal, but he was confident that John Ross would find a way to save their land. Although John was a half-breed, he had the respect of whites and Cherokee alike.

Jade and her father had walked back into their home and found her mother in the foyer. "Sara, please ask the boys to join us in the sitting room. I'd like to discuss our plans with them."

"Yes Charles," her mother had said. "Let me find them and we will be there shortly."

Jade, still holding the nightgown, rolled over on her side and continued to think about yesterday.

Her father and Jade waited in the foyer and had watched as her mother went upstairs to get her brothers. Her mother was so beautiful. She watched her long black braids brush her hips as she walked up the stairs. The dress she was wearing was her newest and Jade admired how her mother had stitched a row of flowers along the bottom. She adorned most of Jade's and her clothes to make them feminine even though they were practical. Jade admired her mother for her creativity. She was not only creative but was also one of the first Cherokee women to learn to read and write English. She spent time with the other families in their tribe to help the women learn so that they could also teach their own children. Jade was proud of her. Her father had commented that her mother was a strong woman and a wonderful wife and mother. He was grateful for their union. She had borne him three fine sons and a beautiful daughter. Jade had blushed when he said that.

Jade thought about her brothers. Joe was seventeen, George fifteen and Michael seven. Joe was intent on staying true to the Cherokee customs, including his braid and dress. George and Michael, being younger, were more inclined to dress like the whites and they kept their hair short. It was a constant topic of discussion. Her parents let the boys decide and did not push their views either way because they understood both sides. They did remind them all that for them to further integrate into the white man's world, it was necessary to make the white men comfortable when they were around them. Most of the white men still regarded the Cherokee as a possible threat, although some had begun to accept them into their communities. Jade thought that Joe would eventually come around to their new ways. She also knew her brothers preferred playing ball games with the other Cherokee boys to working the fields, but they knew when they were needed to help with the harvest. It was the only way to cultivate the crops on schedule and for her brothers to learn first-hand how to manage the plantation. Her father explained that it was critical that the slaves understood the boys were their masters as well as he.

Jade rose from the bed and walked to the window. She put her forehead and her hand on the glass as tears rolled down her cheeks. She could feel the heat of the sun through the window. Were her brothers getting help? Were they coming back for her?

She remembered her mother had gathered the family in the sitting room – all but Michael. "I couldn't find Michael. Does anyone know where he is?" she had said. The children had all looked at one another.

Jade remembered saying that she had seen him walking to the carriage house that morning.

Her father had smiled. "I really want us all here for this discussion. It's important we all understand that we will continue to support our land and enjoy our home as we always have. We need to go over the schedule to make certain we have a successful crop this year."

Then her father had asked Joe and George to get Michael from the carriage house where he was usually whittling tools. Michael was always making tools for everyone and working on various projects for their home so he would feel that even as the youngest, he was contributing to the well-being of the plantation. For a seven year old, he was more responsible and mature than his older brothers. He had an old soul. Jade had told him he had their grandfather's soul inside him.

Joe and George had quickly returned to the house. Their dark eyes were wide and they were out of breath. Joe leaned over with his hands on his beige but somewhat dirty pants, unable to speak for breathing so hard. His black braid had fallen over his shoulder. Jade remembered thinking how long it had gotten. She had looked to the door to see if Michael had come into the house behind them. He had not. George ran to Father and pulled on his arm saying Michael was not in the carriage house. They had searched for him all around the plantation but could not find him. They had even gone to the slave quarters to ask the slaves if they had seen Michael, but most of the slaves were in the cotton fields. Sam, the eldest of the slaves, had been cleaning the horses between the barn and the slave quarters, said he had not seen Michael either. When Joe and George circled the house, they saw some white men in the woods directly behind the carriage house.

They had all heard the stories of the greedy white men coming to take over Cherokee homes.

Her parents had run through the back door, down the steps and around the carriage house, the children all close behind. Standing at the edge of the woods was the white man. He was tall and heavy set. Besides the pistol at his waist, he held a rifle and looked at them through squinted intense green eyes.

"Go back!" her father had said through clenched teeth and motioned for them to return to the house.

Her mother had begun to slowly walk backwards toward the house, arms pulling on the children to retreat with her.

Jade would never forget what had happened next. Her father yelled to the man. "What have you done with my son?"

CINDI CRANE

The man had laughed a short but gruff laugh. "Let's just say, there is one less Indian I have to drag from your home today."

The children and their mother had stopped moving.

Her father had not. He ran toward the man. A loud shot rang out and he stopped in his tracks. They saw another man standing just inside the woods with a rifle pointed, smoke coming from the barrel. He was short and skinny and smiled a toothless smile. Her father quickly turned to look at his family. They all looked at each other. Then her mother had fallen to the ground. Her father ran back to her mother and pulled her into his arms. She had been shot in the shoulder.

Jade shook her head remembering her mother looking at her father, gripping his arm saying, "Protect the children; I will be all right. Run to the house and make them hide. Lock all the doors and windows. Please Charles," she had whispered with tears in her eyes.

The large man had stepped forward. "There is no hiding at this point. The Georgia government has given me this property. I won it fairly in the lottery. It's a shame you didn't take the trail with the other Indians that headed west a few weeks ago. It's not too late. You have until sundown to pack what you can and take to the road, or my men and I will take this land and your home by force."

"Masta Charles! What can I do?" Sam had come running.

Before her father could answer, the white man said, "What is your name, boy?" Sam looked at the man, then at her father. Her father nodded.

"Name is Sam," Sam had said. Sam was extremely muscular and intimidating to look at, however, when he spoke his deep voice had a comforting effect and eased any apprehension one would have towards him. Sweat beaded on his brow; his black skin shining in the sun.

The man walked over to Sam. "You now work for me, boy. So Sam, how many slaves are there here?"

"Jus twelve of us, Suh," Sam replied then looked at her father, concerned, questioning. Jade knew he respected her father and knew he was a fair and honest man.

Her father had provided for Sam's family and Jade had overheard Sam talking with the other slaves saying that her father had treated them more decently then Sam had expected he would, "being an Indian". Her father had bought the twelve slaves seven years ago at an auction. At the time, most had been very thin and sickly. Their prior owner had died a slow death from an illness and the money had run out. What money had been left was spent on the master's family, not on feeding the slaves. So they worked the fields and ate off the land. When Sam's master passed, the master's widow took the slaves to the auction and moved north to live with her sister's family.

When the twelve came to be with her family, they quickly learned that working for Cherokee was nothing like working for the white master. Jade's mother spent time teaching Sam's son, Ben, and the other slave children to read, write and make quilts. They were like their own community and Jade knew that Sam had been at a loss as to what to do about this white man coming to take what belonged to her family. Again Sam looked at her father.

The man spat. "Go back to your quarters and wait there until I come to you and the others. Make them stay inside. If I see any slaves walking the grounds, I will shoot them on site. Do ya hear, boy?"

"Yes, Suh." Sam had lowered his head then turned and ran back to the slave quarters.

Then the man looked at her father. "What are you waiting for?" he had said. "Git back to the house and git your stuff! I'll be back before sundown."

"But what of my son? Where is he?" her father had asked frantically.

— 11 —

"I will return him to you when you have cleared out. Not before!" He turned to walk back to the woods where his men were waiting. They could not see into the woods to see if Michael was safe. They were all afraid the man was lying. Jade prayed Michael was still alive.

Her father had lifted her mother in his arms.

"Oh my god, Michael, he must be so afraid," her mother had cried.

Jade sat back down on the bed remembering the rest of what had happened. Her father had carried her mother back into the house then said, "I'll get you to the house and see how bad your wound is. I need to figure out what to do. I won't risk losing my family, but if we give up the plantation, we will never get it back. This I know in my heart. I wonder if there is a way to get word to John Ross."

Her mother was leaning her head on her father's shoulder and closed her eyes.

Her father had panicked and yelled out her name. "Sara!"

She quickly opened her eyes. "I just closed my eyes to think for a moment. Can we get Sam to run to John Ross to tell him of the situation?"

"The man threatened the slaves if they left their quarters, he would kill them. If he does that he would be losing the slaves he thinks he is inheriting, but it's a risk. I will take you upstairs and get the children to look after you and I will sneak around to the slave quarters to see if we can get one of the horses for Sam to ride out to alert John Ross."

"Be careful, my love," her mother had said.

"I will. Now let's get you upstairs."

Her father then told them all he needed them to be very brave and needed their help. He told Joe and George to run to the well. He told them to get a bucket of water and rags and bring them back so he could tend to her mother's wound. He had told Jade to stay and hold her mother's hand to give her the strength she needed.

Jade had said, "Yes, Papa. I love you Momma. I am here so you do not have to be afraid. We will take good care of you Momma."

The boys had come back quickly. She knew her father had been relieved. In the meantime, he had taken a knife and cut back the part of her mother's dress covering the wound. She had lost a lot of blood and kept closing her eyes.

"Please Sara, don't fall asleep. Please look at your daughter and glean her strength, her love. I will take care of this." Her father had taken the water and rags and carefully cleaned the wound. The bullet was deep. He would not have time to get it out. He had to send Sam to get to John Ross before nightfall or all was lost.

Jade would never forget how her mother looked at her father then said, "Go Charles, we will be fine here. Go talk to Sam."

Her father had looked at each of them then ran out the bedroom door. Jade had heard him go downstairs then slowly open the door and walk out onto the front porch and down the porch steps. Jade had run to the bedroom window to watch her father. She had seen him stop walking and turn around. Then she saw a different white man come into view. He wore a large black hat and a long brown coat. His beard was as black as coal and his eyes were small and close together giving him a look of pure evil. He had a rifle pointed at him. She couldn't hear what they were saying but she saw her father turn back and they both started walking toward the barn. The slave quarters were the next building over. It was not a very large building but housed all twelve slaves with cots and a warming kitchen of its own. Jade put her hands together, praying that he could get Sam's attention. She could see Sam just inside the barn. It was clear that the white man yelled something then lifted his rifle to Sam.

Jade could tell her father was pleading with the man to not shoot. She saw the man lower his rifle a bit. Sam had then disappeared into the barn; she hoped to ride out the back to find John Ross.

Her father picked up two wooden crates that were sitting outside the barn and he and the evil looking man walked back around to the front porch. Her father then went up the steps and into the house. Jade had looked back towards the barn just in time to see Sam riding down the trail toward town. Relieved, she had run to the bedroom door just as her father had come back up the stairs. He had said he believed the white men hadn't seen Sam riding away. Her father explained to them all that the leader of the group did not plan to miss out on the opportunity to own a plantation. He knew without the lottery, he would never have been able to afford property like this. Governor Lumpkin authorized the lottery giving forty acres of Cherokee land to him and he would take what was now his, at any cost.

When her father had returned to the bedroom, her mother's state had worsened. The pain was apparent on her beautiful face and she was breathing very fast. He knew then they had no choice but to leave their home. Her father worried aloud about how the trip would take a toll on their mother. If only John Ross and his brothers would arrive in time. But he explained to them all he could not risk his family's lives on that hope. They would have to deal with the white men once the family was safe in town.

Jade remembered sitting on the bed next to her mother holding the cool rag to her forehead. She was trying not to let any of them see her tears. George was sitting on the other side of the bed holding her mother's hand and Joe was staring out the window. Then her father had said, "You are all being very brave. We must do as they say for now until John Ross comes to tell the men that we still have five weeks before the deadline for removal. Hopefully, things will resolve and we will be back in our home soon. Children, go get two days worth of clothing. I will get your mother's and mine. Move quickly! Let's not test these men's patience."

"But what about Michael?" Joe had yelled.

Her father had looked at them all. "The man said he would return Michael to us when we were ready to go, so go now!"

They had filled their small packs and her father had gone downstairs to the barn to get horses for their trip. Jade had followed him down the stairs to ask him a question and as he walked out on the porch again, the large white man with the searing green eyes was standing at the bottom of the steps with his rifle.

"Your boy Sam disobeyed my order. We have taken care of him. I have men positioned in the woods along the road that leads to the plantation in the front as well as the men situated in the back behind the carriage house. Don't test me again."

Jade covered her mouth with her hands and her father had said, "Did you kill him?"

The man had walked up the rest of the porch steps to look her father directly in the eye. "I told him not to leave his quarters. If you sent him for help, this is on you." Then he had sneered. "Now you have thirty minutes to get your family out of this house."

"I was just heading to the barn to prepare the horses for our trip."

"Who said you could take the horses? They belong to me now so git your family and head out on foot."

"But my wife, will you at least let me have one for her? She is very weak from the gunshot!" her father had demanded.

The man then raised his eyebrows. "I am surprised she is still alive. I had not intended for her to be shot. If you had done what you were told, that would not have happened. You can take that small wagon over there, but you and your sons will have to pull it yourselves." When he saw her father's dismayed look he had added, "If you prefer, I can lighten your load." He looked past her father at Jade on the stairs. "Leave the woman and girl with me." Jade remembered gasping. Her father then turned and saw her standing on the stairs listening to them. Then he turned back to the man.

"No! You will not have them. I will get them quickly and we will take the wagon. What of my son? Will you bring him to the front now?"

"Your son was a fighter; you would have been proud. He lasted about twenty minutes with my men."

That news was like a knife to Jade's heart. Her father looked at her again and she saw the despair and fury in his deep brown eyes. He closed his eyes, gritted his teeth and clenched his fists. Then he took a deep breath. They knew then the men would do anything to take this land and their home. Her father raced back up the stairs, grabbing her arm as he went. This time everyone could see the panic in his face. She knew he tried to put the thought of Michael's death out of his mind so he could save the rest of his family but she had cried.

Her father gathered up her mother in the blankets and told the children to stay close behind him. "Let's go. They are giving us a wagon to transport your mother in. Boys, I will need your help pulling it."

"Where is Michael? We can't leave without him!" her mother had cried.

Jade remembered her father shaking his head. "He is already with the gods. We must move quickly." Her mother had cried out and buried her head in her father's shoulder. The boys had looked frantically at each other. Then they all walked out onto the porch and down the steps.

Jade buried her face in her hands remembering all the details of yesterday; the day she lost her family. Then she put on her clothes, opened the door and slowly descended the stairs.

Chapter 3
June 9, 2010

"It's not exactly what I had in mind," said Carolyn as she and Josie walked out of a small vacant restaurant on Canton Street. "Kacey and I had hoped for something historical. We'd really like something that had a fascinating story behind it because we believe that would draw some interesting clientele. Don't you agree?"

"Yes, I do and I understand. Well, it's up to you. They just do not become available that often in Historic Roswell. You know, Canton Street is a highly sought after area because of the atmosphere and the trendy restaurants and shops in the area. When a property comes open, it doesn't stay on the market for very long. If you would be willing to look at the side streets, you might have more luck," said Josie. She had been selling and leasing real estate in the Roswell area for almost twenty years. She was starting to think Carolyn's goals were out of reach. She was on a mission to find a very specific house to renovate and turn into a restaurant. That seemed to be a much harder way to start a restaurant than to find a space that had been a restaurant prior. Well Lord knows, so far she hadn't found it for her but that's what she did best. Having a happy customer was what her business was all about, she thought and put her best smile on. That's how she had continued to be successful in this competitive market and ugly economy.

"I really appreciate your patience with me, Josie. I guess I would be willing to look at the side streets if you can find the right place. We'd really like it to have a nice front porch and yard I can turn into a patio for tables with umbrellas. People really enjoy eating outside especially spring through fall. It needs to at least be an easy walk to Canton Street." Carolyn insisted.

"Well let me do another search," Josie said. "I need to get to my next showing, so I will catch up with you later."

"Ok, let me know what you find." Carolyn sighed as she looked at the vacant restaurant one more time. Was she being too picky? This place was right on Canton Street, but it was really small and no outdoor space. Would it work as an eclectic wine and small plate restaurant/bar? It was certainly safer, starting small. She wanted Kacey to look at it before she nixed the idea, but Kacey was in Mississippi visiting her mom. Should she just grab it so they could get their business started? Or was she procrastinating because deep down she was really afraid to start her own restaurant? Hell, she'd never even worked in a restaurant! Ok, don't start that again, she said to herself. You gave up your cushy job in the corporate world to do this, so you are going to see it through! Besides, Kacey was going to be a fantastic partner. Not only had she worked in bars and restaurants in the past, but she was very financially savvy. It also didn't hurt that her husband managed restaurants. I couldn't have gotten luckier when Kacey asked me if I would consider being her partner, Carolyn thought. Kacey had confidence in Carolyn's marketing and sales abilities and thought that her management experience would help their business be successful.

"I'll tell Kacey about the place and see if she can look at it this week."

"Alright, and I'll expand my search to see what else I can find. I'll call you." Josie turned to walk away and then had another thought. "Actually, there is this one place that has sat vacant for a couple of years, but it's not for sale, at least not that I know of. I have approached the owners in the past and they weren't interested in selling or leasing. That was two years ago though. I'll try them again. It could be a beautiful property although it's overgrown now. It might be too big for what you are looking for. It's actually considered a plantation. I think they may even talk about it on the ghost tour! I haven't been able to figure out what the story is on the house. Maybe I should call Dianna who runs the ghost tour and see what she knows about it. She knows just about everything about the historic homes in this area. I'll do some digging and get back to you. In the meantime, if you want to do a drive by, it's at the end of Millstone Drive. You won't be able to miss it. Take Rock Way and then make your first right. It's the only house on the street. It's very dark and run down at this point. It would be a five minute walk from here. In fact, you should walk there to see if you think it's walkable from Canton Street. Take a look and let me know if you want me to pursue it. I'll talk to you tomorrow?"

"Sounds great. I'll check it out," said Carolyn. Josie waved and walked down Canton Street to her car, saying hello to several friends as she went. She was well known in this area and Carolyn knew that the fact that she hadn't found the right property yet was not a reflection on Josie. She could see Josie's turquoise jacket from where she stood. Turquoise must be her signature color, Carolyn thought. She had worn something that color the last six times she'd seen her. Josie was very approachable. It didn't hurt that she was blonde and beautiful. The real estate business really suited her personality. She asked a lot of questions about what Carolyn and Kacey wanted in the property they were looking for. Carolyn definitely thought if anyone could help her find her dream place, it would be Josie. But Carolyn, she thought, six times? Really? How long are you going to drag that poor woman out to show you properties before you make a decision?

Thinking about Josie now, she hoped she would be as charming when she finally opened her restaurant. She knew it was going to be important not only to get her clientele in the door the first time, but to keep them coming back. Well that and the food. Yes, there was that. They would have to start looking for a chef soon, but not too soon because their business plan only worked if they didn't have to start paying their staff too far in advance of when they opened. It was a little worrisome thinking about this house that Josie had just mentioned. It sounded like it would take a lot of work. Timing is everything if they are to make a profit the first year.

Carolyn waved to Josie then turned to walk down to Rock Way. It was a gorgeous day and the people were out in abundance. She absolutely loved this town. She knew in her gut it was the right place for their restaurant. As she walked past The Chandlery, one of her favorite gift shops, she saw a Vera Bradley bag that caught her eye. Kacey would love that, she thought. Kacey's birthday was next week and she wanted to get her something special, something she could use while they got their business going. She went into the store for a closer look. It was perfect; big enough to carry her laptop and files and her "Opening a Restaurant for Dummies" book but whimsical enough to fit Kacey's style. No, that wasn't the right word; hippy enough was more like it. Kacey is definitely a hippy at heart; she thought and laughed to herself.

When Carolyn approached the counter to pay for the bag, she was greeted by one of her tennis teammates checking out. "Hey Carolyn, how are you?" asked Lucy. Lucy was purchasing a diaper bag. She was six months pregnant and adorable.

"I'm great Lucy, how are you doing? You look wonderful. That's a really sweet bag. Getting excited?" asked Carolyn.

"Yes, I know I should wait until after the baby shower before I buy things for myself but I couldn't resist. Are you by yourself? Want to grab a coffee and sit down for a little while? My back is killing me!" said Lucy rubbing the small of her back.

"Sure. Let me pay for this and we can go across the street to Katy Kelly's and sit on the balcony. Sound good?"

"Yeah, in fact, I'll go on over and get us a table."

"Ok, thanks, I'll be right there," Carolyn replied. She paid the cashier and headed to Katy Kelly's. What a terrific place. It was unique in décor and the menu choices were fabulous. It was one of the two restaurants on Canton Street that had a balcony. It sort of reminded her of a New Orleans style restaurant with the wrought iron railings. She joined Lucy at her table.

Lucy saw Carolyn approaching and was envious of her fit body. How long would it take to get back in shape for tennis, she wondered. Carolyn tucked some of her blond hair behind her ear as she sat her bags down and took a seat. "Thanks for joining me. I really needed to sit down, but also wanted to talk to you about the match tomorrow. I wanted to get your opinion on if I should play you and Kacey at line one or two. You know if we take three points tomorrow, we will definitely be in second place and would go to the playoffs." Lucy was the captain of their tennis team. She was really good at it. She had just the right mix of putting together a competitive line up and at the same time, being sure she played everyone at least two times to be fair to all the players. She was also one of the few captains that asked her players their opinion on the lineup before she sent it out.

"Well, thanks for asking, but you know we will play either line. It's really up to you," said Carolyn. "Who else are you going to put in the lineup that could play line one if we play line two? Sally and Debbie?"

"Yes. So I could really go either way. I just want to make sure we take three lines so we make it to the playoffs. If you are ok with it, then I will put you and Kacey at line two so that it will be a sure thing. Kacey gets back from Mississippi tonight, right?"

Carolyn laughed. "Yes, she will be back tonight and that sounds

— 21 —

good, no pressure, huh? By the way, are you going to make it to Kacey's birthday dinner Wednesday night? Girl's night out!"

Lucy laughed too. "Yes, I will be there, although since I'm not drinking, it will probably be a short night for me."

Carolyn finished her coffee; Lucy finished her iced water and left the restaurant. They said their goodbyes and Carolyn again set out toward Rock Way. She was anxious to see the place. As she walked to the corner of Canton and Rock Way, she admired the store fronts and began daydreaming about the restaurant and what it would be like to be an integral part of the community she loved so much.

She turned onto Rock Way and walked past the antique store. Right behind the store was Millstone Drive. She took a right and looked down the street. About 300 yards away, she could see the house. What an incredible home, she thought. Josie was right; it looked empty and unlived in. She felt the urge to see more so she kept walking. She could see that it was two stories, had a porch with a balcony over it and each had four white columns. The front yard was quite large and had a black wrought iron fence. As she passed a gardenia bush, she could smell the fragrant flowers. The gate was open so she continued in. She walked up the path and went up the porch steps.

It is so quiet, Carolyn thought. She peeked in the windows alongside the front door and could see the foyer and the staircase. She had an eerie feeling and looked around. I guess technically I'm trespassing, thought Carolyn. I wonder why they don't live here. She heard a creak behind her and jumped. Turning, she saw a young teen-aged African-American girl standing on the second step. She had on a red shirt, jean shorts and flip flops. She wore a peace sign around her neck and her hair was curled.

"Oh honey, you scared me!" cried Carolyn, and then laughed.

The girl looked at Carolyn suspiciously. "Can I help you?"

"I was curious as to if the owners would sell it. Do you live around here?"

She pointed at a small white house next door. "Yes, we live next door. My house is old too and it's been in my family for many years. It's not as big but it's pretty. I like this yard better because it's so much bigger but sometimes I get the creeps when I am here. Papa doesn't want me to hang out over here." She looked back toward her house. "I have to get going."

"Ok, maybe I'll see you again. My name is Carolyn. What's your name?"

"Wanda. Sorry, I have to go." She ran off in the direction of her house.

Carolyn smiled. I'd probably be nervous living next door to a vacant house too, she thought. She walked back down off the porch then decided to peek around the corner. She saw a barn and a small building next to it. She wondered if the small building was a cook house or slave quarters. It certainly was old enough to have had slaves at some point. She continued around the side to the back and saw what looked like the remains of a carriage house; beyond that, some very dense woods. She could see another house peeking out behind the woods to the right. Staring at the woods she felt something but couldn't quite put her finger on it. Okay, your mind is playing tricks on you. And you are full blown trespassing at this point, she thought. She walked back around to the front of the house, down the path and out the gate. Carolyn turned to look at the house one more time. Restaurant? Maybe. Her husband's renovation project? Yes, it was definitely worth looking into.

Chapter 4
April 20, 1838

Joe and George ran as fast as they could to town. They went to the country store that was owned by the Williams; a Cherokee couple and described to them what had happened. The Williams immediately sent a rider to John Ross to explain the land takeovers were beginning. The whites who had won the land lottery were taking possession with the blessing of the president and the governor. It was only a matter of time before the rest of the Cherokee would be removed to the West.

John Ross, without delay, rode to the store to see the boys. He dismounted his horse and tied him to the hitching post. Joe and George frantically explained that their brother, Michael and their parents had been killed. They also told John the white men had kept their sister, Jade.

John immediately, for fear of what they would do to Jade, left the store and headed for the plantation. As he rode down the gravel path to the home, he was greeted by multiple men with shotguns. David Greyson came out of the house onto the porch. "You have two minutes to turn your horse around or I will shoot you for trespassing."

John pulled up his horse, stopped about twenty feet in front of the porch and dismounted. "Do you know who I am?" he said intensely.

"I know you are an Indian and you need to get on the road west. That is all I need to know," sneered David. "I am within my rights to remove you myself from this property if I have to."

John stared at the man then looked around at all the faces of men he could not understand. Greed was a terrible sin. But today his concern was getting Jade back. It was up to him to make a difference. "I am Chief John Ross. I understand you have been awarded this land by your governor. All I want today is the girl. Please give me the girl and we will be on our way." He never took his eyes from David.

David was impressed by John Ross' articulate speech and his sophisticated manner. He could barely tell he was Indian. He remembered hearing that he was a mixed breed; that his mother was white. His dress was that of a gentlemen and he held himself in a way that read authority. "I don't know what you mean. We came to stake our claim and told the Indian family that it was time for them to move on and they did. They left several hours ago." One of his men was holding Jade inside the home, hidden from view and gagged.

John Ross narrowed his brow. "I have just spoken with two of the sons. They say that you killed the parents and the youngest boy and kept the girl. Where are the bodies? And I will ask you again to give me the girl. I will take her with us."

The men cocked their shotguns and moved a few feet closer to John. John continued to stare at David. David stared back. He did not want to shoot John Ross but he was not going to give up the girl or admit to the killings. He was told to take the property by force if needed. He assumed that meant by whatever force necessary, although he felt he would probably suffer repercussions if he killed the Indian chief. "As I said, there are no bodies and the girl left with her brothers. Now please leave my property before my men get twitchy. I don't want to kill you, John Ross. Go west. Take your tribe and build new homes."

A shot rang out. "Don't shoot!" said David. One of his men had fired a warning shot. "This is your last chance. Leave now."

John slowly backed up to his horse and mounted, never taking his eyes from Greyson. He reluctantly returned to the store and explained to the boys what had happened. "Stay with the Williams. They will accompany you to the west where you can begin again."

Shortly thereafter, federal troops and state militias forced the remaining Cherokee out of their homes and into stockades along the border of Tennessee awaiting their removal to the west. Many of the Indians died of starvation and illness while in captivity. John Ross had tried to overturn the contract that John Ridge, the prior chief had made to give them $4.5 million to help the tribe start over in Oklahoma. John Ridge and about two thousand of the tribe had already gone west. John Ross had hoped that either Andrew Jackson would finally agree to the Supreme Court ruling stating this land was Cherokee land, or that there would at least be enough delay so a new U.S. president would do so. That wasn't going to happen in time. And in the end, the president, Martin Van Buren, had General Winfield Scott put the removal into action.

John Ross worked out an agreement with General Scott to allow the Indians to lead their own way on the Trail. The white soldiers would accompany them but not guard them. The Cherokee would no longer be prisoners. They were separated into groups of a thousand each and the first Cherokee-led march began on August 28th. The last party would leave the first week of December.

They started in Georgia, traveled through Tennessee, Kentucky and southern Illinois, crossing several rivers, including the Mississippi. Crossing the Mississippi River was treacherous and caused considerable fear amongst the travelers. They moved through southern Missouri into their new land, called Park Hill. It would later become the state of Oklahoma. During the first month there was a drought which brought its own set of problems. Finally at the end of September, the rain came, but so did the mud, then the harshest winter in years.

As the later groups traveled over the land they would come across graves, excrement, and little to no food. Depression was rampant as they continued to mourn their lost loved ones, their homes and way of life.

Of the approximate twelve thousand Cherokee that took the trail, only about eight thousand made it to their new land. Now called "The Trail of Tears", a quarter of the Cherokee died from starvation, freezing or disease. Unfortunately, George Hawkins never made it to Oklahoma. He had tried to help several of the elders and children and broke his leg when he slid into a river bank. He had contracted an infection that eventually led to a paralyzing fever. Joe buried his brother along the trail under rocks and sticks and vowed to someday make it back to Jade.

Chapter 5
June 9, 2010

"Wanda, what were you doing over there? I told you not to go over to that house. There is no reason for you to be snooping around that house. You could get hurt and it's trespassing." Frank shook his head, but knew he couldn't stay mad at his beautiful daughter. Those curls got him every time.

"But Papa, there was a lady over there. She was the one that was snooping!"

"What do you mean? Who was over there?" Frank demanded.

"She said her name is Carolyn but she said that she was wondering if the owners would sell it. You think she is going to buy that place Papa?" Wanda peered out the window and saw Carolyn walking down the path.

Frank shook his head then followed his daughter's eyes out the window. Seeing a tall attractive white woman, he decided to see what the visit was about and walked outside.

"Miss? Miss! Can I help you?" yelled Frank as he strolled across his lush green lawn. He was proud of that lawn. He usually got "Yard of the Month" from the neighborhood garden club. He was a tall, stocky man. Wanda came running up behind him. She wasn't about to miss out on something happening involving the house next door. Hopefully the lady has lots of kids, Wanda thought.

"Oh, hello!" Carolyn said as she started toward Frank and Wanda. "My name is Carolyn Kane."

"Hi, I'm Frank Jones and this is my daughter Wanda. Can we be of assistance?"

"Maybe. My realtor mentioned that this house has been vacant for a couple of years, but in the past they weren't willing to sell. It doesn't look like they come around much. Do you know the owners?" Carolyn asked.

"Yes," said Frank. "The Greyson family has owned this property for many years. The current children have all grown up, moved out and don't seem to take interest in keeping it up. Last time I talked to Daniel he said that it's a money pit but since it's been in his family for more than a century, he felt guilty about selling it. Christina, his sister, moved to New York and rarely comes back. She is in the magazine business and Daniel is an investment banker in downtown Atlanta. I have their phone numbers if you would like them."

Frank pulled out his iPhone and read off the numbers to Carolyn who plugged them into her cell phone. She thanked Frank, waved at Wanda and headed back toward Canton Street. She hadn't mentioned she was thinking about turning the place into a restaurant. She wasn't sure how the neighbors would respond. Frank was obviously very meticulous with his own property; fresh paint and beautiful landscaping. She assumed the plantation home was zoned for commercial, but she would have to check that with Josie.

Carolyn reached her car and drove back to her house. She and Scott, her husband, had purchased their home two years ago and were almost done with the remodeling. The house was about two miles from Historic Roswell. It was built in 1930, and needed just about everything replaced. Carolyn loved the Craftsman style, so they enhanced it with some of the newer Craftsman accessories. She could sit on the front porch for hours reading or working on her restaurant business plan. It was also where she and Scott would enjoy a glass of wine and talk about their day.

They were coming up on their tenth anniversary. Scott was just as handsome, if not more so, than when she first met him at a charity event. With his dark hair, strong defined jaw line and round glasses, her first impression of him was that he looked kind of GQ. She assumed he was from New York or Chicago. When he spoke to her, she almost laughed out loud because he had one of the strongest southern accents she had ever heard. It turned out he was born and raised in Atlanta, which was uncommon these days.

She pulled her car into the garage and went into the house. She was immediately greeted by the other two loves of her life, Diamond and Ruby, her Miniature Schnauzers. You would have thought she had been gone for weeks. They jumped up and down in a frenzy; happy to see her. In fact, Diamond barked and barked while Ruby just kind of mumbled in the background. Carolyn laughed. Ruby never tried to out bark Diamond. Did that make Diamond a diva or the Alpha Dog? She played with the girls and threw their toys for a few minutes then gave them a treat. Satisfied, the dogs returned to their beds.

"Hey Honey!" Scott yelled out when he came in through the back door.

"So how was golf today? How did you play?" Carolyn asked as she gave him a hug and a kiss. She loved hugging his broad shoulders.

"I won a beer," Scott said proudly. "I played really well on the front nine, not so hot on the back nine but I was still able to pull it out."

"That's great, Scott. How was work this morning – oh, did your certificate come in today?" asked Carolyn expectantly, taking off Scott's hat and running her hand through his messy dark hair.

"Not yet, but it should be here any day. You know, I don't have to wait for the certificate to come in to start doing my searches and research. Having a license to restore historical homes is important, but until I find the right property, the certificate is a mute point," said Scott as he opened the refrigerator. "What's for dinner?"

"Actually, what if I told you I may have found us both the perfect place? Don't get too excited, but I did find a historical home this afternoon, actually Josie found it, but it's currently not for sale." Carolyn proceeded to tell Scott about the house and meeting Frank and Wanda. "Frank said it is owned by the Greysons. Maybe you can do some research to find out more about them since the house has been theirs for many years, according to Frank. I don't know what "many years" means, but it looks about the same age as Barrington and Bulloch Hall. I guess it was built sometime in the 1800s."

"You are talking about the house off Canton behind the antique mall, right?" Scott asked.

"Yes, you already knew about it?"

"Yes, we learned about it in the training class. It's one of the plantation homes that was left standing after the Civil War but it is actually older than the Bulloch and Barrington plantations," Scott said as he continued to peer into the refrigerator.

"Really? Wow, that is interesting. I don't remember much about the land lottery but wasn't that when the Georgia governor did a lottery to split up the land that was originally owned by the Cherokee Indians?" Carolyn was very excited that Scott seemed to be aware of the house and its history.

"Yes. I don't remember what year it was built but it had to have been at least several years before the Indians were sent west. Remember the Trail of Tears?"

Carolyn opened a bottle of Chardonnay and poured them both a glass. "A little. I remember that the Cherokee Indians were sent out west and that the white men got their land, but I don't really remember the details. Let's go sit on the porch for a few minutes and you can tell me more about it. Then we can go hit number six." Carolyn had listed all of the restaurants in old Roswell and numbered them.

She wanted to check them all out to be sure that she had thought of everything in her business plan and to see what worked and didn't work well in her competitors' restaurants. Number six was the Mexican restaurant and she knew Scott would definitely be up for that.

"Which one is number six?" Scott asked. When Carolyn told him, he smiled and walked out on the porch. Taking a seat in one of the large, cushioned chairs that bounced, he put his head back and sighed. "I really do love it here and it would be so nice to have us both working close to home."

"So you will consider the Greyson house?" asked Carolyn excitedly.

"Well, yeah, I will consider it, but not sure we can afford it even if it is for sale, but with our investors, it's a possibility. Talking the owners into selling it may be difficult, but it's worth a shot. There aren't a whole lot of homes left standing that are that old. In fact, the house that, what did you say his name is – Frank, lives in definitely isn't as old as the Greyson house, but it would be important to find out more about that house too. It's always interesting to find out about the history of the ancestors, you never know whose descendents you come across and how the neighbors knew each other. So you said it was run down? Because if it was already restored, I am not sure how much more I could do with it unless of course, they didn't restore it accurately. Then I would have to redo some of the work they may have already done. The idea is to get it as close to the original as possible." Scott was on a roll now, excited about the possibilities.

Carolyn smiled. She loved to see him grab onto an idea and make it his. She knew that he would be excellent at restoring historical homes. He owned his own contracting firm for the last seven or so years and with the market down like it was he was trying to find something else to subsidize his remodeling business. Restoring historical homes was a whole different ball game. It took more money but could be so much more rewarding. It was also hard to find homes worth remodeling these days. They either had already been restored or were so dilapidated it wasn't worth it. It was still unclear if she would be able to turn it into a restaurant.

Carolyn had a thought. "So let's just say that the Greysons were willing to sell it, and you restored it. Would you be willing to let me use it as the restaurant? I guess we have to find out if it is zoned for commercial."

Scott looked at Carolyn, "Actually, since it has already been identified as a Historical Home, per the Historical Society, it is automatically zoned commercial. If we bought it, we would be sure to use the right contracts, etc. when we closed on it. Which means the Greysons, would have to agree to let it be used for something other than a home. As you know, the other plantations are set up as museums but also as event facilities. We could do the same thing, have it be a restaurant, but also allow tours. I am really interested in taking a look at it. I saw the picture of it in my class but I'm not sure if I have been by there. Want to do a drive by on the way to Mexi's?"

"Absolutely," replied Carolyn. "Let's go!" She had forgotten to ask him more about the Trail of Tears, but they could talk about that later. In fact, she knew it was a very depressing story, so putting it off until a later date was fine with her. She didn't want anything to diminish their new excitement about this wonderful find.

Chapter 6
June 9, 2010

"Surprise!" the girls yelled when Kacey walked in with Carolyn right behind her.

"What? This isn't a surprise! I planned it myself!" Kacey chided. The girls all laughed. The band was playing soft rock and country and there were a few people dancing.

Lucy walked up and said, "Great idea to have it here, I haven't been here since before I got pregnant and it's nice to get out and party with my girlfriends - although, as you can see, I'm drinking sparkling water with a lime." Lucy smiled and looked around the bar. She was adorable in her maternity top and skirt with flip flops. She looked so happy, Carolyn sighed. She and Scott were in their early thirties, so they still had time to start a family, she told herself. It definitely wasn't the right time until they got the restaurant underway and manageable, and Scott had completed his first historical renovation. If they were lucky, their two projects would be one and the same. She couldn't help but think about the Greyson house again.

"Let's get a drink," Kacey said.

"Of course, it's on me birthday girl! You are looking good by the way! I love the new short do, it makes you look like Audrey Hepburn," said Carolyn. She moseyed up to the bar and said, "Two proseccos, please, dry if you have it. I am so glad you turned me on to this sparkling wine. It's delicious."

The bartender sported long blond hair with a purple streak, a tattoo of Betty Boop (what was that about?) and multiple piercings. She smiled. "You got it! And the birthday girl's first drink is on the house!"

Kacey and Carolyn took their drinks over to the table to join their friends. Angel, the massage therapist, was looking beautiful, tanned and of course, buff. She had made quite the stir in Roswell. Angel was a single girl in her early thirties with a young son, Jimmy. She had recently moved up from Tampa to open a Spa right in the heart of it all. Her father and mother had both recently passed away and her marriage had only lasted three years. Angel wanted a new start close to her best friends in the type of historical area similar to the area where she had lived in Tampa. Canton Street was right up her alley, so to speak. She was already known for her deep massages and unique techniques using a bar hanging from the ceiling so she could massage with her feet. She called it "Extreme Massage" and it certainly was. One massage and you'd be sore for days, but once the toxins worked their way out, you would feel like a new woman. Carolyn sighed, thinking about it. Scott had tried it once, but only once. That was all the proof Carolyn needed that her pain tolerance was higher than his. That information might come in handy some day, she thought smiling.

"OK, so here's to Kacey, world's best tennis player, world's best Mom, world's best entrepreneur, world's best friend – not necessarily in that order!" shouted Mia. "Cheers girlfriend! How does it feel to be the big 3-5?" Mia wasn't sure she would like it when it was her turn next year. She had just finished her degree in veterinary medicine and felt like her life was just getting started, but she was already teetering on "middle age". Mia was a conflict of realities. She was a striking woman with big blue eyes and blond hair. She was extremely intelligent and had gotten her bachelor's in three years, graduating as valedictorian. She worked part-time as a vet tech at an animal hospital to pay for her degree. She had already invented a doggy popsicle, she called "Lickers". She had sold the concept based on the fact that large dogs tend to over drink in the hot months and can be at risk of their stomach's flipping. Her medical solution was to give them something that would cool them down and at the same time, quench their thirst. She was trying to determine what was next in her life.

The five girls toasted and talked animatedly for hours. They danced together and at one point all five took off their shoes and put them in a pile. They stood in a circle on the dance floor in their bare feet, adorned with a mix of polish, toe rings and a blister or two and Carolyn took a picture of the ten feet, fifty toes and one ankle bracelet. This picture would go on to be a symbol of their friendship for years to come.

"So tell me how it went with Josie," Kacey said. "I got back Sunday afternoon and haven't had a chance to call you. When I got back from Mississippi, it seemed like all hell had broken loose with the boys. Mike had forgotten their Boy Scout meeting was Monday night and they didn't get their Pinewood Derby cars completed. The five of us spent about three hours in the garage Sunday night - just what I needed after a three hour drive!"

Carolyn laughed. "Sorry, don't mean to laugh, I can just see you lining the boys and Mike up like an assembly line and whipping those cars out."

"We got them done but it took awhile. Who would think that a bunch of guys would be so particular?" Kacey exhaled and put her forefinger to her temple like a gun and pretended to shoot. She rolled her eyes with the biggest grin on her face. She was obviously proud of her boys and pleased with herself that she could hold her own in a house full of men.

"You are amazing Kacey!" Carolyn laughed.

Kacey looked distracted as she looked through the crowd, obviously recognizing someone. "At least they didn't show up empty handed and they learned a little bit about how resourceful their ole Mom is and how they need to plan better next time! Is that Josie over there?"

Carolyn looked in the direction Kacey was pointing. "It sure is and I think she is heading over here. That's great, but let me tell you real quick. I wasn't thrilled with the space that opened up on Canton, but I still think you should see it. Maybe you will see something about it that I couldn't. But I am dying to talk to you about this old plantation home that Josie told me about. Hi, Josie! How are you?"

"Well, I have had the craziest day! It started out with me accidently popping the lid off of my half-caf-half – decaf-skinny-vanilla chai latte, dumping it down my brand new Yves Saint Laurent suit and onto my three inch Jimmy Choos! However, on my way home to change, I got a call from a seller accepting the offer one of my clients made last night! I just finished the paperwork and decided to stop in for a dirty martini. They have gorgonzola-stuffed olives here, my fave!" Josie beamed.

Carolyn clapped. "Congratulations! Another reason to celebrate! It's Kacey's birthday tonight too! The big 3-5 and she was able to get Mike to keep the boys so we are celebrating as well! In fact, I was just getting ready to tell her about the place you found on Canton but I also want to find out if you heard anything about the plantation home on Millstone." Carolyn looked at the dance floor to see Mia and Angel cheering Lucy on as she tried the limbo. That didn't look easy, especially with the baby belly she was carrying. But Angel and Mia had her back so Carolyn wasn't worried.

Kacey said to Josie, "Tell me about the place on Canton first. That's really where we want to be - location, location, location!

What's it like?"

Josie looked at Carolyn and replied, "It is right in the heart of the district, but it's very small. In fact, the restaurant that occupied it prior moved down the road because they wanted more space. It could be a good start. You can always expand or move later once you have your business established."

"That's not a bad idea," Kacey said looking at Carolyn. "She has a really good point. We are both nervous about starting our new place. In fact, with our focus being appetizers and wine, we want it to be intimate, right?"

"I know you are right," Carolyn said. "I just keep picturing a front porch or patio so we could sit outside. But why don't we go look at it together and see what you think. Maybe you will see the potential I missed."

"Ok, I definitely want to see it, if for no other reason than to try to gauge the size and determine if we should keep looking. After we look at it together, I'll get Mike to go by it and do some measurements. You know, he is the best person to figure out if there is room for the kind of bar and seating areas we are thinking of and still have room for an effective kitchen," said Kacey, giving Carolyn a "please?" kind of look.

"Ok, Josie, can you show us tomorrow at lunch time? Obviously, we can't risk losing it, if it turns out to be the right spot."

Josie pulled out her iPhone and checked her calendar. "Yes ladies, that works for me. Say noon?" Kacey and Carolyn nodded as they clinked their glasses and drank a swig of their prosecco.

Carolyn was a little dismayed thinking about the plantation home. But then she had a thought. "Actually, what you said earlier may be just the answer! If we get the smaller place, get our reputation for spectacular cuisine and atmosphere out there, when not if we need more space, we can move to the plantation home! By then Scott will have the renovations done, like in a year or two." She beamed.

Kacey shook her head and said, "That sounds like a great plan and if we end up not needing the extra space, maybe you and Scott could turn it into an event place, or a bed and breakfast or something else." Carolyn raised her eyebrows and grinned, nodding her head.

"Well, now girls," Josie started then sipped her martini, "let's not get ahead of ourselves on the plantation home. I haven't even gotten a call back from the family that owns it yet although I have left two messages. I'll keep trying though."

Carolyn was disappointed but said, "I figured that might happen. When I stopped by the other day, their neighbor, the only next door neighbor, said they take very little interest in the place but feel guilty about selling it since it's been in the family for over a century. I will see if Scott can do some digging too. He finally got his historical renovation license and knew a little about the home. We'll keep approaching it from that end and see what we turn up. There must be some way to make them feel comfortable selling it, especially if they don't have time to keep up such a beautiful, important home. Well, I need to head out, but I will see you girls tomorrow at the Canton Street place." Carolyn hugged them both then walked to the edge of the dance floor in time to see Angel doing one-handed pushups on the floor. The crowd was counting out loud and cheering her on. Carolyn put her hands over her mouth to keep from laughing then got Mia and Lucy's attention and waved good night.

Chapter 7
June 10, 2010

J osie met Kacey and Carolyn on the corner of Canton and Webb. As the girls approached, Josie thought maybe today was the day they would make the decision to go for it. There weren't going to be many more chances. Most of the restaurant and store front space was under lease for years and were long standing successful businesses. The last restaurant in this spot moved because they wanted more space, but she felt confident these two ladies could make the space work with their concept. They communicated and compromised really well and were similar in some ways but had just the right amount of differences to keep it interesting and creative.

"Is that it across the street?" Kacey asked.

"It sure is, Hon. I wanted you to get a glimpse of it from in front of one of your competitors! Folks come to this restaurant," pointing at the competitor's restaurant, "because it's been here a long time, has great food and service. But the patrons will see you building out your space across the street and their curiosity will get the best of them. They will be sure to try it. I don't know much about running a restaurant," Josie smiled, "but I do know what I like. Yummy food, smooth wine and a hip atmosphere and the place will be hopping. You know I will be a frequent customer and of course I will spread the word! It's the perfect location."

Carolyn laughed. "Thanks Josie, that's good to know! So let's take a look and I'm not going to say anything. Why don't you walk Kacey through the place and she can come to her own conclusion and then we can talk about it." Carolyn had only to look at Kacey's face to see that her wheels were already turning. She looked extremely focused. She was probably trying very hard to make the space work because of the location. Josie did have an excellent point about that. Carolyn hung back a little while the two women walked across the street.

Josie began her tour. "So the first thing you will notice is the awning and the bay windows. From the outside those are two features that capture the passerby's attention because they protrude out farther than the two adjacent store fronts. Now the door should probably be replaced. It's a little worn, but I do like that it has a window from top to bottom. I think that is really important because the space faces west and you will get the afternoon sun in through the bays and the door." She turned to look at Carolyn who was walking slowly behind. She smiled at Carolyn knowing that she had to sell them both in order to get them to move on this place. "Carolyn, I know you want a patio or porch, but if you really work these bay window spaces well, you can still get the feel of being outside. I recommend you put tables in the bays. I would bet those would be prime seating areas. You may even want to consider making the windows the kind that you can open. That will give the feel of bringing the outside in."

Carolyn raised her eyebrows and nodded in agreement. "That's a good point," she said. She looked at Kacey, who was already looking around and up and down with a look of curiosity on her face. Carolyn realized this wasn't just her dream. She needed to be a good partner and really pay attention to what Kacey wanted as well. Kacey looked over at her then at Josie. Josie looked away so she could give the women a moment to communicate. She could tell that Kacey wasn't ready to say anything out loud yet but wanted to at least give Carolyn the look that said, "It has possibilities". That was a start.

The restaurant was one large room that had been gutted. It was only still considered a restaurant because the prior tenants had left the hood and the grease trap. The good news was it was a clean slate. The bad news was they would have to buy all new appliances, build a bar, and equip the kitchen.

Kacey walked around looking, tilting her head, making notes. She even looked out the back door.

"Ok, you are killing me!" said Carolyn. "What are you thinking?"

Kacey looked at Carolyn and slowly her grin grew to a full smile then to a pleading look as she walked over to Carolyn. "We can make this work. Humor me here." She turned and started showing Carolyn with long brush strokes with her arms, where she thought the bar would go, where the tables would be placed, where the kitchen would be built out. "I really think Josie has an excellent point about the bay windows but did you look out back? The alley actually is very open and quiet. We could consider building a patio out there too. That would give us some outdoor space when the weather is just too nice to be inside. We could make it private and romantic with the right kind of lighting and fencing. We could even add a fire pit, like you want. I figure we could seat forty people comfortably including the bar stools then another ten if we build the patio out back. That would get us to the income we had agreed we would need to move forward. That is of course if we can keep them coming in. But we have to start with the space and I really don't think we should risk passing it up. Are you still concerned about the size, Carolyn?"

"Well, you know what they say, "Size does matter!" But you are right, if we can get forty people in here that would meet our minimum space requirement to meet our target revenue. Why don't you and I go to my house and do our Benjamin Franklin."

"Benjamin Franklin? What does that mean?" asked Kacey.

"Oh right, sorry, that's an old sales tool. You put the positives on the left hand side of a piece of paper and you list the negatives on the right hand side and see which one outweighs the other. I have a feeling I already know the outcome but it would be important to document why we thought we could make a go at it here and then hopefully one day soon, we will be looking back and realizing we had made the right choice. Let's go over the business plan again too now that you have done a quick layout of bar size, tables, and the kitchen. Thanks Josie, we will give you a call by tomorrow morning. Thanks again for your help and your patience!" With that, Carolyn put her arm around Kacey's shoulders and said, "Let's go partner!"

Back at Carolyn's house, the two sat at the kitchen table with a glass of ice tea and chicken salad sandwiches. Kacey looked around the kitchen. "You two have really put a lot of work into this place. It looks fantastic. I like what you did with the brick over the stove. Now that you are just finishing your home are you sure you are up for renovating a restaurant and helping Scott with the historical home as well?"

"Well that's really the question, isn't it? Are we talking about one restaurant slash historical home, or are we talking about two different places. The historical home will mostly be Scott's responsibility unless we think we want to turn it into a restaurant down the road. I am really looking forward to hearing more about what he has uncovered about that house. I can't believe it's been in the same family since the 1800's. That's amazing! You know, with my Navy brat upbringing, it's hard for me to imagine staying in one town more than a couple of years. And our family is spread out all over the U.S.; I can't wait for my parents to come in town next weekend. Anyway, I digress. Why don't we start with the business plan and plug in the forty seats, we'll use that as a minimum and see what that does to the revenue and the expense calculations. Obviously, with a small place, we won't need as many employees as we had originally thought."

"I agree. Carolyn, I really do have a good feeling about the space on Canton. It's ideal from a location perspective. Smack in the middle of the shops. And even though we would be right across the street from the most popular restaurant, I agree with Josie, that gives us more visibility. Our concept is different from theirs so it should be friendly competition. In fact, people can come to our place when they can't get in over there because the wait is too long! They can also come to our place for either a glass of wine before their dinner at another restaurant or for dessert afterwards. That's even more reason to be in the middle of them all. I say we go for it. It's the right price to get started quickly." They updated the business case, and then put the Ben Franklin down on paper.

Kacey stopped talking then and sat back. As Carolyn had always joked, "Don't sell past the close!" She needed to give Carolyn the time to think it through and not pressure her. The decision needed to be both of theirs and they both had to be confident in the success.

Carolyn took their plates to the sink and then turned to Kacey. "Ok, I think I am there. The business case works, the Benjamin Franklin is a no brainer, but I promised Scott that I wouldn't make any decisions without at least telling him what we have decided before we sign anything. I will talk to him tonight. You go home and talk to Mike and then give me a call. We can call Josie first thing in the morning. Sound like a plan?"

"Sounds like a plan!" Kacey grabbed her new bag that Carolyn had given her for her birthday, gave Carolyn a big hug and Diamond and Ruby a pat on the head. Then she waved as she walked out the door.

Chapter 8
June 10, 2010

Daniel Greyson stared out over the Atlanta skyline from his thirty-fifth floor office. He couldn't believe it had been two years since the tornado tore through town and busted out many of the windows in the Westin. He also couldn't believe they still hadn't replaced them; something about how hard the windows were to make because they were rounded. Expensive too, he imagined. He was glad he wasn't in their rotating bar or outdoor elevator at the time. That had to have been scary as hell, he thought. His office building had sustained a little damage, but it had long since been repaired. Appearance is everything.

His Executive Assistant Holly, said through the speaker, "your sister is on line one, Mr. Greyson."

Turning from the window Daniel took a seat in his high back leather chair behind the desk. "Hello, Christina. How is New York?"

"New York is FAB! I think I might be getting the promotion to assistant editor! Just imagine, a southern belle like me, running one of the top fashion magazines in the country!"

"So being Assistant Editor gives you that much power, huh?" Daniel chided.

"It's just a stepping stone. I'll be running this place before you know it! Anyway, I got your message. What's up?" Christina was multi-tasking as usual. Her boss had sent her out for the samples at Ralph Lauren, so she had stopped at the Panera Bread on the corner. The line was long as usual so she thought she would call her brother to scratch that one off her to-do list.

"I got a call from a realtor in Roswell asking about the house. Apparently, there is a potential buyer who is thinking about turning it into a restaurant. I know we agreed to sit on the property but it is taking a lot of time for me to keep it up and I could really use the cash with the market as it is right now. I have got some pretty sizeable international funds I would like to invest in, but I'm afraid to dip into my reserves again. This last recession really hurt." Ok, so maybe he wasn't taking a lot of time, in fact any time on the house, but she didn't need to know that.

"But Daniel, we promised Mom and Dad that we wouldn't sell it. We promised that we would keep passing it down. And they stated that in their will. Of course, we have to have someone to pass it down to and that doesn't look like it's going to happen anytime soon since neither of us have a significant other."

Daniel laughed. "You know, twenty-five is right around the corner, not that the clock is ticking loudly."

"Thanks for reminding me. What about you? You will be turning thirty next year. Anyway, I don't have time to get my hair done much less a guy. Ha, that was pretty funny, don't you think? I still don't know if I could sell it and let them turn it into a restaurant. Great Grandpa would turn over in his grave! I don't think so. If anything, I picture it being a museum like the other plantation homes. I would be afraid that the restaurant wouldn't succeed, and then what? It would get sold over and over, remodeling it every time. Chinese one day, Italian the next? I say no to the restaurant idea."

"Ok, I have to agree with you there. I'll let the realtor know. Well, little sister, I need to get back to my clients and I am sure you are in the middle of something really pressing as well. I'll talk to you soon. Don't be a stranger. Love you."

Daniel and Christina hung up just in time for Christina to place her salad order.

The realtor had also made a comment about the place looking pretty run down. I guess I better get by there and check on it, Daniel grumbled to himself. I don't understand how that can be. I pay a fortune to take care of it. Daniel dialed the number to the house. No answer. Then he dialed his caretaker Clint's cell phone number. Again, no answer. He left a message for Clint to call him back then went about his business.

Later that afternoon, Daniel realized he still had not heard from Clint. That's odd, he thought. He decided to drive out to Roswell and see what was going on. Did Clint quit and I didn't get the memo? He put his things in his briefcase and headed out of the office. "Forward my calls to my cell, Holly. I have to run out to the plantation. I will see you in the morning."

"Will do, Mr. Greyson." Such a shame, thought Holly. He was so cute but obviously not for her since he was her boss. She loved that dark hair and those doe eyes. Just her luck, she thought as she shook her head.

Daniel made his way up 400 to Northridge then over to Roswell Road and headed north. He couldn't imagine living this far OTP. There was an acronym for everything these days. "Outside the Perimeter", he laughed to himself. I wonder who came up with that one. Maybe they should look at selling the place. He certainly wasn't spending any time there and who knew when Christina would be back in town for any period of time. He could really use the money. They would make a fortune selling it. He first needed to figure out what was going on with Clint. If he skipped town without even giving Daniel a heads up, he definitely would have his head. The whole point of letting Clint live there was to keep it up to date and clean; ready for anyone to visit, just in case.

He made his way up Canton Street and turned left on Rock Way then right onto Millstone. He couldn't believe his eyes. He could see the house at the end of the street and the landscaping was overgrown. How could this have happened? There were vines growing out of control up the front of the house and weeds in the front yard. It actually looked pretty creepy. How long had it been since he had been by? He figured it had been at least six months. Well shame on him. He pulled up in the circular drive to the front of the house and ran up the porch. He used his key to let himself in. He tried to turn the light switch on and nothing happened.

"Clint? Clint! Are you here?" There was no sound except the sound of his footsteps on the hardwood floor. It was almost dusk at this point, so it was very difficult to see in the foyer. He went back to the front door and left it open hoping for a little light to guide his way. He went to the hall table and opened a drawer looking for matches. He was in luck. He struck a match and found a candle in a candlestick on the small table and lit it. He picked up the candlestick and walked toward the kitchen in the back of the house. The smell was horrendous.

"What the...," he scrunched up his nose in disgust at the smell. Clint had obviously left food on the counter and it had spoiled. Where was Clint and worst yet, how long had he been gone? "Clint, are you here?" Again, no answer. He heard a creaking noise above him. He decided to look upstairs. He slowly climbed the stairs, getting more nervous by the minute. "Clint?" he muttered. No longer with the intensity of the last few times he had called Clint's name. "Come on Clint, this is not funny." He decided to check out a couple of rooms then get out of there and come back when it was light out. He figured he needed to call an electrician to see what the problem was. He noticed that a window was open and a shutter was hanging by one hinge. That must have been what the creaking noise was. After looking quickly through a few of the bedrooms and sitting rooms, with no luck, he swiftly made his way back to the staircase and flew down them. He went back out the front door, locked it, got into his car and headed home to his house in Buckhead.

"How soon can you get over there?" asked Daniel.

"I could meet you there between nine and noon tomorrow morning. Will that work?" asked the electrician.

"Is that the best you can do? Can't you narrow it down a little? I am a very busy man."

"I'm sorry that's the best I can do, but it will probably be closer to noon than to nine, if that helps."

"Great," said Daniel sarcastically. He had to get this mess straightened out. He was still feeling uneasy about his visit to the plantation. He had the chills. He picked up the phone and called the realtor back.

"Josie, this is Daniel Greyson calling you back about your interested party. I have spoken with my sister and we have decided that we can't sell the place if it is going to be turned into a restaurant. It just wouldn't be right. Our parents were adamant that we keep the house in the family, although it is just Christina and I at this point. If you do come across someone that would keep it as a home, we might be interested in discussing that."

"Well, I know my client will be very disappointed. However, I may know someone that might be interested in keeping it as a home. Can you give me a ballpark on what you would be willing to sell it for?"

Daniel gave her a number. "I am a little flexible on the number since I haven't had the opportunity to research what it might be worth right now."

"I can help you with that by researching some of the other similar homes in Roswell that have sold in the last year. I will see what I can find out. Let me talk to my clients and I will call you back." Josie hung up and called Carolyn. "Carolyn, have you and Kacey decided on the space on Canton Street?" She was hoping that they would move forward with that property and then it wouldn't be such a blow that the Greysons weren't interested in turning the plantation home into a restaurant.

"Yes, in fact, I was just about to call you. We went over our business case and also spoke with our husbands and we are all in agreement that at least as a start, this is the right property for us. We would like to lease the space. Did you ever hear back from the Greysons? I would really like to at least keep that as an option for down the road." Carolyn was glad that a decision had been made to move into the heart of Historic Roswell. It was going to be quite the challenge but also very exciting. She couldn't help but want to hang onto the idea of owning a plantation home and turning it into something spectacular though.

"Actually, I just spoke with Daniel Greyson. They do not want to sell it to someone who will turn it into a restaurant. I'm sorry, Carolyn. It's really not an option as a backup plan. Do you want me to let the landlord know that you will take the Canton Street property as is?"

"Well that's a shame. But yes, let's move forward with Canton Street. Wait a minute. You said that they don't want to sell it to someone who will turn it into a restaurant. Does that mean they are open to selling now?"

"They will consider speaking with someone who would renovate it and keep it as a plantation home. Does anyone come to mind?" Josie kidded. She knew that Scott had just received his historical renovation license and he would be looking for his first project. The question would be if he could afford something this size. It would clearly be a remarkable adventure for him. She knew his goal was to purchase a historical property, renovate it, then sell it and move onto another historical property with the profit he made from the first and so on.

Carolyn smiled, knowingly. "I think I might."

Daniel Greyson got out of his Porsche in the plantation's driveway. He looked around and not seeing the electrician's truck, decided to pay Frank a visit. He walked across the lawn and rang the bell. "Hello, Frank. Long time, no see."

"Hello, Daniel," Frank responded, sounding disappointed. He peered at Daniel, surprised at the visit and still irritated about the shape the house next door was in.

"Do you have a minute? I have been trying to reach Clint and he has not been answering my calls. When was the last time you saw him? I'm thinking he must have taken off, but he didn't let me know, and he didn't even cash his last check."

Frank did not invite Daniel in and stood squarely in the doorway. "Well, it seems like the last time I saw him was about two months ago. He was carrying some Home Depot bags into the house. I assumed he was doing some repairs and then I was surprised that I didn't see him again. I thought you let him go. You know he usually parks his truck around back by the old carriage house. Did you look to see if it was there?"

"Actually, no. I hadn't thought about that. I figured since he wasn't here, his car wouldn't be here. That's a good idea. I will take a look out back. Thanks, Frank. How is your daughter by the way?"

"She is just fine, thank you," said Frank, matter of factly.

The electrician had pulled into the drive. Daniel thanked Frank for his time and walked back to the house.

The electrician held out his hand. "Thank you for your patience, sir. My name is D. Just D."

"Ok, D. I'm Daniel Greyson. It's no problem. Let me show you into the house." Daniel and the electrician walked down the hall leaving the front door open again for light and Daniel stopped at the door to the basement. "The electrical box is down there. Not my favorite place in the world. Why don't you take a look and I will be back in a few minutes. I need to check something out." D. nodded and pulled out his flashlight, opened the basement door and headed down the stairs.

Daniel walked through the kitchen, noting the rotten food again. He went to the back door and looked out. He was surprised to see that Clint's truck was there by the carriage house. He had an instant feeling of dread. He went out to the truck to inspect it. The door was unlocked and nothing seemed out of sorts. He stood there scratching his head when D. yelled out. "Mr. Greyson! I found your caretaker. Well, what used to be your caretaker, I assume."

Chapter 9
April 21, 1838

Someone was pounding on the door. When Ben opened the door he was surprised to see the new master with Jade. She was looking at the ground. Ben moved aside so they could enter.

"You will keep her here," said David Greyson as he pushed her inside.

Jade stood right inside the door and didn't move, only continued to look down at the floor.

Ben felt his stomach twist. He led her to the table and pulled a chair out, motioning for her to sit down. She did.

Theresa came into the room drying her hands on a towel. "What is it?" she said eyeing David and the girl.

"You will keep her here. Make room for her. I will need her at the house from time to time and I will come get her when I do," responded David.

Jade continued to stare at the floor.

David left the slave house and went back to the plantation house.

Theresa went over to Jade and asked her if she was alright. She was terrified at the thought of what David Greyson had been doing with this young Indian girl since yesterday. Oh, where was Sam? Why had he not returned from town? She prayed that he had not been caught, but she had no way of knowing. She couldn't ask their new master. He had said that he would kill any of them if they left the slave house. She had done her best to keep the rest of the slaves in the house and from being restless. Please Lord, please let him be alive. How will we go on without Sam? She couldn't think about that right now. She nervously smoothed her hands over her hair insuring that her bun was still tidy.

Theresa carefully pulled Jade up out of the chair. "Come with me Jade," Theresa said, and guided her out the back of the slave house to the outhouse. "Stay right here. I will be right back." She walked over to the well and drew a bucket of water. She took a rag and went back to the girl. Jade began to tremble. Theresa said, "It will be alright. You are safe with us. We will take care of you, Jade. I know you have had a terrible loss but things will get better. You are safe." Theresa wondered at her own words. Could she make such a promise? The words seemed empty.

"Are you in any pain?" Theresa asked as she cleaned Jade's skin with the rag and water.

Jade didn't answer. She just continued to look at the ground and sob quietly.

"Please honey. Please tell me if you are feeling any pain. I want to help you and keep you safe." Theresa's voice cracked as she tried not to picture the horrendous ordeal that this girl had been through. She had seen both of her parents killed and had learned that Michael had been killed as well. Then her two older brothers had been sent away. She must feel completely alone. And then on top of it all, she may have been abused. Would she ever recover? She cleaned Jade up as best as she could. She pulled Jade into her arms to try to comfort her against her large bosom but Jade froze, stiff in the embrace.

Theresa walked Jade slowly back into the slave house.

Ben had made a bed for her in the corner, near Theresa's bed. He had understood correctly that Jade would need to be close to someone whom she trusted. He wasn't sure if Jade trusted his mother, but it had to be a far cry from being with the master. He did not want to know what the master had done to her in the main house or why he said he would bring her back from time to time. He felt sorry for Jade that she had lost her family yesterday. He stood watching her with his hands in his pockets, shuffling his feet.

Theresa helped Jade lay down on the bed that Ben had made. She touched her forehead and then ran her hand down her hair. Jade pushed her hand away and rolled over to put her back to her. She began to sob again. The crying went on for another hour or so before she finally drifted off into a fitful sleep.

Theresa awoke to find Jade standing at the open front door staring at the place in the yard where her parents had been killed. She was no longer crying but her shoulders were slumped. Theresa came to stand next to her and lightly touched Jade's shoulder. Jade pulled away. Theresa went to the kitchen and made breakfast for everyone. They all sat around the long table in the kitchen area and spoke in soft voices. They were respectful of Jade's pain and were also still afraid for Sam since he had not returned. Jade would not eat or even come to the table. When Theresa looked up, Jade was no longer standing at the door. Theresa got up from the table and looked outside but she did not see her. She went into the room where they all slept and found Jade curled up in her bed facing the wall. Theresa figured she was exhausted and needed some space. She prayed that this girl would find peace. Sally, one of the young slave girls brought over her blanket and laid it over Jade. Ben came up beside Theresa and took her hand. He looked up at her and Theresa saw the sadness in his eyes. He was a good boy and was becoming so much like his father. Ben and Jade were the same age and she knew that Ben would protect Jade as best that he could.

Jade dreamed of her parents and happier days. They were a family again living in their plantation home and she was showing off a new dress. Her mother had sewn flowers across the bottom. Her father and mother clapped and she spun around and around. Then suddenly someone grabbed her arm and turned her around. It was him. He laughed a loud, evil laugh and started dragging her up the stairs. She screamed for her parents to save her, holding her arm out to them, begging them to help her. Her mother and father reached out their arms to her then slowly faded away.

Jade woke with a start. It was a nightmare - one of many to come.

Chapter 10
June 20, 2010

C arolyn, sitting in one of the chairs on her front porch, put her head back and took a deep breath. "It's always good to win the division, but just once I'd like to make it to State," she said scrunching up her nose in frustration. She was relaxing on the porch with her parents and Scott. Her parents had come up from Pensacola for the weekend.

"You should be proud, Carolyn. You and Kacey played really well and won all of your matches this season. You really can't do any more than that. And think about it, you two have only been playing a few years. Most of the girls played in high school and college." Scott was proud of her and really enjoyed cheering her on. That was more fun to him than playing eighteen holes. He wasn't sure how much tennis or golf they were going to get in once they started the restaurant, but time would tell. Hopefully, they would be successful enough to hire a manager and take Sundays off. "Are you going to take a nap?"

"No, I am tired but I really want to talk about the house more and you never did tell me the rest of the story about the Trail of Tears. Are you two interested in hearing about it too?" Carolyn asked her mom and dad. The four of them were very close. Her parents really liked Scott and respected what he did for a living. Her dad was retired Navy and was always doing projects around the house, just like Scott. Scott thought that was one of the reasons they got along so well. Her mother liked him too because she could see how much he loved Carolyn.

"Yes, you told us about the restaurant, but I do want to hear more about the historical home," her Dad said, putting his newspaper down. Since he had retired he made it a point to stay up on the latest news. He put his hand over her mother's. They were both fifty-five, very attractive and healthy and had been married since they were nineteen. The older they got the more dedicated they seemed to be towards each other. Her father had reddish-blond hair and blue eyes and her mother was just starting to color her dark hair blonde since she was going grey. Carolyn always pictured her mother in her dark hair and then was surprised to see her blonde when she came to visit. She knew she would eventually get used to it and regardless, her mother was beautiful either way. Carolyn had been blessed with her mother's big brown eyes.

"Me too. Are you sure you two aren't getting in over your heads?" asked her mom.

"Well, we definitely don't want that either. I heard from Josie and I don't see how we can afford the house. Even with the investors, I am not sure we want to go that much into debt, especially with you opening the restaurant in a few months," Scott said looking at Carolyn. "I think it's too much to take on right now," sounding disappointed. "But I did send the investors the details and we'll see what they say."

"I hope it works out," replied Carolyn. "There is just something about that house that makes me feel like it needs us. Tell me more about it. You said the other night you were looking up the information about it?"

"Yes, it was built sometime around 1830. There is no exact record of the date it was built because it was built by Cherokee Indians who were sent on the Trail of Tears. The Greysons won the land and the plantation home in the land lottery in 1838. Apparently, there was a Cherokee family living in it at the time and they were kicked out and sent west with the other Indians. There are no details about how all of that happened. Just that it belonged to a Cherokee family, named Hawkins, and then it belonged to the Greysons."

Carolyn furrowed her brow. "That's terrible. I don't understand how they could have won the land that belonged to someone else, Indian or not. Who allowed that to happen?"

"The story behind the Trail of Tears began when gold was discovered in Northwest Georgia, including Roswell. Gold is what enticed the whites to move into the area. Andrew Jackson, who was the president at the time, must have been a greedy son of gun because he was the one that started the whole thing. He told the white folks to just take the property. But the Indians fought back. I don't know if you know this, I didn't, but the Cherokee Indians were actually very sophisticated and educated. They were believed to be the one tribe that was actually able to integrate with the whites because they had sincerely made an effort to live like the whites."

"Really?" asked Carolyn. "I didn't know that. I always pictured them in loin cloths and feathers with bows and arrows living in tee-pees. That's not how they were?"

"No," her mom interjected. "I read about it. Scott is right."

Scott smiled. It was always a good thing when your mother-in-law thought you were right. "In fact, they had developed their own alphabet and were the only tribe that could read and write and that helped them to learn the English language so they could communicate. They really tried hard to assimilate to keep the peace. Obviously, never realizing it wouldn't matter, and eventually, they would lose everything anyway. Their Indian chief had gone to the U.S. Supreme Court Justice protesting the takeover of their land. The Supreme Court ruled in their favor but Andrew Jackson defied

CINDI CRANE

it. According to some information I read, he is the only president in our history who has ever defied a Supreme Court ruling. Jackson told the governor to give out the land in a lottery, so Wilson Lumpkin, the governor, did just that. He basically split up the land into forty acre plots and conducted a land lottery. The Cherokee even had some mixed marriages. In fact, the Cherokee chief that ended up being the chief for about forty years was a half breed and he married a white woman. That might have been why he was able to negotiate some relief for the Indians. When they finally got to Oklahoma, this chief, John Ross, helped them build a new life. So I guess in the end, at least they had a place to start over. But don't you think that's sad about them losing their homes right here where we live?"

"Yes, you are right it is sad," Carolyn's dad said. "I didn't realize the Cherokee land came this far south. I thought it was further north in Georgia. That's interesting."

Carolyn nodded. "It is also sad that there aren't any tributes to the Indians in Roswell. I rarely hear any stories about them other than they were here before the Trail of Tears, obviously."

"Well, there are several Indian mounds up in Northwest Georgia that have been preserved and there are parks around them that tell the story," Scott said. "There is also a town called Cherokee in North Carolina, where some of the Indians fled, so they wouldn't have to go west. But yeah, not a lot is talked about them here in Roswell. The City of Roswell didn't become the City of Roswell until after the Indians were gone and the original white founders either built their plantation homes on the land they won or lived in the Indian's homes. The Cherokee owned plantations and slaves and were farmers too. Barrington, Bulloch and Smith plantations were built in the late 1830s. That's why this Greyson house is even more interesting. If this is an original Cherokee Indian built home, that's even more reason to preserve it. In fact, just talking about it makes me want to do something about it. I'm going to call the investors and get their

— 60 —

thoughts on it first thing tomorrow morning."

Carolyn looked at Scott and realized that they had to find a way to make this work. She hoped that her opening a restaurant wasn't going to ruin his plans after all of his hard work getting his preservation license. It would be wonderful to truly make a difference with this house. It would also be important to make it known, that this was originally a Cherokee Indian home. That would be in a very small way, a way to give back – a bit of redemption for Roswell.

The foursome relaxed on the porch for a while and then Carolyn and her mom went inside to look at the new quilt book her mom had brought up from Pensacola. She had been making beautiful, intricate quilts for years. She refused to sell them but made sure her family enjoyed them year round. She had just finished making several for Carolyn's brother's family in Maryland so it was Carolyn's turn for a new one. Carolyn had asked her to make this next one a historical quilt where the fabrics were reproductions. They both wanted to surprise Scott with it in honor of his certification. They knew that being wrapped in a quilt made from love and history would inspire Scott.

Chapter 11
June 21, 2010

That Monday, Carolyn's parents headed home. Carolyn and Scott promised to keep them updated. Scott spoke with the investors who informed him that although they were very interested in restoring historical homes, especially in the Roswell area, the funds were not available for such an expensive project. They asked him to find additional investors or a smaller property. Apparently, they were willing to put up about a quarter of the price of the house. Scott was extremely disappointed and called Josie to let her know he was going to have to find more investors with the price being what it was. Josie had informed Scott that she would let the owners know.

When Josie contacted Daniel Greyson, Daniel was also disappointed because now that Clint had perished on the property, he had to find another caretaker and deal with the local police as they were investigating Clint's accident. The police had assured Daniel they would move expeditiously, but they needed to be thorough. So far, they had not uncovered anything other than what appeared to be an accident.

Daniel called Christina to tell her what had happened to Clint. "Ok, so maybe I haven't paid enough attention to the house. It's very difficult working downtown, living in Buckhead and taking care of this monster of a house in Roswell. I wish you lived here so you could help me."

Christina made a huffing noise. "Well, let's talk about me. Not only did I not get my promotion to assistant editor, god knows what they are thinking, they gave the job to James, who has half the experience I do! I think I have hit the proverbial glass ceiling. It is so unfair. Do you think I should sue?"

Daniel was actually pleased with the news. "Not only should you not sue them because it would be very difficult to prove and tie up more of your funds but it would also take a lot of time to work through the case. If you sue them, it could give you a bad rep in the business. I think you need to come back home. There are plenty of opportunities here and you can help me take care of this damn house!"

"Daniel, is that the only reason you want me to come home? I have really tried hard to build a life here in New York and going home makes me feel like I am going back with my tail between my legs. I wouldn't be able to face all of my friends after I made such a big deal about making it in the Big Apple and how small town Atlanta really is," Christina protested.

"No one will think less of you. It's a tough time right now. It's not like you got fired or even laid off; you just didn't get the promotion you wanted. You don't even have to tell anyone about that. You know, I have been thinking about what you said about turning the house into a museum or events place. How about if you get back here and make that happen? I think we owe it to Mom and Dad to do something with this house. Leaving it vacant with some caretaker living in it isn't what they had in mind."

Christina was quiet for a few minutes. "Hmmm. That's actually not a bad idea. Once I got the place up and running, I could start my own magazine. Maybe a travel magazine or a magazine about the history of Roswell and events in Roswell. That would drive people to our place, of course. Alright, let me think about it for a few days and I will call you back."

The next day, the police called Daniel to tell him that they were ruling Clint's death an accident. One of the steps had a nail that was sticking up and based on the amount of paint cans around Clint when they found him, they deduced that he had tripped over the nail head and lost his balance, tumbling down the stairs. Since it was Clint's responsibility to care for the property and the fact that no one else had visited the home in months, there was no reason to believe that there could have been anyone else involved. The policeman then laughed and told him, "Unless you believe in ghosts." Daniel didn't think that was funny, because he did in fact believe in ghosts. How could he not, growing up in a house that old? He didn't want to think about that though.

Daniel paid for the funeral arrangements for Clint and attended the small service the next day. There was only one other gentleman at the funeral who said that he was a long time friend of Clint's. He then asked Daniel for a job. At first, Daniel was offended that this man would solicit him for his friend's job before he was even six feet under, but he realized he still needed help at the house at least until Christina made up her mind about what she was going to do. He gave the man his card and asked him to call in a few days.

"Well, the more I thought about it, the more excited I got," Christina said. "For one, it's nice to know that my big brother needs me. I think this is the first time you have even admitted that you do. But secondly, it would be great to honor Mom and Dad this way. I think they would be really happy knowing we care about the house and making it something special. And thirdly, I do miss my friends and maybe it would be a way to meet someone and start a family. I always thought if I did ever have a family, Roswell would be the perfect town to do that in. You think there are any new guys there?"

"How would I know since I haven't been spending any time there? But they say Roswell is one of the fastest growing cities in

Georgia, so it would make sense that there would be more guys. I am really glad to hear about your news and I can't wait to see you. When are you coming home?" Daniel relaxed feeling things were falling into place.

"I should be there at the end of the month. That way I will have given my employer two week's notice and I can leave on good terms. I do have a question though. Where are we going to get the money to make the renovations and turn the house into a museum or events facility? I haven't decided yet which way to go but either way, I definitely don't have the money to do that and as you know, I can't get into my trust fund for another five years."

"Interesting that you would ask that. The realtor that has been calling me called yesterday to tell me the guy that wants to buy the place and restore it historically, doesn't have what he needs to buy it, much less restore it, so he was not going to be able to make an offer. Why don't I set up a meeting with him and see if we can hire him to do the renovations, and also see if we can get his investors to invest with us?"

"This seems too good to be true!" Christina sounded more excited than she did when she thought she was getting the promotion. Daniel felt really good about that. "Do you know if this guy is single?"

"I don't know anything about him, but we both will when we meet him. I'll see if I can get a meeting with him the first week of July. Christina, I am really glad you are coming home."

Chapter 12
July 2, 2010

"Honey, I am so sorry but I am going to be about fifteen minutes late. The leasing agent was running behind on his last appointment. Go ahead and order me an unsweet tea and a grilled Chicken Salad. I will be there as fast as I can. And Scott, I love you. I am so happy!" beamed Carolyn. It was all coming together. She hung up with Scott and looked at Kacey and Josie who were sitting across from her in the waiting room and they all grinned. "Are you nervous?" she asked Kacey.

"A little, but more thrilled than nervous. I can't believe it's really happening. Just think, in about three months, we will have our grand opening. I have an interview this afternoon with two chefs. I know you have your lunch meeting, but as soon as you finish come to the restaurant to meet them okay?" Kacey asked.

"I will. I'll need to run home and let the dogs out, but I'll get there as soon as I can. I am very glad they were able to lease the space to us instead of selling it to us. This will give us a chance to make a go of it before we get in too deep over our heads. Thank you so much Josie for all of your help."

"And patience!" chimed in Kacey.

"It has been my pleasure and I wish you the success that I know is coming your way," replied Josie.

The leasing agent poked his head in the room and said, "Kacey and Carolyn?"

"That would be us!" said Kacey.

"Well, I have all the paperwork prepared if you two are ready to sign," said the agent. "Josie was very helpful in assisting me to get these ready so that we can have a quick meeting. I understand you two are very busy ladies."

"Bring it on," replied Carolyn. "We couldn't be more ready." Paperwork completed, Carolyn and Kacey said their goodbyes and Carolyn rushed to meet Scott and the Greysons for their lunch meeting.

"Hi, I am so sorry I am late but it is very nice to meet you!" Carolyn shook hands with Christina and Daniel and kissed Scott on the cheek. Carolyn could tell that they were brother and sister. They had dark hair and warm brown eyes and were both very attractive.

"It's not a problem," Christina said, "we were just talking about where we went to college. Turns out you and I both attended Georgia and the guys both attended Georgia Tech. So you must know what I go through during football season every year! It's a major competition between Daniel and me!"

"I know what you mean. We wear our jerseys, order a pizza and rib each other all through the games. It's a blast. I am not sure how much time we are going to have to watch this year, much less attend any of the games with the projects we are taking on, or in this case, hoping to take on. Did Scott tell you that I decided to lease some restaurant space on Canton Street for our restaurant?"

"Yes," Daniel replied, "he just mentioned it. I guess congratulations are in order. You just signed, right?"

"Yes, with my partner, Kacey. We are ecstatic to be getting it going and right in the heart of Roswell. I had concerns at first because I had hoped for a historical place where we could have a patio. But we have some ideas on how to "bring the outside in" as our realtor put it. I will definitely let you know when we have our grand opening. I hope you can join us."

Scott smiled. He was extremely proud of Carolyn for following her dreams. Now it was his turn. "So, we know you don't want to turn your home into a restaurant and we definitely understand. Can you tell me about this idea you have?"

"Absolutely," responded Daniel. "In fact, Christina, why don't you tell them what you have in mind?"

"Ok. It turns out that I am homesick. I love New York, but it hasn't worked out quite the way I thought it would. I have three years of excellent editorial experience under my belt, but it's time to make a change. When Daniel called me about your interest in our plantation home, my first thought was we couldn't sell it because that would be defying our parents' wishes. They both died in a car accident five years ago."

"I'm so sorry," said Carolyn.

"Thank you, it's been very difficult. Their estate was tied up in probate for the first two years. The family they hit sued us in a civil suit, even though the police ruled it as an accident. Our father had a heart attack while driving and his car swerved into the other lane and hit the family head on. The mother was killed instantly and one of the children died later at the hospital. The father and the daughter were obviously grief stricken. We settled out of court but not because we felt that Father did anything wrong. We know the accident was not his fault. However, we felt that we wanted to give them some type of financial support for their losses. Our parents died instantly." Christina's voice quivered. "It was a terrible couple of years, wasn't it Daniel?"

"It was. The accident affected so many lives. I guess the shape that the house is in reflects how we have been feeling. Pretty much disheartened; down in the dumps, so to speak." Daniel looked away momentarily. He had really tried to help his little sister, but it was so difficult considering he couldn't seem to get himself out of a rut at the time either.

"So although we will never forget how wonderful our parents were, we really haven't done anything to honor their memory. The more I thought about this project, the more I realized this is a way to do just that. I know they are looking down on us, guiding us down this path. There are so many right reasons to do this. So you ask, what is "this"? I'll tell you. Daniel and I have decided to restore the house to its historical true self and then open it to the public. But I would like to do things a little differently than the other plantation homes. Instead of just having it be a museum or an events facility, I would like to do a combination of both. In fact, I would like to take your restaurant idea and have a patio café incorporated as well. Kind of like they do at the Biltmore House, but on a much smaller scale. We'll have to figure out how and where to do the cooking, because we wouldn't want the kitchen in the house used for that purpose. I am hoping you will tell me that either the barn or the old slave quarters will do the trick. We are ok with renovating either, or both of those buildings to be used for the café and for the events. In fact," looking at Daniel for confirmation, "I think the barn is big enough to hold a good sized party in it." Daniel nodded. "I love your idea of having people be able to eat outside too. The grounds are so gorgeous, or at least they used to be," she frowned at her brother then smiled and patted his arm. "But we need your help."

Daniel jumped in. "As you can see, my sister has high hopes and the energy to go with them. I understand Scott that you are a historical renovator?"

Scott looked at Carolyn. He wanted to be up front. "I would like to say that I am a historical renovator, but considering I just got my license, I would prefer to use the term "Historical Property Consultant". I don't want to oversell my experience, but let me tell you what I have been doing. I have owned my own contracting company for over seven years. My specialty is in residential and retail remodeling. I have renovated several restaurants and have excellent references. Two years ago when the economy started to tank and the business wasn't coming in consistently, I decided to take the time and get my Historical Renovation Certificate. I finished the course about a month ago and got my license last week. My instructor would be happy to give me a reference as well. We had to visit a number of historical homes in the Atlanta Metro area and review them. Our final certification required that we tell the instructor which ones were truly historically restored and which ones were just restored. I passed with a perfect score; the only one in my class. I am very meticulous and I assure you that if you award me the project, I will get this house back to its original appearance as much as feasibly possible. I assume you want to leave the electricity and plumbing in place?"

"Yes! We wouldn't be able to survive without that," Christina laughed. "Daniel mentioned something about you having some investors that may be interested in helping as well? I know that your original plan was to buy a place, but would you be interested in becoming a partial owner? We would pay you for the renovation work, of course."

"That would be ideal. I never would have thought that an opportunity like this would present itself. I will definitely talk this over with my investors, but I am fairly confident that they would be delighted to be a part of this venture. I would want Carolyn, to also be a part owner with me. Do you see that as a conflict with her having the other restaurant?"

Daniel and Christina looked at each other. Daniel spoke up. "Actually, it might be a real pull to have the two places linked, advertising for each other. They will be so different; I don't see it as a problem. Do you?" he asked Christina.

"No, I don't. I think it will be a lot of fun for the four of us to work together, especially utilizing the different talents we all bring to the table. Can you send me your references? I'd like to call them right away so we can make a decision. I called the Roswell Historical Society and they gave me a list of other historical renovators, but I am not sure I want the same person renovating our place that did the others. I'd like someone with fresh ideas to look at our property and someone who is very motivated to make it work out well. I feel really good about both of you. When can you talk with your investors?" Christina asked.

"Is this afternoon soon enough?" asked Scott as he smiled.

"As you can see, my husband is like a bulldog with a bone," Carolyn laughed realizing the inference to the University of Georgia's mascot.

"You didn't just say that," chided Scott.

They all laughed. They seemed to be becoming fast friends and felt comfortable with the conversation so far. They told a few more stories about the college days as they finished their lunches then parted ways.

Carolyn and Scott walked to their cars, barely able to contain themselves.

"What do you think?" asked Carolyn. She wanted to scream but figured everyone would think she was crazy.

"I just can't believe our luck. You know if you hadn't found the plantation home and pushed to turn it into a restaurant; we wouldn't have had the conversation we just had. I really like them both and it's going to be extremely rewarding to do this project in light of their parents' deaths. That was really sad, wasn't it?" Scott shook his head and sighed heavily.

"It is really sad. And you are right, that gives us another reason to make this a successful project. I think they are going to award us the business, don't you? I mean your teacher loves you, so that should be a no brainer."

"Yeah, I feel really good about the whole thing. And congratulations, honey on signing your lease." Scott pulled her into his arms and kissed her. "I think this calls for a celebration! Where do you want to go for dinner?"

"The next restaurant on my list of course! Number seven - Relish."

That evening over dinner, Scott told Carolyn about the calls to the three investors. Two of them were on board, but the other wasn't interested. Scott felt that was still doable since he and Carolyn would also be investors and of course the Greysons would still be part owners as well. They didn't want too many hands in the pot. "Kaitlyn is going to fly in from Tampa to look at the place, but she thought it was a fantastic business case. Kevin asked if I could see if the Greysons wanted to meet for a drink to talk about the plans. I think he was really more interested in seeing Christina. He said he remembered her from high school, but didn't think she would remember him. I told him we could meet at Blue Roads tomorrow at 5:30. Is that okay with you?"

Carolyn smiled. "Way to get with the program! Did you know that is number eight or was that just a lucky coincidence?"

"Of course I knew." Then he rolled his eyes. Carolyn was so easy to please. "I called Christina and Daniel and told them about Kaitlyn and Kevin. They were both really happy and they said they would see us tomorrow at 5:30 at Number Eight, I mean Blue Roads," he kidded.

"Did they check your references yet?" Carolyn asked.

"Not all of them, but Christina talked to my teacher. She called him first. She said he was exceptionally complimentary and unless one of the other references comes back bad, they were ready to make me an offer. I guess I need to get a price together for the renovation. I want to keep that separate from my ownership portion of the deal."

"This is so exciting. Think about how much our lives just changed in one day," Carolyn replied. "Oh, and Kacey and I met with two

chef candidates this afternoon. Let's just say, we need to keep looking if we are going to make an impact. Although we are doing small
plates, appetizers and desserts, they need to be different and absolutely scrumptious to bring people in before and or after they go to
another place or why would they come? We also need a chef that is a
wine connoisseur. So it was a bit disappointing that they didn't work
out, but nothing could put a damper on today. I love you. Why don't
we take this celebration home..."

Scott quickly paid the bill and they were out the door.

Chapter 13

July 3, 2010

At 5:30 sharp, Carolyn and Scott walked into Blue Roads. They saw Kevin sitting at the bar drinking a martini.

"Hi Kevin," Scott said. "How are things going?"

"Fine, thanks. Good to see you. How are you, Carolyn?"

"I don't think I could be doing any better, thank you. Are those blue cheese stuffed olives?"

Kevin laughed. "Yes, would you like one?"

"No, I am going to order the same thing, that's my favorite." Carolyn waved at the bartender. "Can I have a Greygoose, dirty martini, up with blue cheese stuffed olives, please? And he will have a Bud Light."

"Actually, since we are celebrating, make that a Jack and Ginger instead of the beer," said Scott.

"Hi everyone," said Christina waving as she walked up to the bar. "It's good to see you again," she said to Carolyn and Scott. "And you must be Kevin? You look familiar, have we met?"

Kevin smiled and looked at Scott. "Yes, we went to Roswell High together. We had the same algebra and history classes." He remembered her beautiful brown eyes.

"Oh wow! What a small world. Did you used to have long hair?" asked Christina.

"I did. That was me. I guess I was the school hippie, when being a hippie was out of style," Kevin said, taking a drink of his martini. "Can I get you a drink?"

"Yes, I will have a chardonnay." He was very good looking, Christina thought. He had thick dark hair, blue eyes and a nice voice. "Oh, here is Daniel. He was a few years ahead of us so I don't think you would have met. Hi Daniel, this is Kevin." Christina noticed how tall Kevin was when he stood up.

"Hello, pleasure to meet you Kevin. Carolyn, Scott, good to see you again. What's everyone drinking? Well, it looks like a smorgasbord! Actually, I will have a scotch and water."

Kevin reached for the bill and Daniel said, "No, let me get the tab. I appreciate you all getting together on such short notice. Let's go get a table so we can talk a little more privately."

The hostess showed them to their table. The five chatted for awhile, really enjoying each others' company; then they got down to business.

Daniel started. "Here is our proposal. Christina and I will continue to be the majority owners of the home, but we would like to split the remaining forty-nine percent with each of you and potentially your other partner from Tampa. Kaitlyn, I think you said her name is?"

Scott nodded.

"I will leave it up to you four to determine how you will split the forty-nine percent. Is that agreeable?" Daniel asked.

Kevin, Scott and Carolyn looked at each other, agreed with the forty-nine percent and to discuss the split later.

"So, let's talk about the plans," Christina said. She looked at Kevin, smiled and then looked at Carolyn. Carolyn got the feeling that there was some interest there. "The house has not been kept up for about a month, so there is general clean up and a lot of growth in the yard. I have already called a landscaper to come take care of the yard. There are actually vines growing up the house! I couldn't believe how fast it grew. I think its Kudzu," she rolled her eyes. "So as soon as we get the ownership squared away, I'd like to begin looking at the plans for the renovation - Scott that would be your department. When do you think you can come by and take a look so you can come up with the plan?"

Scott leaned forward in his chair. This was the exciting part to him. "I have a couple of remodeling jobs I am finishing up, but I can definitely start on the plans. I do need to come by and look around. It would probably take me a few hours to really look at each room. Is your plan to renovate all of the rooms back to their historical accuracy, or do you want to separate your living quarters? I am assuming, Christina, that you will live in the house?"

"Yes, that is my plan. Although I have to say, I am a little nervous about being there by myself. I'll see how that goes. If it gets too crazy with the renovation, I may get an apartment while we are having the work done."

"That makes sense. I will know more after I have had a thorough look at the house as far as how much work it will take. I'll let you know if I think it's livable while the work is going on. In addition, in doing my research on the house, I understand it is the only plantation home still standing that was originally owned by a Cherokee family prior to them being relocated. That house has an incredible history. If only walls could talk! Did your family document anything about the house at the time and do you have your family tree documented?"

Carolyn could see that Scott was very in tune with this project and she was so proud of him.

Daniel spoke up then. "We do have our family tree documented and we have some letters that talk about our family growing up in the plantation home over the years. They named it Greyson Manor. I guess we should continue to use that name and even put a sign up so everyone knows. We didn't do that when we were living there. My parents were actually pretty humble and continued to live in the house to keep it in the family. They had talked about getting a townhome to downsize, but the accident took that decision off their plate." He choked up for a minute. It was clearly still difficult to talk about their parents. "I agree with Christina that this project will honor them and their dedication to our family, our family home and the community."

Carolyn noticed he didn't mention anything about the Cherokee Indian family that originally owned it. That part fascinated her and she was sure it would be a big driver for visitors as well. "Daniel, do you have any information about the Indian family that owned it before you?"

Christina started to say something, but Daniel cut her off. "No, other than my family won the property in the land lottery that the Georgia governor conducted. It was how things were done at the time. You may know that Andrew Jackson was the one who forced the Cherokee west, so we try not to dwell on that. In fact, if you notice, there isn't a lot of talk around here about the Cherokee Indians other than to explain that they had owned the land before the land was given away in the lottery. It is a very sad tale and not one we are proud to have been associated with. My understanding is all the Cherokee went west or to the Carolina mountains and their tribes are still there to this day. So I guess all that ends well…." Daniel sort of half smiled trying to lighten the conversation.

Kevin said, "Actually, turns out the government ended up taking a lot of the land they had given them in Oklahoma as well. I am part Cherokee myself, so I have read the story and believe I understand it pretty well. In fact, did you know that Roswell was established in 1836 but wasn't incorporated until 1854? It would be interesting and important for the tours to understand where your family came from. The original families that built the magnificent homes, the town, churches and mills came shortly after 1828, when Roswell King was attracted to the area by the gold rush. He contacted some friends of his from the east coast of Georgia and some from up north and they began to build the town. He built the mills, called the Roswell Manufacturing Company in 1839 shortly after all of the Cherokee had been removed from the area. The other plantations, Barrington, Bulloch and Smith were built in the late 1830s. Obviously as the mills grew, more families settled in the area. There are stories of several white men that married Cherokee Indian women and those women were obviously permitted to stay in Roswell. We have been able to trace our family back to the 1830s where one of the store owners married my great, great, great grandmother, a Cherokee Indian. At the time, the Cherokee were really trying to co-exist and took on the white men's dress, language, church, etc. trying to fit in - for all the good that did." Kevin shook his head.

Daniel peered at Kevin. "Is your Indian background why you are so interested in our home? You aren't going to try to sabotage the project are you?" he half laughed and looked at the others.

"Of course not. I just think the history is very interesting and important and I am glad to be a part of this project. I do believe though that we need to try to understand the history of the house all the way back to when it was built. That is what the visitors will want to know and I am not okay with leaving out the details of the fact that it was originally owned by a Cherokee family. It will attract interest, so it's good for business, but I also feel an obligation to my roots. Are you okay with that Daniel and Christina?" Kevin put it back in their court.

All the while, Scott and Carolyn sat listening intently trying to understand the undercurrent of the conversation from both sides.

Christina put her hand on Daniel's arm and said, "We are very proud of our home, and will be more proud when it's fixed up." She smiled at Scott. "I agree that the facts are important and I will go through our family records to see if I can find that information. It's too bad none of our parents or grandparents are still around to fill in the blanks. But I am sure that there are records. I'll see what I can find out."

Scott looked at Carolyn then back at Christina. "I already know who originally built the home. It was in the records that we had to research in our Historical Renovation course. A Cherokee family named Hawkins owned it until the land lottery and then David Greyson was awarded the property. I guess he was your great, great, great grandfather? That's all I know. I don't think he was married at the time, because they didn't list his wife's name, unless they just didn't do that back then. I could probably find that out, but you said you have your family tree, right?"

Christina nodded. "I will have to find those records. I really never paid that much attention to the names."

Chapter 14
May, 1838

Jade and Ben carried their baskets into the cook house. Ben noticed again how careful Jade would empty the basket. She had hardly spoken since that terrible day, but she seemed to be accepting of her new life. She did what she was told and tried to blend in with the slaves. They were growing to love her and understood her pain. They could relate in one way or another. At dinner they would tell their stories and read the Bible aloud. Jade would listen intently but still did not join in the conversation. Sally would always sit next to her trying to make conversation. Sally was eleven and looked up to Jade like a big sister. She brushed Jade's hair when Jade would allow it.

Theresa watched the children as she cleaned the clothes. Ben was obviously becoming very protective of Jade and she hoped that was a good thing. She was almost like a hurt fawn, licking her wounds, keeping to herself, staying quiet. So far, Master Greyson had not taken her back to the house. She prayed that he never would again.

Theresa called to Ben, Sally and Jade. "It is time for your studies. We are going to work on our writing today. Please go get your paper and pencils and bring them to the table." She was determined to continue the lessons that Ms. Sara had started with them. Ms. Sara had said reading and writing was what would bring the world together and would help our children grow into successful people. She was eternally grateful that Ms. Sara had included Ben in her classes. Sally's parents were grateful as well. Theresa missed Sara so much. It had been a dream come true when they came to work for the Hawkins. Their lives had all changed from being in an abusive environment to a loving community that worked together for the good of all. Yes, they were still slaves, but the Hawkins treated them as part family, part employees. They had been abused their whole lives before they came to live with the Hawkins. Theresa prayed once David Greyson took a wife, his wife would help bring peace back to their plantation and he would grow less anxious and more calm and fair.

There had still been no word from Sam. She assumed when John Ross came to call, Sam had been the one to ask him to come, but now she thought it must have been Joe and George. She was fairly certain that she would never see Sam again. She didn't want to think about what could have happened to him. She began to cry.

"Mama," Ben said. "Papa will come home. I know he will. Please don't cry." He wrapped his arms around her and they clung to each other for a few minutes.

Jade stood watching them and tears rolled down her cheeks. She missed her family terribly. How could this have happened? Theresa and Ben and the others had been very nice to her and she hoped that the Master never came for her again but she lived in fear he would do just that.

They spent about an hour practicing their letters and forming sentences. It was difficult since Theresa did not know how to read or write herself but Ben, Sally and Jade remembered enough from their studies and had the workbook Sara had given them to work from. After Ben and Sally had gone back outside to help gather vegetables, Jade continued to write. Theresa let her be. She wondered if Jade was writing anything in particular or just practicing her letters. She seemed very intent about it. Jade looked up and saw Theresa watching her. She put her papers in the workbook, took them back to her bed, placed them under her pillow then went outside.

"There you are!" said David Greyson.

Jade turned and looked at him. Terrified she tried to run back into the slave house. David grabbed her around the waist. "Oh no you don't, you are coming with me."

Jade screamed. Theresa, Ben and several of the slaves came running. Sally hid behind a tree.

"Please Master Greyson. Please leave her with us. We are taking good care of her."

"I see that, but I need her with me for awhile. I'll bring her back tomorrow."

Jade cried out her first words since it had all begun. "Please help me!" she begged Theresa. Theresa lowered her head and cried. She ran into the slave quarters as David carried Jade into the house.

Ben went running after David. "No, you can't have her. Take me! Leave her alone!"

David turned to look at the lanky slave boy. "Well now that just won't do," and he pushed him to the ground. "Get busy, boy. Isn't there some cotton you can pick?" He carried Jade kicking and screaming up the steps and into the house. Jade never took her eyes off Ben.

The next day David brought her back to the slave house. This time she had on clean new clothes. Theresa assumed they were her own clothes. He must have bathed her. She looked like a doll. But when she raised her head to look into Theresa's eyes, Theresa knew what the night had been for Jade. This continued for several years.

Chapter 15
July 7, 2010

"Knock, knock, I'm here!" called out Kaitlyn. "Hi sweetie, I missed you!" she hugged Carolyn.

"Well, come on in! How was your flight? Let me take your bag," offered Carolyn. She was so happy to see her old friend. Kaitlyn was looking good too. "You look fabulous by the way. I like the highlights!"

"Thank you. I like them too. The flight was fine. Sure makes Atlanta seem closer since the flight is only one hour. It's the drive up here from the airport that's the killer! It took me longer to get my rental car and drive to Roswell than it did to fly from Tampa! Wow, that airport and traffic are insane!" sighed Kaitlyn. Then she grinned. "But it was worth it. I can't wait to hear all about your news."

"Ok, I am putting your bag right in here. This is your room. Let's grab a glass of wine and sit on the porch. It's really nice out."

"It's actually kind of chilly, but I have a sweater," Kaitlyn said while she grabbed her sweater from her bag.

"Chilly? It's July and it's seventy degrees! Oh yeah, you're a Florida girl. How could I forget? Well let's just sit on the porch and see how you feel and we'll take it from there." Carolyn grabbed a quilt for Kaitlyn. "First of all, Kacey and I signed the lease on our restaurant. I think I told you that and ever since we have been trying to get all of the pieces in place. We have interviewed a few chefs, but have not found the right person yet. Since it's a small plate and wine bar, we really need both a wine connoisseur and a chef rolled into one. You wouldn't happen to know anyone would you?"

"No, but do you really need that? You and Kacey know a lot about wine and your wine reps could make recommendations for you," suggested Kaitlyn.

"Hmmm, I hadn't thought about that. Maybe you are right. At least we should start talking to some wine reps and see what they recommend. They may even have a suggestion for a chef who knows his wine. That is a great idea. In fact, one of Kacey's neighbors is a wine rep. We were going to talk to him. I'll get her to set that up right away. Thanks! See you are already adding value and you just got here! Mia and Angel are coming over shortly. They can't wait to see you. It's been a long time."

"So it sounds like the restaurant is at least moving forward. Have you built it out yet?"

"No, but Scott and Mike are helping us with that. Kacey and I are going to pick out furniture and dishes tomorrow. It's so exciting! I can't believe it's finally happening. We are trying to have our Grand Opening party on Labor Day. That is really pushing it though. Good thing we applied for our liquor license six months ago. It just came in the mail. Anyway, the restaurant is on track."

"Did you decide on a name yet?" asked Kaitlyn.

"Yes, "Southern Charm", what do you think?" Carolyn beamed.

"I like it. It's perfect. It says, cozy but sophisticated, just like Kacey and you."

"Oh thanks! We liked it too. We ran through a bunch of ideas, but kept coming back to that. So, about the plantation home, let's talk about that before the girls get here. I think you will really like the Greysons and Kevin. Scott and I feel we are going to make a strong and amicable partnership. The Greysons want to keep the majority share of the house. We don't blame them and quite frankly, I don't think we could have gotten in on the partnership if they hadn't. Scott and I talked about it and we thought we would like to put in nineteen percent and if you and Kevin could put in fifteen percent each, we would be there." Carolyn told Kaitlyn what the amount would be. "Can you swing that much?"

"Yes, I can. When Aunt Bess left me as her sole heir - I still can't believe she did that - she asked that I put it into something that would make a difference in the world. She was always very philanthropic, but as you know, I have always been more entrepreneurial. This opportunity seems like a little bit of both. I love the historical aspect of this project. And when I told Ken about the idea, he supported me as well. Now that the boys are almost through college and the remainder will be covered by their scholarships and what's left in their college funds, we really don't have a lot to worry about. As soon as the boys finish school and get their careers going, Ken and I are going to sell the house, buy a condo on the beach and maybe another condo here depending on how things are going with the plantation home at that point. We're probably looking at about a year and half before we do that. So of course we would spend most of our time there in the winter and here in the summer. You know I can't take the cold!"

Carolyn shook her head and laughed. "I am just so grateful to you that you are willing and truly interested in helping us. Thank you, old friend." Her eyes teared up and they hugged. "I have to say, I am impressed that you have so much figured out already and I am also really glad that Ken is on board. We would never want this to be a burden or ask you to do something if he wasn't for it too. No one knows better than me how important it is to have the support of your spouse before you jump into something that could be intense and stressful. But of course that is why it will be so rewarding. Don't you agree?"

"I do, and to your point, I wouldn't be doing this if we both didn't believe in it. And to know that it is also helping you and Scott achieve your goals is just icing on the cake. When can I see it?" Kaitlyn took a sip of her wine and bounced in the chair. This was just what she needed after the harrowing drive from the airport. These chairs are so comfortable, she thought. Hopefully she would get used to Atlanta traffic, although she doubted it. Did anyone ever, really?

"We are meeting Christina at the house tomorrow at nine. I guess we should start calling it Greyson Manor, from now on. That is its name. Do you want to see some of the pictures that Scott took?"

"Yes, that would be great. You mentioned something about a Cherokee family having owned it before the Greysons. Is that right?" She put her wine down on the table and began looking through the pictures.

"Yes," replied Carolyn. "Supposedly, it's the only plantation of its kind still standing that is that old. Most of the others were built a few years later by the white families who won the land in the lottery. Most of the Cherokee homes on the property the white men won were torn down. I am assuming they either weren't as grand as the new owners wanted, or they just didn't want to live in a home that an Indian lived in. The thing that gets me is that we came to America, took over their land, demanded they live like we do, they tried to, and we just kept taking and taking from them. I think that is so heartbreaking - definitely not one of our finer moments in history."

"What is this "we" thing? I know we are white, but we can't take blame or credit for that matter for what our ancestors did. All we can do is try to make it right now," Kaitlyn said seriously.

"You know, you may have hit on something. You are right, of course, but what if we could somehow find the descendants of the Hawkins family? That was the Cherokee family that built Greyson

Manor but were kicked off their land and sent west. Do you think we would be able to find their descendents in Oklahoma?" Carolyn asked.

"Wow, that would be wonderful, wouldn't it?" Kaitlyn nodded. "That sounds like a project in itself, but worth it, if it's possible. I wonder, since they still have tribes, if it's easy to look them up on the internet or at least just make a call out there. Let me look into that. I brought my laptop with me, and now that I am not selling real estate in Tampa, I will have time to do that. Do you mind if I take on that part of the project?"

"That would be fantastic. We are all busy with the renovations and the restaurant so that would be great. Oh and you may want to talk to Kevin about it too. I didn't realize it, but he told us the other night that he is part Cherokee. Apparently, his family lived in Roswell and his great, great, great grandfather married a Cherokee woman, so he has a vested interest in that part of this story. I will say though, Christina and Daniel didn't seem quite as excited to talk about that fact. I got the feeling they feel ashamed that their ancestors won the land the way they did. They didn't seem to know a lot about it though. Kevin said he wanted to look into the story more so we can document it for the tours. Scott learned the family's name was Hawkins in his Historical Renovation class. See if you can find them in Oklahoma. Oh here come the girls! Hey Mia and Angel!"

The girls all hugged and talked for hours. Then when Scott came home, Carolyn made some pasta and they all sat around the table talking about old times, what they were each doing now and about the exciting times they had ahead of them. Carolyn went to sleep that night in Scott's arms, feeling very content. She had a feeling that she was going to continue to learn more about the town she loved and the plantation home that she was falling in love with. She couldn't wait to find out all of its secrets and share them with the world.

Chapter 16
July 8, 2010

Kaitlyn, Kevin, Carolyn, and Scott met Christina at Greyson Manor at nine that morning. Christina greeted them on the porch.

"Daniel has a meeting at work this morning. It's with one of his biggest investment clients. He couldn't move the meeting, so let's go ahead. I can show you around and hopefully answer any questions that you have. Would you like to start inside or out? As you can see, I had the landscaper remove the Kudzu. Well, he said it wasn't Kudzu, but I still think it must have been since it grew that fast. I mean I know my brother wouldn't have allowed vines to get so out of control. It wasn't *his* fault." Christina winked sarcastically.

Carolyn spoke up. "Do you mind if we start in the house? I need to leave at 11:00 to meet Kacey today, and you all can stay as long as you like, if that is okay. I have already seen the barn, the slave quarters and the carriage house in the back - definitely worth checking out."

"So you have already seen all that, huh?" Christina asked teasing.

Carolyn blushed. "Yes, you could say I was nosey the day I came by to check out the house. I couldn't get in, so I did some snooping around. I hope you don't mind."

"Not at all. Let's go inside. Did Daniel tell you about the caretaker?"

Kaitlyn spoke up. "I haven't heard, what about him?"

"Well unfortunately, he fell down the stairs to the basement and broke his neck. Apparently, he died instantly - poor guy. We aren't sure how long he was down there. It took several weeks before Daniel realized there was an issue and came by which is why the house got overrun with weeds. The Caretaker's funeral was a few weeks ago. Isn't that terrible? According to Daniel, he didn't have any family. Why don't I show you the main floor first and then I can take you upstairs. See this beautiful winding staircase? As far as we know it is the original. At least that is what my father told me. I guess you need to verify that Scott."

"No worries, I will verify all the major architectural pieces and let you know if any need to be replaced or restored. It does look like someone added some linoleum in this half bath off the foyer. Do you mind if I pull that up? Hopefully, the original flooring is under it."

"Go for it. I never liked that anyway. So come through the foyer to the kitchen and the keeping room. Obviously, we have had appliances added over the years. Is there any way to keep this separate from the tours so we don't have to rebuild the cook house? I remember my mother telling me the cook house had burned down many years ago. Apparently someone had left the fire going."

"Yes," said Scott, "we should keep the kitchen separate since plantation homes didn't really have kitchens back then. They had space to eat – I see there is a formal dining room and space to prepare the food, typically in the basement. They sometimes called them warming kitchens. The food was cooked outside or in the cook house, away from the main house since they had to use real fire and then the food would be brought in to the warming kitchen to prepare. Is that still there in the basement?"

"Yes, but it is used for storage. It is an interesting space and many of the antique pots, dishes and furniture are still down there. I don't think it would take much to clean it out and restage it," responded Christina.

"Then let's keep the main floor kitchen off limits from the tour but show the warming kitchen in the basement. In addition, why don't we focus on the foyer, the staircase, the living room, the library, and a couple of bedrooms upstairs that we can rope off to keep the visitors only in those rooms. Then we can take the rest of the tour outside. I noticed that there is a Mason's symbol at the top of the house. That may be what kept the Union soldiers from destroying the house during the war. That would be good information to add to the tour as well."

"Really?" asked Kaitlyn. "What does that mean?"

"Many of the houses were burned when Sherman and his Union troops came through in the 1860s. They stayed in the mansions and used them for quarters and hospitals. When they were ready to move on they burned the homes down, unless they had a Mason symbol. The legend is that General Sherman was a Mason so he left those homes intact, for the most part. Christina, did your parents tell you any stories about the house?" asked Scott.

"Yes, they did. I do remember my father telling me the same story you just mentioned about the Mason symbol. They told me a lot of stories about the house and the area. I think we can have a meeting to go over the stories and I can document the ones we want to tell on the tours. Why don't we go upstairs and check out some of the bedrooms? There are several that we didn't do anything with and just kept them closed up because there were only four of us but there were seven bedrooms. The one at the end of the hall always gave me the creeps. I would go in there when I was playing with my dolls, just pretending they were on a trip to another country, and I would get a weird feeling in that room. I actually think that is why I kept going back. I think I thought I would figure something out eventually as to why I felt so strange going in there. I kept looking for a ghost. I never did see one but the feeling was always there. I think it would be a great room for the tour though. It's pretty much been untouched and I am not sure why. I guess I just came to accept that it wasn't needed, so we didn't use it."

They walked down the hall and Christina opened the door. It was very musty inside and had antique furniture in it.

"Could this possibly be the original bedroom set?" Kaitlyn asked.

"I don't know that for sure but it's possible. Should I get an antique appraiser to come look at it and tell us how old it is?" asked Christina.

"Yes, that is an excellent idea. In fact, have them inspect all of the furniture and see if she or he can tell us how old it all is. That would be quite the find, if it turns out that some of this is original," Scott said. "I am willing to bet that it is. I am sure the owners of the antique mall around the corner can send someone over here."

"Please let me take on that project. Christina, if I get the appraiser lined up, can I call you and we can take him through the house to see the furniture?" asked Kaitlyn. "I really want to contribute some of my time to the project."

"Sure, that would be very helpful. Just call me when you are ready," responded Christina. "That is an excellent idea. Any other questions?"

Scott shook his head no, and then continued through the bedrooms taking pictures and making notes about the architectural details.

When they finished exploring the house they went out onto the front porch.

Scott said, "I definitely want to see the slave quarters and the barn. I know you want to use them as part of the event facilities, which is a great idea. I just want to check them out and make sure that we don't corrupt anything that should stay as is."

They walked throughout the other buildings commenting on

how well they were constructed, but how depressing it was to think that slaves were actually kept there and worked the fields. It appeared that the slaves must have all slept in the same room. The slave quarters also had a small kitchen area.

They all knew it was a sign of the times, but Carolyn thought about what Kaitlyn had said the night before. "As Kaitlyn reminded me last night, it's not on us to take the blame for what had occurred in the past, but it is on us to try to make things right now." They all agreed. "I have to go meet Kacey. Scott, will you take Kaitlyn home before you head back to your office?" Scott nodded yes and kissed his wife goodbye. "Thank you for meeting us this morning, Christina. I will call you. Goodbye, everyone." Carolyn went back out to her car and noticed that someone at Frank's house was looking out the window at them. The curtains were then pulled shut. I guess they are just curious as to what's going on, thought Carolyn. That's understandable. She would be sure to talk to Christina about letting Frank know. He seemed like a really nice man and they would need him on their side as the work began on the house. He may not be thrilled with all the construction or the events that will take place. It was better to address that up front.

Christina walked over to Kevin. "I noticed you have been very quiet during the tour. Is everything okay?"

"Yes, I am just taking it all in. I am trying to picture what it must have been like over one hundred and seventy years ago to live in this place at that time. I consider myself quite fortunate that I am a part of this project. It will be very worthwhile and it also has allowed me to see you again, Christina," Kevin said. He looked at her dead on to try to see if he could tell if she felt the same way.

Christina blushed. "Yes, I can't wait until the renovations are completed and we are open for business. I believe that will give us all a great sense of accomplishment and something we can feel good about at the end of each day. I know my parents would be proud that we are taking this step." Then she added, "It's nice to see you too, Kevin."

Kevin didn't want to rush things so he left it at that. Eventually, he wanted to take her to dinner to get to know her again. He hoped that what he had revealed about the original Cherokee family and his heritage didn't scare her off. She was someone that he really wanted to know better.

In the house next door, Frank sat down in his recliner and pulled out his Bible. He opened it up and pulled out the journal pages. He started to read them again and as usual, he was transported back to an earlier time on this same land, when a young girl became a woman much sooner than she had ever wanted.

Chapter 17

April, 1841

J ade walked slowly down the porch steps that morning and walked past Ben without a word. Ben shook his head and stormed off. Sally ran after him. Theresa was standing in the doorway to their quarters and moved aside to let Jade pass through. Theresa watched Jade go straight to her bed where she stayed for about an hour even though it was midmorning.

When Jade got up, she went to Theresa to ask what she was needed to do that day then went out to the cook house. As usual, she didn't mention what had gone on the night before at the Greyson home. But Theresa knew. She wondered how a sixteen year old girl could deal with what was happening to her. Theresa herself had her first child at the age of fifteen, but that was by choice. Jade didn't seem as afraid of Master Greyson as she once was. She seemed to have found a way to deal with his frequent visits requesting her to come to the house. She no longer fought him but she clearly was a very unhappy girl.

There was also a riff now between Ben and Jade. Where it once seemed that they were becoming friends, Ben avoided Jade and blamed her for not putting up more of a fight. Jade on the other hand seemed resigned to the fact that she had no choice but to go with Master Greyson. Theresa knew that to be true. What a cruel man. Theresa obviously had no idea what exactly was going on in the house. For all she knew, he had his way with her, that she had no doubt, but he also must be feeding her and bathing her because she always came back without an appetite and very clean and well dressed. She supposed the lack of appetite could be due to what she was enduring throughout the night. Theresa thought Jade was beginning to accept her position in this community of sorts but she worried for her because the light seemed to be fading from her eyes.

Theresa knew Jade still missed her family terribly but Jade had never tried to escape. Master Greyson never told any of them where they buried Jade's family, so Jade made three crosses and put them in the ground near the edge of the woods behind the Carriage House. Each time she would go back to pray by the crosses, they would be gone. She assumed Master Greyson didn't want anyone questioning whose graves they were. So Jade would make new ones and again put them in the ground near the edge of the woods.

Theresa often wondered if her brothers would ever be able to come back to retrieve Jade, but so far that had not happened and she assumed that at this point, Master Greyson would never allow Jade to leave. Theresa realized that not only did Jade miss her family, but she was only one of three Indians left in the area. The other two were Cherokee women who had married white men before the rest of the Cherokee were forced west.

They had all heard the stories of the horrible months the Cherokee endured in the stockades before they were finally sent on what they were now calling, "Nunna dual Tsuny", "The Trail Where they Cried". Theresa hoped and prayed that George and Joe had endured the hardships of the trail. She wished that Jade had some contact with the other Indian women that stayed. Would that bring her some sense of belonging, some sense of peace?

She saw a coach coming up the path to the manor. Riding alongside the coach, was a tall black man on a large brown horse. They pulled up in front of the manor. Master Greyson came out and quickly made his way down the steps towards the coach, smiling broadly. He opened the door on the far side of the coach. Theresa could not see who was getting out. The black man looked around and then noticed Theresa. He smiled and tipped his hat and she looked back at Master Greyson. The driver of the coach jumped down and pulled several large trunks off the back of the coach and handed them to a couple of the slaves that David had called over. He directed them to take the trunks into the house. They clearly struggled with the weight of them but finally got them up to the porch and through the front door.

Master Greyson then began walking up the steps with someone holding his arm and as he did, the person he had helped out of the coach came into view. It was a woman. Her dress was the most exquisite dress Theresa had ever seen. Theresa heard a light gasp and turned to see Sally looking at the dress as well. The light blue fabric shown in the sunlight and the white lace was so beautiful it took Theresa's breath away. When Master and the woman got to the top of the steps he leaned over and said something to her, she laughed and they both turned to look out over the property and the slaves that had all stopped what they were doing to watch. She smiled.

"This is Mrs. Kay Greyson - my new wife, your new lady of the manor. Please welcome her to her new home. If she needs anything, do not hesitate to give it to her," Greyson said proudly. Kay giggled and raised her hand to her mouth. She seemed shy but happy to be there.

When had he taken a wife? Not that he had to tell Theresa anything, but she was surprised that he had not mentioned getting married. She would have thought he would have wanted her to prepare the house for the new mistress. Perhaps he had taken care of the arrangements himself, or more likely, he hadn't thought to at all.

"This is Joseph," pointing at the tall black man. "He is now a part of our community as well. Joseph, go with Theresa and she will find you a bed." David winked at Joseph and then looked knowingly at Theresa.

Oh no, she thought, horrified. She glared at her master and then at Joseph. She was in no mood to take in a man. At this point, she knew with certainty that Sam would not be coming home. She would find this man a cot but it would not be with her. She summoned him with her hand to show him inside and as she turned to go into the house, she saw Jade standing by the door staring at David Greyson and Ms. Kay. Theresa followed Jade's gaze back to the porch and saw an odd look in David's eyes. Almost a look of smugness. He seemed to hope that this woman would make Jade jealous. Could he really be that arrogant and demented? Theresa looked back at Jade and saw her lower her head and walk back to the cook house. Ben waited outside the cook house and looked at Theresa. He had seen the same look. He followed Jade into the cook house and shut the door. Theresa turned so abruptly that her long grey skirt swirled around her.

"Was that an Indian girl David?" asked Kay.

"Yes."

"How is it that she is living here?" Kay asked.

David's eyes turned cold for just a few seconds when he looked at her and then he recovered, smiled and said, "She was orphaned and when they took the Indians out west, she begged me to let her stay here. I didn't have the heart to send such a young girl on her way when she clearly didn't want to leave her beloved land. You know this was Indian country at one time, don't you?"

"Yes, I do know that, which is why I am confused. Unless they were married to a white man, they were all sent west. I would have thought she would have wanted to be with her tribe, especially since she was orphaned." Kay looked toward the barn then back at David, questioning.

David began to get irritated. He knew she would have questions, but he didn't expect to have to go into any detail, she was his wife. Who was she to question him about anything? "Don't you worry, my dear. She lives with the slaves and seems happy there. I haven't told anyone about her because I was trying to help her and I was afraid someone would come and take her away. She was just a young girl at the time. I felt bad about winning her home in the lottery, so I was just trying to make her happy. Let me show you inside. I have asked that your bags be put in the third bedroom, but of course you will sleep in mine."

She swallowed obviously and turned back one more time to look at the barn, then decided against asking any further questions for now. There may be a story there that she didn't really want to know. David put his hand on the small of her back and gently guided her into the house.

Chapter 18
July 8, 2010

C arolyn met Kacey in front of their soon-to-be restaurant. "I thought it would be a good idea to try to buy the furniture, glasses, etc. at the antique mall and some of the local shops. At least as much as we can, or a few interesting pieces worst case. That would show our fellow shop owners that we want to give back. It would also be great advertising for them. Obviously, we need as many people coming to Roswell to spend their time and their money," Carolyn smiled. "Do you mind if we start with the antique mall?"

"Not at all. That is a fantastic idea. And besides, we want the place to be eclectic. A couple of good antique pieces with some funky lighting and pictures would look great together. In fact, I had an idea about the pictures for the walls. Remember when we went to that Cork and Canvas party and we painted for the first and last time? Remember how surprised we were about how great our paintings came out?"

"Uh oh, I think I know where you are going with this," Carolyn's eyebrows scrunched together.

"What if we painted pictures of wine glasses and bottles in a lot of different funky perspectives and bright colors? That way, since the walls will probably be dark to set the tone, the pictures could brighten up the place. We can even use metallic paints to make them shine – almost like they were sconces and we can get lighting to shine on each picture."

"Wow, you have put a lot of thought into this! That's a fabulous plan and I guess it's worth trying. It would be cool that we actually painted them ourselves. It would make the place more personal. I like it! The other thing I was thinking is that we should have some track lighting and some really pretty pendants as well. You agree?"

Kacey high fived Carolyn. "I do! Let's head over to the antique mall and get busy. You know, I have even seen some pictures in magazines where all the glasses and dishes were different - really eclectic."

"I like that suggestion too and it will make it easier to buy them in bulk. Let's go!"

Kacey and Carolyn spent the day in the various Roswell stores and acquired several interesting pieces. They called the paint shop and set up a party for that evening deciding to invite some of their closest friends to help them paint the pictures of the wine glasses and bottles. They had planned to get together anyway, so the timing was perfect. When Kacey arrived at the paint shop, Mia, Angel and Lucy were already there. Carolyn swung by the house to pick up Kaitlyn. She let Diamond and Ruby out and fed them.

"So how was the rest of the tour? Did you see the barn and the slave quarters?" Carolyn asked.

"Yes, we did. I am so glad I was able to get up here to see the place in person before I invested," Kaitlyn remarked.

Carolyn looked at her in alarm. "Have you changed your mind?"

"No, not at all. I just wish I could be here more often so that I can be a bigger part of the project. I am definitely going to suggest to Ken that we get a condo here as soon as possible. I am so excited about how this is going and how it's going to all end up. It seems like such an important endeavor and I never would have found out about it if you hadn't been interested in opening a restaurant here. Have you thought about that? I mean what a fluke. But what a great fluke! Christina and Daniel seem very nice, although I haven't gotten to spend much time with Daniel to get to know him. He seems very busy with his job. It doesn't seem like he will be as involved as Christina. Don't you think?" asked Kaitlyn.

"I think that is the plan. Apparently, Christina gave up a really amazing job in New York to come back to their plantation home and make something of it. I am just glad she is opening it up to allow all of us to be a part of it as well. Oh, before I forget. I noticed that she and Kevin seem to be getting reacquainted in a very friendly sort of way. Have you noticed that?" Carolyn looked over at Kaitlyn as they pulled into the paint shop parking lot.

"Yes, in fact, I saw them talking together while we were exploring the property. That could be interesting, as long as it doesn't cause any riffs in our project and investments."

"I agree. They seem to be taking things slowly and they did know each other in high school. I'll keep my fingers crossed for them. One other thing – our realtor, Josie would be great to work with to help you find a condo. Let me know when you want to start looking and I will get you two together. She can help you long distance as well and if you see something you want me to look at for you when you are back in Tampa, just say the word," Carolyn offered.

The girls joined the rest of their party and they spent the evening painting their hearts out over wine. Could it have been more appropriate? Carolyn asked Kacey to set up a meeting with her wine rep so they could start talking about inventory and more importantly to see if he had any ideas on finding a chef that really knew his or her wine. Maybe they wouldn't need a wine connoisseur but they definitely needed someone who could make recommendations on the fly and could help create a menu that would pair particular wines with their appetizers. Kacey agreed and said she would call her wine rep friend the next day to schedule a meeting. While they painted and sipped their wine they talked about the schedule and when the build out would be complete. They still planned to have their grand opening party on Labor Day and it seemed everything was falling into place to make that happen.

Carolyn shared with Kacey how things were going at the plantation home and how happy Scott was to be involved with this project in particular but to also be doing something different than his typical remodeling jobs. She reassured Kacey he would stay on schedule to complete the renovations for the restaurant.

"Here are my masterpieces as my contribution to your new place girls," Mia said proudly showing her two paintings.

"These are beautiful!" Carolyn said. "I really like how you made them like close-ups so you don't see the whole bottle or glass in the picture. Can you ask the instructor how we add metallic paint without messing up what you have already done? We want them to really shine when the light is on them."

"I'll go talk to her. I'm sure she can help with that. Looks like Kaitlyn is done too. It is so good to see her. It's been too long this time," Mia said.

"Oh, Mia. There is someone that I have met recently that you may be interested in. He is very nice, about the same age, is a Financial Analyst and very good looking," said Carolyn.

"Really? How did you meet him?"

"He is one of the owners of the plantation home we are renovating. His name is Daniel Greyson."

"Hmmm. That's a possibility. But you know I am uncomfortable being set up. Maybe next time you have a bunch of us together, you can invite both of us and we will see how it goes." Carolyn agreed and Mia walked over to talk with the instructor.

"Kaitlyn, those are terrific! They look Van Gogh!" Kacey exclaimed. "I think we should put them in groupings when we hang them up. I am so happy we did this! This was such a good idea if I do say so myself!"

Angel and Lucy's pictures turned out very different but just as interesting.

Carolyn applauded. All of the pictures turned out to be very personal expressions and very appropriate for their restaurant. "Okay, gather around girls. You can go back to finishing your pictures after I show you something." Carolyn pulled the ten by fourteen out of the bag she had brought and showed the picture to the girls. They gasped then they all cheered and laughed. It was the picture Carolyn had taken of their feet in the bar. "I am going to hang this over the bar to symbolize several very important things. Our friendship most of all, but I think the circle of feet also represents our never ending ability to help each other when we need each other. The naked feet represent our willingness to bare our "soles", get it?" They all laughed. "I have a copy of this picture for each of you. Kacey and I want to thank you for being so willing and able and available on short notice to do all that you have done, and will do," she winked, "to help us follow our dreams." Carolyn put her arm around Kacey and they raised their glasses. "Here's to you, dearest friends."

Chapter 19
July 9, 2010

Frank saw through his window that Christina and the same man that was there the day before were on the porch talking. He wondered if she was having some work done. It looked like they were reviewing some plans. He walked outside and picked up a watering can and started watering plants on the right side of his property hoping Christina would see him. She did.

"Hi Frank, how are you?" yelled Christina.

Frank looked up from his watering and nodded with a pleasant smile. "It's good to see you at home Christina. Everything okay?"

"Yes, in fact, I need to talk to you. Do you have a minute to join us?" she asked.

Frank put the can down, walked around the fence down the drive and met Christina and Scott on the porch.

"Hi, my name is Frank Johnson." Frank said as he stuck his hand out towards Scott.

"It's a pleasure to meet you, Frank. Scott Kane."

Christina jumped in. "Scott is doing some historical renovation work on the house. We are trying to return it to its original state - at least a large portion of the house."

"Really? Why is that?" Frank asked.

"Well, that is what I wanted to talk to you about. I have moved back to Roswell permanently. My plan is to restore most of the main floor, the basement and some of the bedrooms. I'm going to turn it into a museum for tours, like Barrington and Bulloch Halls," she continued, hoping to get it all out before he objected. She had a feeling he wasn't going to like the idea. "I also plan to turn the barn into an events facility and the slave quarters into a working kitchen." She stopped then waiting for his response.

Frank looked from Christina to Scott and back again. He hadn't expected this. He was not happy they had not been keeping up with the place but didn't expect them to do a complete one-eighty. "Well, that's some news."

Christina hesitated, waiting to see if he had more to say. "Frank, I know there will be some construction going on and I will apologize up front for the commotion. But there will also be events, like weddings for example on Saturday evenings and maybe even other nights that will have music. I feel bad that it might be disturbing to you. What do you think about that?"

"I am not sure what to think. It never crossed my mind that ya'll would make a change like that, although, I can't say that I blame you. I know your home is the oldest of the bunch and it definitely has stories to tell. Stories you probably don't even know." Frank chuckled.

Christina frowned. What did he mean by that? "You know stories about the house?"

Frank replied, "Well sure, I told you my family has been here a long time as well."

Scott asked, "Exactly how long has your family lived in this area Frank?"

"I can honestly say that I am a descendant of slaves - literally, slaves that worked this very land."

"Can you prove that?" asked Scott.

Frank looked at Scott offended.

"I don't mean to question you, but part of what we are doing with this project is documenting stories and researching the history so that we can tell it as part of the tour. Do you have documentation of your ancestry? That would be an incredible find, of course if you are willing to share your stories with the world," Scott hoped.

"I do indeed," said Frank. "I taught history at Georgia State for the last twenty-three years. I retired when I thought I was ready, but I must say, I have learned that landscaping can be both relaxing and rewarding, but flowers don't talk back. At least not like my daughter," he chuckled. "I would be honored to share my family's history with you, on one condition."

"What would that be?" asked Christina. She looked at Scott with excitement in her eyes. What a find!

"If you allow me to conduct some of the tours, I will share my stories with the other tour guides to tell as well. I don't need a big paycheck since I have a pension, just a little something to get my daughter some nice things from time to time and to buy my flowers with. I have been told that I have a very distinguished voice," he smiled.

"You do! You absolutely do! And it's a deal! Wow, so you are ok with some music playing into the evenings and on the weekends too? I really don't see any way around that," said Christina.

"I am sure Wanda will be thrilled with the activity. Being an only child and since her mother left us a couple of years ago, she gets bored just being with me. As you know, there aren't a lot of families in this neighborhood anymore since so much has turned commercial. When would you like to sit down and discuss my stories? I can pull together my family records and we can discuss what would be interesting to tell. I will say though, being a descendant of the slaves that ran this plantation when the Cherokee Indian family built it and then continuing to serve the white family that won the home in the lottery, I do have several decades I can reference. My great, great, great grandmother was probably around your age, Christina, when the white men, your ancestors, took over the home. She was apparently an amazing woman. She kept all the slaves together, except for her first husband.....oh, I apologize, I can go on. I know you were in the middle of something. Anyway, just let me know when you would like to schedule a meeting and I would be happy to accommodate," Frank said. They made plans to get together the following week and shook hands.

"Well, that turned out very different than I thought it would," said Christina.

"Yeah, who would have thought? It is incredible that both descendents stayed in the same places, on the same properties, all these years. That is very rare these days. I can't wait to hear about his great, great, what did he say, great grandmother? Should we get back to looking at the plans?"

Christina was still watching Frank walk back to his house and seemed to be in deep thought.

"Christina?" asked Scott.

"Huh? Oh, sorry. Yes, I am interested to hear these stories too. I hope we aren't opening a can of worms here. You never know what we might find when we start looking into the details of the lives of those that came before us. I guess we will soon find out. Yes, let's get back to the plans and then I want to call Daniel and fill him in on our good fortune."

Christina and Scott worked on the plans for a few more hours and then Scott headed home to make the changes. Christina called Daniel.

"Daniel, when was the last time you talked to Frank?" she asked.

"Well, I talked to him when I went through the house and ended up finding our poor soul of a caretaker. I actually went over to ask him if he had seen Clint and unfortunately it had been several weeks since he had. Frank always seems to be home, you notice that?" Daniel asked.

"Yes, but apparently that is because he retired from Georgia State a couple of years ago. Remember that he was a history teacher?"

"Yeah, I do remember that. What are you thinking? He may be able to help with the house?"asked Daniel.

"Well not the house per se, but I explained to him what we are doing and was bracing myself for him to complain but he seemed very pleased. In fact, he went on to say he is related to the slaves that worked the plantation. Did you know that?"

"Now that you mention it," Daniel started, "I do remember Dad saying something about that. But Mom and Dad were always embarrassed about that so they didn't talk about it much. You know how they were; they didn't have a prejudiced bone in their body."

"Well, we have to stop worrying about that. This is our chance to try to make some good from bad with this project. Now not only can we tell the world that a Cherokee Indian family owned this place before our family did, but we can also say that the descendent of the slave family is working with us to share the stories of the time. I think it's wonderful. But I hope Frank doesn't have any ulterior motives. You don't think he would make our family sound bad do you? He said that he is willing to share his stories if we hire him as a tour guide. Can you believe that? That's either really good luck or really bad luck depending on the stories!" exclaimed Christina.

"Did he tell you the stories? We should definitely have a caveat that if in any way the stories are ones that we are not comfortable telling, he doesn't tell them, although I don't know how we would stop him, freedom of speech and all of that. But he will be working for us, so that does give us a little bit of editorial privilege. I guess we will have to hear what he has to say and then take it from there," Daniel said.

Sitting in his den, Frank thumbed through his Bible and the journal pages that were hidden inside. He would have to decide how much he should tell. What he had to say would definitely draw a crowd, but would Christina and Daniel be able to live with the knowledge? That was the question.

Chapter 20
July 15, 2010

"All right, I am taking minutes so let's begin this meeting of the investors and potential employee for the Greyson Manor Plantation Home Tour and Event facility," Carolyn announced as she wrote down the date and participants' names. They had met for lunch at the famous Mittie's Tea Room Café, named after Martha "Mittie" Bulloch Roosevelt, the mother of our famous and adventurous President "Teddy" Roosevelt. The restaurant, a quant converted farm house, was in the heart of Roswell, literally and figuratively. It was also number twelve on Carolyn's list of Roswell restaurants to visit.

In attendance were Christina and Daniel Greyson, Kaitlyn Jonas, Kevin Miller, Frank Johnson, and Carolyn and Scott Kane. "The agenda for today's meeting is to discuss the house plans, the barn and slave quarter conversions, the financial update and Frank's stories for the tour. In fact, Frank, why don't we start with you so that you can go on with your day," Carolyn stated.

All eyes turned to Frank. Not only did he have a distinguished, deep resounding voice, he was a handsome man. He was tall, wore silver-framed glasses, had salt and pepper hair and a close cropped beard. He looked to be in his mid to late forties.

"I would be happy to begin." Frank pulled a very old, worn Bible from his briefcase. He opened it up and the group could see that there were several old looking, loose papers inside. They were yellowed and looked like they had been handled and read many times.

"These papers are a sort of journal that was collected back when the slaves worked the plantation. They were written by an Indian woman." He stopped to let that sink in. He looked at each of them. There was definitely confusion as they were trying to grasp the sequence of events.

"So you mean, the Indian woman that ran the plantation prior to my family taking it over?" Christina inquired.

"You would think so, right?" Frank nodded and looked at each of them for impact.

"Ok, Frank, you have our full attention." Daniel interjected.

"The story is that my great, great, great grandmother, Theresa, took care of an Indian girl that was left behind." Immediately, shock crossed their faces. "My great, great grandfather, Theresa's son, Ben, was very close with the Indian girl as well."

"What do you mean she was left behind? How is that possible? Scott and I have been reading about the Trail of Tears and we understood that unless they were already married to a white man, they were all sent west other than the Indians that escaped to the mountains in North Carolina," Carolyn pointed out and looked at Scott for confirmation. Scott nodded in agreement.

"Yes, that is true," Frank began. "And that is the mystery that is solved in these journal pages. Apparently, the girl's mother was teaching her children and the slave children to read and write, and Theresa continued with the lessons, which is how the journal came to be."

"So you are saying that the Indian family just left their daughter with the slaves? Sorry, Frank," Kevin jumped in. It was a little uncomfortable discussing slavery with an African-American man. He would try to be sensitive to that.

Daniel peered at Frank. Something wasn't right, here. He was dreading what Frank was going to say. He could tell it wasn't going to be pretty because he was dragging it out. "Let's just let Frank finish. What do the papers say?"

Frank took a deep breath. "Apparently, only two of the three sons took the Trail of Tears."

"What happened to the rest of the family?" Kaitlyn asked. This was getting interesting.

"According to the journal, the third son, the youngest son, was killed by David Greyson's men."

Horrified, Christina and Daniel stared at Frank. The rest of the group stared at them. No one spoke.

Frank continued. "The journal also states, that the parents were killed as well, on the property," for emphasis, "before they left to go west." Frank stopped and looked intently at Christina and Daniel who looked dumbfounded. "Would you like me to continue?"

They both nodded. Carolyn and Scott looked at each other, concerned. Did they really want to know this? Should they be hearing this with Christina and Daniel as they were hearing it for the first time?

Frank swallowed hard. "Her name was Jade. She witnessed the murder of both of her parents. Theresa and Ben saw the killings as well, according to Jade's journal. Charles and Sara Hawkins were the parents. David Greyson had taken Jade and told Charles and Sara that he was keeping her. She was thirteen at the time. They fought back and were gunned down by David's men." Frank hesitated, looked at them over his glasses, and waited to see if they wanted him to continue. He knew this would be hard to comprehend.

Tears welled up in Christina's eyes and Daniel shook his head and put his face in his hands. This was a terrible story, Daniel thought. Frank looked around the table. The rest of the group was wide-eyed and stunned. Carolyn put her hand on Christina's back.

Christina composed herself. "Go on, Frank."

"Like I said, the two older brothers Jade believed, went west with the rest of the tribe. To read the journal, she didn't blame them, but she never got over being left behind. She always felt like an outsider, not being black or white. She grew up in the slave quarters with Theresa and twelve other slaves - at least most of the time."

Daniel put his hands on the table. "What does that mean? Most of the time?"

Frank took another deep breath and didn't respond. He shook his head and this time it was he who looked uncomfortably down at the table. He wasn't sure he should go on.

Scott was taking it all in, but this was not sounding good. He was trying to stay unemotional about it but could they really talk about this on the tour, he wondered. He doubted that the Greysons would allow it.

"Tell us, Frank. Just tell us the damn story. We might as well know the whole thing at this point," Daniel grumbled, his leg nervously twitching.

"David would come for Jade every few months. He would take her to the house. As Jade explained it in the beginning, he would hurt her, then send her back to the slaves. As she grew up, she explained that she eventually came to accept her fate."

Christina got up from the table and quickly walked to the ladies room.

"Should I stop?" Frank asked Daniel.

Daniel stared at Frank. "I will need to read those papers myself. I hope you understand."

"Yes I do. I made a copy for you." Frank pulled a file from his briefcase and handed it to Daniel.

"Is there more?" Daniel weakly asked.

"Yes. There is more."

Daniel looked toward the ladies room and then at Frank and

then at the rest of the group who was sitting quiet. "We will have to adjourn this meeting and reconvene at a later date. Frank, thank you for telling us. I will read the papers and then let you all know when we can get back together." He got up from the table and walked toward the ladies room. When Christina came out, he put his arm around her shoulder and they walked out the door.

Frank looked at the rest of them. "Maybe I should have told them in private."

Kevin responded intensely, "Ya think?"

Frank gathered the papers and put them back in the Bible, stuck the Bible in his briefcase and got up. He nodded to the group and walked out of the restaurant.

Chapter 21
July 15, 2010

The table was very quiet. They finished their lunches and the waitress cleared their plates. "Does anyone want coffee or more tea?" she asked. The group looked at each other.

Carolyn made the decision. "Yes, let's get refills of our tea and finish our meeting, agreed?"

The four agreed.

Scott took a deep breath. "Well, that was interesting. I am sure that Christina and Daniel were mortified to hear that story. Frank did confirm what I had found out in my historical renovation class, in that the original Indian family's name was Hawkins. I am not sure how you prove the stories though, just because they are written like a journal. Regardless, they have hired me to do the renovations. Let's proceed assuming they will still want the work done. We will have to let them decide what they want revealed in the tours. I can go back over this with Daniel and Christina later. Christina and I have finished the walk through and she told me which rooms she wants to renovate and include on the tours. I did the floor plan and documented the changes needed. I have them with me. Would you like to see them?"

"Yes, now that the other three left we have more room to spread out," mentioned Kaitlyn. "In fact, let's get the waitress to clear the table. I really want to see what you are doing, since I need to get back to Tampa tomorrow." She called the waitress over.

Scott rolled out the plans and began to go over the details. "The home's architectural style is called Federal. I am not sure if you noticed, but the windows are Palladian and there are some round and elliptical windows as well. Those are some of the characteristics of a Federal style home. It was structured after Chief James Vann's house, which was built in 1804. The Vann house was considered the most elegant of all Cherokee Indian plantations. It was considered the 'Showplace of the Cherokee Nation'. Many of the Cherokee plantation owners tried to replicate the style and grace of Chief Vann's home. Clearly, that was what the Hawkins' had tried to do with their home. This home was built in 1830. It was the last plantation home in Roswell built in that style. When the founding families of Roswell moved here, they built their homes in the Greek Revival style. Let me know if this is more information than you were hoping for," Scott inquired, looking around the table.

"No, this is very interesting to me, don't you agree?" Kevin asked Kaitlyn sincerely.

"I agree," responded Kaitlyn. "Tell us more. We need to know so we can help promote Greyson Manor."

"You know I agree," smiled Carolyn, proudly.

"Okay, most of the changes that we will be making are cosmetic. Nothing structural really needs to be replaced except the fireplace mantels. Those were fancied up over the years, but the materials are too new. I will replace those with intricately carved wooden mantels from the 1830s. The original iron crane hangs in the ten-foot-wide fireplace in the parlor, which is a real coup. The thick oak plank floors are the originals as well. The old box locks and brass knobs are on the forty-inch doors. In the parlor, the wood baseboards are painted black and splattered with white paint to look like marble. That was a popular practice back then. There is no crown molding in the house but there are chair rails and that was also common. The bricks for the house were made on site and came from the red clay located on the property. Stone was used for the foundation and to line the well. They have a very elaborately carved stairway—this is one of the items that was copied from Chief Vann's house. It's the oldest example of cantilevered construction. I won't bore you with the details of the type of framing, but it's called balloon framing." Scott looked up from the plans and looked around the table. "Too much detail?" he asked.

"No this is good and it gives you a chance to run through it once with us before you present it to the Greysons," replied Kevin. "Can you tell us how it gets certified as historic?"

"Sure. What we will be filing for is a COA, a Certificate of Appropriateness. It's an application outlining all of the specific material changes. Since I am a contractor and a historical appraiser, I can do the initial review. I will ask that another qualified and certified historical appraiser give the final approval since this is my first historical renovation. That way there is no conflict of interest. Since the house is already "Locally Designated", the COA will give it more protection. Christina and Daniel's parents had gone through the nomination process and it was approved to be included in the National Register of Historic Places, back in 1984. In case you are interested, the Secretary of the Interior has four standards for the treatment of Historic Properties. They are preserving, rehabilitating, restoring and reconstructing. We will technically be "restoring" Greyson Manor. That means we are going through the process of accurately depicting the form, features, and character of how it was built by removing features from other periods, like the linoleum in the half bath. They allow limited upgrading of mechanical, electrical, and plumbing systems and other code-required work to make the property functional. Make sense?"

The rest of the group, engrossed in Scott's description of the work, nodded their understanding.

"Scott you are doing a fantastic job." Kaitlyn patted his arm. "I can't believe this is your first historical restoration. You have obviously done your homework. If you are done going over your plans, I thought I would share with you what I found doing my homework assignment this week. Carolyn, remember when you asked me to see if I could find the Cherokee Indian family in Oklahoma? Well, the story Frank told about Charles and Sara being killed makes sense now. I couldn't find records of a Charles Hawkins there, but I did find a Joe Hawkins, whose deceased father was a Charles. This has to be the same family because the records also said that his brothers George and Michael were also deceased. There was no record of a Jade. Do you think that Joe didn't list her because he was ashamed that she was left behind and wasn't sure if she was still alive?"

"It's very possible," responded Kevin. "As I think Carolyn told you, I have some Cherokee Indian blood as well and have done some research. There is a lot of misinformation because of incidents like that and also later in the census polls. A lot of the Indians would list themselves as either white or black because they were afraid that the government would take their land if they knew they were Indian. Can you blame them? So it's very hard to trace your bloodline. I've been struggling tracing mine. I am really only going by what our family says they were told by our ancestors. It's really hard to prove. In fact, they have these DNA tests now, but I have heard mixed reviews on them as well. I'm thinking about doing that though since I have hit a wall as far as research. I guess it couldn't hurt to try it."

Kaitlyn continued. "I found Joe listed on the Dawes Final Rolls list. It's the list of the Indians that were granted land when they got to Oklahoma. It was part of their payment for moving west. This whole thing is so sad but I am really glad we are doing something to help. My opinion is we do tell the true stories during the tours. It's part of the history. I think it's fascinating. Obviously, we will have to wait and see what Christina and Daniel think. They may need some time to get over this initial shock, don't you agree?"

"I agree," murmured Carolyn. "I wonder what the rest of the story was Frank was eluding to. I guess Daniel will read all about it. We'll have to wait to see if he is willing to tell us."

"The other assignment you gave me was to see if we could have the furniture appraised," Kaitlyn said. "I was able to find an appraiser through the Antique Market and he met with Christina and me. He made a list of which pieces are from which decade. I have a copy of that for each of you. It turns out that many of the pieces are from the early 1830's, so they could be the originals that the Indian family had bought. We figured if they were pieces dating later than 1840, then the Greysons added those. It was a fun project. Thanks for letting me run with that. I was really glad I could do something more than just invest."

"Well gang, I need to get over to the restaurant. You are coming with me, right Scott?" Scott nodded at Carolyn. "I think your work is done until we hear back from Daniel as to how we proceed. I need you to look at the restaurant appliances that are coming in today. Mike is meeting Kacey and me there as well. Tomorrow we are interviewing a potential chef. It's a woman and she says she is a wine connoisseur. We shall see."

Chapter 22

July 15, 2010

"Did you hear what Frank said?" Christina cried. "How could David have done that?"

"I know there must be some kind of mistake or misunderstanding. I am going to read the journal. I'll let you know what it says."

Daniel had taken Christina back to Greyson Manor. It was pouring down rain and the sky was very grey. Christina was feeling grey herself. She went upstairs to her room and Daniel took the file into the parlor. He laid it on the end table and went over to the bar and poured himself three fingers of Johnnie Walker Black. He took a long swig of the warm scotch then put the glass to his forehead and closed his eyes. He said a silent prayer that he was not about to confirm what Frank had told them. And Frank had said there was more.

He took his drink over to the end table and sat down. He looked around the room. What secrets are you hiding, he asked the house. He opened the file and began to read.

"January, 1841. My name is Jade. I am a Cherokee without a tribe. My family is gone. I live with the slave family and they care for me. I am sixteen years old. Three years ago Papa and Mama and Michael were killed by David Greyson's men. And then Greyson took me back to the house. I will not call him Master. He hurt me. He takes me to the house now many times. It doesn't hurt so much anymore but I hate him."

Daniel put the page down and picked up his scotch then just stared at it. He began to sob. His great, great, great grandfather had raped a young Indian girl. He felt nauseous but picked up the next page.

"April 1841. He brought home a wife. Her name is Ms. Kay. She is beautiful and has a kind smile. How could she be with him? Her dresses are fine. They are prettier than Mama's. He put Mama's things in that room. He says that is our room-the room with the window facing west. I imagine I can see my brothers out west. He brushes my hair with Mama's brush. He bathes me and makes me put on Mama's things. He says he loves me. I wonder if he will still take me to the room now that Ms. Kay has come to live in my house. "

Daniel picked up the next page.

"June, 1842. I saw Ms. Kay rocking on the porch. She was staring at the cotton fields. She was not smiling. Her dress was pretty. Her yellow hair was loose. It is very pretty too. I asked her if she needed something. She looked at me and didn't answer. She just kept rocking and looking at me. I wonder if she knows that Greyson loves me. I went back to work."

"January, 1843. I think she knows that Greyson took me to our room last night. He told me I had to be very quiet. I am always very quiet. He told me that I am pretty. He said he likes my long dark hair. I asked him about her. He said we don't talk about her. I told him she doesn't smile. He said he knows."

"March, 1844. It has been over a year since I have written. It is so hard to have any alone time here. I saw a man come to my house this morning. He was carrying a small black bag. He was a doctor. Ms. Kay is ill. Theresa was at my house all day. She said

that Ms. Kay cannot bear a child. Greyson is mad about that. He wants children to fill up my house and carry on his name. Ben says that it is God's punishment. He says that Greyson doesn't deserve to have children. No one knows that I think I may be with child."

Daniel read the last line again. There it was. That was the "more" Frank referenced. Jade was our great, great, great grandmother. Christina and I are part Cherokee, Daniel thought. Born from a rapist and an innocent Cherokee orphan. He put his head back on the chair and closed his eyes.

The next morning Christina walked into the kitchen to find Daniel there. "Oh, you stayed last night?"

"Yes," Daniel replied pouring himself a second cup of coffee. He looked up at her and she saw the distress in his eyes. "I believe it's true, Christina."

"You read all the pages?" she asked.

"Yes. They span three years. They basically say that David had raped Jade since she was thirteen and that eventually he took on a wife but she couldn't have children. In the last page Jade is saying she is pregnant. There aren't any other pages. I don't know if she stopped writing or if Frank didn't give me all of the pages or if he just never had any additional pages. Maybe she hid them. I don't know if Jade had that child. I am assuming so but don't have a way to prove it. She also said that the bedroom at the end of the hall was where she was with David. Since we know our great, great, great grandmother's name was Jade; I would say that is proof enough for me."

"But why wouldn't anyone have told us that she was Cherokee?" Christina asked.

"I can only assume that there was shame. There should have been. Our great, great, great granddad was a perverted monster."

"Do you think Mom and Dad knew?"

"I don't know. But I think if they did, they would have told us. We're adults. Maybe it's best that they died without knowing. The question is, now what do we do with that knowledge?" Daniel rubbed his temple.

"I think we need to talk to Frank again and ask him if he has any additional information. I wonder if his family wrote a journal or if he has the other pages. Maybe he didn't want us to read more than we could handle in one sitting." Christina made herself a cup of English breakfast tea and sat down at the table. "I want to read the journal pages, Daniel."

"Ok, I'll get them for you. Then let's go over to Frank's, ok?"

Christina finished reading the journal papers and put them back into the folder. She and Daniel walked over to Frank's house. Wanda answered the door.

"Hello Wanda. Is your Dad home?" Christina asked smiling at the girl. It was sad to think that Wanda was actually older than Jade was when Jade…she didn't want to think about it.

"Yes Ma'am, please come in."

Daniel and Christina stepped into the foyer.

"Please, come in. I assume you read the file?" Frank asked as he walked them into the living room. "Please, have a seat."

"Yes, we have both read the pages." Daniel hesitated then added, "Clearly, it's not something we were happy to learn about. Do you know if there are other pages?"

Frank shook his head. "If there are, I don't have them. I would think she would have continued to write but she may have hidden the other pages. Do you think you are related to her?"

"Christina and I are both choosing to not jump to conclusions too quickly. The last entry said that she was pregnant, but we don't know if she had the child, or if it survived, or if there were others. But we do know that our family tree says that we had a 'Jade' in our family in the 1800s. The other question I have is what happened to

Greyson's wife? If Jade did have the child, did David take it and raise it with his wife? Did his wife die? There are so many unanswered questions."

Frank looked tentative. "Have you discussed whether you are going to continue with the renovations and the tours?"

"Is that why you told us this horrid story? Are you trying to get us to stop our project?" Christina demanded.

Daniel raised his eyebrows and looked from Christina to Frank. He hadn't thought of that.

Frank shook his head. "No dear, I wouldn't do that. I just feel strongly that if you are going to turn it into a historical tour facility, then you have to tell the facts. I had never shared the journal with your parents or you in the past, because I, well, quite frankly, I was torn. I knew it would not be welcomed news and there really didn't seem to be a point in dredging it all up. I am sorry you had to learn about this, this way. You do realize that if it is true, then you have Cherokee blood in you. Look at it this way. You could be the direct descendent of the Cherokee family that owned this land. So essentially, they never truly left their land. Isn't that something?"

They were quiet for a moment and then Daniel said, "I guess that is a positive spin on a terrible story. But how in the hell do we tell the true story without horrifying the visitors, assuming we get past it enough to even relay this information. That was a rhetorical question. We need to think about it." Daniel rose. "Come on, Christina, let's go."

Frank watched them leave and with a heavy heart he sat back down.

Chapter 23
July 16, 2010

C arolyn and Kacey met at Southern Charm, "Charm" they were calling it for short. Their restaurant was coming together. The stainless steel appliances had come in the day before and they thought that they had never seen a refrigerator as beautiful. The stove went well with the hood that was there when they moved in and the prep area, also stainless, was spacious. The kitchen was just about complete. Scott promised to focus on building their bar and today was the day. Since they had not heard from Christina and Daniel last night or this morning, they decided to focus on the restaurant for now and give the Greysons some breathing room. Carolyn was sure that the shocking news about the murders of the Indian family members was something they were going to have to deal with as well as determining if they should reveal that information. Carolyn, Scott, Kevin and Kaitlyn all made a pact not to share that information with anyone else.

"Hey girl," Carolyn waved at Kacey.

"Hey you, everything alright? You sound a little down," Kacey asked.

"Yes, I am fine. Just a little tired. It's a lot of work focusing on two large projects at the same time."

"How is the renovation coming along? Have you started the

work yet or still in the planning stages?" Kacey asked as she pulled out her notebook.

"We are still in the planning stages, and you just reminded me that we haven't even started talking about the barn and slave quarter conversions. In fact, let me go say hi to my husband and remind him about that."

Kacey yelled out as Carolyn was walking away, "okay, as long as you don't distract him from the job at hand!"

Carolyn looked back and smiled at her friend then walked over to where Scott and Mike were working on the bar. Scott was using a large noisy sander and was wearing goggles. "Hey handsome," she said and leaned over and kissed him. "We're getting ready to have an interview. Should we take her somewhere else or can you guys take a break?"

"We can take a break. I need to go check on some parts out back." Scott wiped the sweat from his brow and he pulled the goggles off.

"Man, you look sexy in those things!" Carolyn purred.

"Get a room!" Mike called over his shoulder walking out back.

"Oh, I also wanted to tell you that we totally forgot to talk about the barn and the slave quarters yesterday. I know you haven't finished the plans yet, but should I go ahead and set up another meeting to discuss the event part of the business?"

"Actually, I need a little more time to put the plans together and you told me to focus on your bar, honey, so that's what I am doing. I'm also thinking we need to leave the Greysons alone for awhile. Let's see if they call us in the next couple of days. You know they must be devastated."

Carolyn frowned and shook her head. "You are right, babe."

"What? Did you just say I was right?" Scott winked.

Carolyn punched him in the arm lightly, laughing. "Very funny! Ok, looks like our interviewee just walked in the door, so I will talk to you later. Go play with your tools!" Carolyn winked back.

"Hi, Gabby? I'm Carolyn Kane and this is my partner, Kacey Burton."

The ladies greeted each other and shook hands.

Kacey pointed at the new table and chairs that they had set up in the bay window. "Let's sit over there and try out our new set up."

They had Gabby sit facing into the restaurant hoping to entice her. Kacey and Carolyn faced Gabby and the window trying to get the feel for the experience their patrons would soon have in their "bringing the outside in" space.

"So Gabby, we have reviewed your resume," Carolyn started. "You have an impressive background. Looks like you worked at three different restaurants over the last twenty years. Why don't you tell us about your experience and what you think you can bring to our new restaurant." She liked Gabby's demeanor so far and she was definitely a beautiful woman. She was thin and had shoulder length medium blond hair. She had huge green eyes, Carolyn noticed. Her looks would be a plus behind the bar. She had been thinking more about wanting to make sure that Charm would attract men as well as women. She had read several articles on the internet that said that men drink at least twice as much alcohol as women. She knew the appetizers couldn't be too prissy and they had to sell beer in addition to wine.

"Kacey explained to me that your concept is a wine and appetizer restaurant/bar. What I think I can bring to your restaurant/bar more than anything is business. New business and continued business. Because ladies, no disrespect but, I know this is your first place and you need someone that A) you can trust and B) that is going to bring in the cash. Am I right?" Gabby questioned them both.

Kacey and Carolyn looked at each other. This was an interesting start. Gabby had turned the conversation back to what was important to Kacey and Carolyn instead of launching into an "all about me" conversation. So far, so good and as Carolyn knew, that was

Sales 101; important for any industry.

"You are right Gabby," Kacey agreed. "So how would you make that happen?"

"Well, first of all, I need to gain your trust and once I do that, the rest will follow. Here is how I propose letting us all get to know each other better and giving you the opportunity to see me in action. Kacey, you had mentioned that you need someone who knows food and drinks, so I am assuming, especially now that I have seen the size of the place, that you need someone who is also very organized and efficient. What if I put on a little sidewalk taste test? Samples of some of the items I propose we include on the menu. Obviously, we can't include alcohol, but we could show a list of some of the wines. I also have a suggestion. I love your concept, but you have to have a way to pull in the men as well. For instance, you could play on the idea of providing free snacks and discounted beers while their wives shop. Then their wives can join them when they are through. It has to be attractive to both genders to bring in the 'dough', if you know what I mean."

Carolyn smiled at Kacey. "I haven't had a chance to talk to you about this, but Gabby is right. I did some research and supposedly, men drink twice as much as women. We need to find a way to bring them in too."

"Ok, as long as it doesn't turn into a casual sports bar with peanut shells all over the floor. I would give up a little revenue to keep that from happening. Remember the place is called 'Charm'," Kacey insisted.

"I agree with you Kacey, but remember, it's called 'Southern Charm' and so we want to attract southern gentlemen as well."

They both looked thoughtful and turned back to Gabby. "Tell us more about the sidewalk taste test. What did you have in mind?" inquired Carolyn.

"Kacey told me that you want to have your grand opening on

Labor Day, right?"

They nodded.

"What if Saturday, July 31st, we have a taste test right outside on the sidewalk? That's a month ahead of the grand opening. That would give you a chance to try me out and still have time to find someone else if you don't like what you see and taste. It will give you two weeks to advertise it and get folks to come out on a Saturday. You think the bar would be done by then? It would be great to let people peek in the windows to see what's 'coming soon'."

The girls agreed that it was an excellent idea and talked through the details. It would also give their patrons the chance to give them feedback about what would bring them in for a drink and appetizers or desserts. Gabby gave them several references and talked about her experience with food and wine pairings.

Carolyn lay in bed that night, next to her very tired husband, listening to his deep breathing. He had fallen asleep the second his head hit the pillow. They were both working very hard at their new ventures and not bringing in any money yet. She knew she would look back on this time with fond memories, thinking through the effort they were all putting in to make their dreams come true. She didn't want to rush it. Her last thought before she drifted off to sleep was thinking about Jade, the Indian girl that one hundred and seventy years ago, lived at Greyson Manor. What were her dreams about, she wondered?

Chapter 24
June, 1844

Theresa walked slowly back to the slave house. She went in, sat down and cried. Ben came in after cleaning up. It had been a long, hot day in the fields. The heat was unbearable but they had just had their first cotton bloom of the season.

"Mother, what is the matter?" Ben kneeled down next to her. "What can I do to help you?"

Theresa was wringing her handkerchief. She looked up at her son and saw the love there. Her heart ached for Ms. Kay. "It's Ms. Kay. She has lost another child. The doctor came today and told her that she cannot have children and that she should stop trying or she will die." Tears streamed down her cheeks and Ben hugged his mother.

"It's that damn Masta Greyson. He is forcing himself on her!" Ben gritted his teeth.

"Ben, he is her husband. It is her duty to bear children and clearly she feels a failure for not having done so. She has a faraway look in her eyes. I hope wherever her mind has gone that she comes back to us. She has a sweet soul."

"But Masta Greyson doesn't deserve children. How could you even think that a child could have any kind of happiness with him? What about Jade?" Ben stood up and went to the window and looked out, deeply disturbed.

Theresa understood that her son had deep feelings for Jade. She wasn't sure of the nature of them but he was very protective of her. He must be thinking that he hasn't been able to protect her from the Masta, she realized. "My son, come here and look at me."

Ben turned and looked at his mother. He dropped his head and came back to her side. Then he looked her in the eyes.

As she looked at him, she realized she had been right. There was pain in his eyes, but more so there was love for Jade in those eyes. "She will survive this, my son. She is a strong girl. She has survived worse, at least in her mind. Seeing what happened to Charles and Sara right in front of her; that will never leave her. You have been a good friend to her, Ben."

They heard a carriage leaving the barn and went to the window. Joe was driving and he pulled up in front of the manor. He jumped down when David came out with Kay. David was holding her elbow. She looked unsteady. Joe and David helped her into the carriage then David went around the other side and climbed on. He tapped the horses and they went on down the road toward town.

"Kay, darling, are you feeling any better?" David said, with very little concern in his tone.

Kay looked straight ahead and didn't answer.

"Kay, I asked you a question," he ran one hand through his hair and glared at her.

Kay continued to look ahead and did not answer.

"I believe your father has asked us to attend the cocktail party in honor of the Dunwodys this evening because he wants to know that you are doing well since marrying me. You haven't visited him much in the last year." Kay said nothing. "When we arrive at your father's this morning, you will meet with the other ladies for tea and I will meet with the men about the mill and then with Dunwody's architect. Apparently, the goal is to discuss how to help the Dunwodys with their plans to rebuild their plantation home. The fire at their house warming party two Christmas' ago has really spooked them. They are talking about building it with brick and stucco this time. It is still horrible to think about how many people got burned during that fire. It's a lesson to all of us to not throw debris down the chimney! Anyway, we will enjoy the party tonight and return home tomorrow. Do not mention anything about your miscarriages. It will just break your father's heart and put too much focus on us. I have an idea I will tell you about in good time that I believe will make you very happy."

At that, Kay looked at Greyson. "There is nothing you can do to make me happy," she said and looked back at the road.

Greyson squirmed in his seat and shook his head. He would not allow her to suck him into her pathetic self pitying. For god's sake, she was living in a huge manor and wanted for nothing. He had to think of the business at hand. He was set to make a fortune this year. He planned to talk about getting additional help from the slaves owned by The Roswell Manufacturing Company. The faster he could harvest the cotton crops, the faster they could grow the mill. There had been talk of adding a second mill eventually.

They pulled into the Temple plantation. Kay's face lit up when she saw her father standing on the porch and then her expression went stoic again.

David patted her on the back. "Cheer up my dear, it will all work out." He jumped down and went over to her side helping her out of the carriage. She immediately ran to her father and flew into his arms. Her father had a look of alarm on his face.

"There, there, my girl. Let me look at you. You are looking quite pale my dear, what is the matter?" her father asked her, concerned.

"Oh Father," Kay put her head on his shoulder weeping.

David quickly went up the porch steps to stand with them. He put his hand on Kay's back. "She has missed you terribly, sir, and she is a bit under the weather." He tightened his fingers on her dress and she looked up at him. She saw the anger flash in his eyes. She pulled herself out of her father's arms.

"You must think I am a silly girl, Father. David is right. I just miss you. I will be fine." She brushed her tears away and smiled at her father. Then she walked past him into his home. Her mother had passed away several years earlier from Scarlett Fever, which is why she assumed her father had made a fairly quick decision on giving her hand in marriage to David. He always seemed to be at a loss for what to do with her. She heard the other ladies in the sitting room and joined them there. She was happy for the space between her and David. What had he meant when he said he had an idea that would make her happy? He had to know how much she wanted a child. She would have to think of that later. For now, she would enjoy the company of her family and old friends.

David joined Robert Temple and the other men who owned stock in the mill; "The Colony", they called themselves. They were enjoying a smoke and a drink in the parlor.

"Gentlemen, David has joined us," stated Robert. David proceeded to shake hands and offer his greetings. Robert watched him as he did so. Something seemed amiss with his daughter. It really was no longer his business, but he couldn't help wanting to understand how she was truly doing.

"Greyson, join us for a drink. We are celebrating a very successful month. The mill is now producing tenting and rope in addition to the clothing and flannels. Much of our success is due to the vast amount of cotton you have been able to harvest. Cheers!"

"Cheers!" they all raised their glasses then drank.

"Greyson," a heavy set man asked, "How does it feel to be profiting to such a great extent off an Indian plantation?" the man laughed. Some of the other men laughed but not as energetically.

Greyson laughed with them. "Let's just say, it was the luck of the draw!"

"Cheers, cheers," yelled the burly man.

"As you know, Greyson, the rest of us had to build our own homes whether we won the land or bought it from the lottery winner. Do you have no self-respect? How could you live in a Cherokee house?" asked another man sternly.

"Henry, how many times are you going to ask me that? I know you didn't fare as well as I did in the drawing, but it couldn't be helped. There is no reason for me to destroy a perfectly fine plantation house, just to satisfy your prejudice." David laughed and shook his head. The other men laughed as well. Turning his back on Henry, he started to walk over to get another drink.

Henry looked irritated. "What of the Indian girl?"

David stopped in his tracks. He slowly turned to look at Henry. "What did you say?"

"I said, what of the Indian girl?"

"I don't know what you are talking about," and he turned back once again. The room was silent. All but Robert had heard the rumor.

David poured himself a stiff drink and drank it down. All eyes went to Robert while David had his back to the men. Robert grew furious. His thin face turned red and he pulled his shoulders back, which seemed to make him look a bit taller than his normal short height.

"Greyson, tell me you don't have an Indian girl," Robert said through clenched teeth, then he pulled on his long grey mustache.

David stiffened once again. Time to come clean. He turned and looked at the crowd. "All right, I will tell you. Her family left her behind and it was too late to send her out west. She was just a little thing at the time and I just couldn't in my right mind turn her over to authorities. She has been living with my slaves. I haven't mentioned it because it is really not that important."

Robert glared at David. "How old is she now?"

"I have no idea. I would say she is a young lady at this point. I really don't see her often." Then David looked past Robert with wide eyes. Beads of sweat appeared on his wide forehead. Kay was standing in the doorway.

Robert turned to see what David was looking at. His daughter stood staring at David. "My dear, you really shouldn't be in here. You don't need to hear about the business we men are discussing. Are you all right?"

Kay took a deep breath and saw David take one as well. "Father, it is true. We do have an Indian girl living at the plantation. She is nineteen now, according to the slave mother. She keeps to herself and is a good worker. I didn't see any harm in her staying. In fact, I had heard she was orphaned and didn't want to leave her home. Please don't worry yourselves about her. I plan to start spending more time with her. Apparently, she knows how to read and write. I want to introduce her to Mrs. Moore and Mrs. Gordon so that she will have an Indian connection here. I think you gentlemen will all agree the stories we have heard about the Trail of Tears is that a horrendous injustice was done to those Indians and since we are all directly benefiting from their plight, we need to atone for that. Helping this young girl is one way we can do that, don't you all agree?" She looked at each man, holding his gaze for a few seconds, ending with Greyson.

One man grumbled under his breath. "Damn Indians."

"Excuse me, Mr.?" Kay asked.

He shook his head and walked over to get another drink.

"Father, what do you have to say about all of this?"

Robert continued to pull at his mustache and thought for a moment. He looked at Kay and then at Greyson. "Is this what has been concerning you, Kay?"

Kay looked into his eyes. "Yes, Father." She hated to lie to him, but she needed to for the time being while waiting to hear what David's idea was.

Robert walked over to Kay and kissed her on the forehead. "You have always had such a big heart." He turned and looked at the men. "She was always taking in strays when she was a young girl. I guess this is just a continuation of that kind behavior. I think it is fine and admirable of both of you to make sure this girl is cared for. You could have turned her out and god knows what would have happened to her. I think we all agree, don't we gentlemen?" They all nodded their heads in agreement except the big, burly man. "I repeat, don't we gentlemen?" Robert asked him directly.

"Yes, yes," the man grumbled.

"Thank you, Father." Kay touched his forearm then turned and walked back to the sitting room to rejoin the other ladies. She thought to herself, well at least she would have a daughter of sorts.

Chapter 25
July 1844

"Theresa, I want to ride into town with you, Joseph and Jade." Kay was sitting in the parlor putting the finishing touches on a shawl. She didn't look up from her work.

Theresa was stunned. Did she just say "Jade"?

When Theresa didn't respond, Kay looked up. "Is there a problem, Theresa?"

"Well, Ms. Kay, I thought I heard you say you want to go into town with me, Joseph and Jade."

"I did say that, Theresa."

Theresa had a questioning look on her face.

"If you have something to say to me, Theresa, just say it. You know I respect your opinion."

"Why thank you for saying that, Ms. Kay. Jade hasn't been off this plantation since....since her family was here." Theresa dropped her head. Then she looked back up, confused. "Does Masta Greyson know of your idea, Ms. Kay?"

"Yes, he does. We spoke of it last night. I want to drop off some clothes and household items to help the Dunwodys recover from that horrible fire. I am glad they are finally getting around to rebuilding. I thought it would be the perfect time to introduce Jade to Mrs. Gordon and Mrs. Moore. They are the Cherokee Indian wives of two of the mill workers. Mr. Gordon runs the storefront for the mill and Mr. Moore is an engineer who works with the machinery. You remember seeing them the last time we were in town together, don't you Theresa?"

"I do, Ms. Kay. Oh, Ms. Kay, Jade will be so happy to see other Cherokee, I do believe." Theresa put her hands together and did a slight hop.

Kay smiled at Theresa's enthusiasm. "Well all right then, go and collect them and ask Joseph to bring the carriage around front. Once he does, tell him to pick up the crates in the foyer. They are full of clothes for the Dunwodys. I want to leave straight away. Run on now." Kay folded the shawl and took it out to the foyer and laid it in one of the crates. There was no reason Ms. Dunwody couldn't have something nice to wrap around her shoulders when the weather turned cool. Maybe it would help alleviate some of her sorrow for losing her home. She stood looking around Greyson Manor. She appreciated its beauty, but she also couldn't help but think of the Cherokee family that lived here prior. She had been afraid to ask David which story was the truth. Did they go west or did they die? She couldn't bear the answer either way, so it was best to not think of it at all. She went to find David.

"David, can we talk for a moment?" She found him on the back porch sharpening a blade.

"Yes dear, what can I help you with?" He stopped what he was doing and looked at her. "You look lovely today."

"You haven't told me your idea yet."

David looked at her then leaned back against the porch railing. She seemed in much better spirits since seeing her father. She seemed stronger somehow and with purpose but he knew she was still grieving for her second lost child. He decided to broach the subject. "We could adopt."

Kay raised her eyebrows. Then turned away, tears in her eyes. She collected herself then turned back to him. "I know how desperately you want children of your own. You have mentioned the word 'heir' many times. Would you consider an adopted child, your heir?" she asked hopeful.

He folded his arms, leaned back against the railing again and crossed his legs. He looked straight into her eyes, wanting her to understand what he was saying. "Only if the child was my own."

Kay's face dropped. "What do you mean? If I can't have a baby...," she suddenly understood. "You mean you would have a child with another woman and then raise it with me?" Was he having relations with someone? Just then Jade caught her eye as she was crossing the yard heading towards the slave quarters. David followed her gaze, seeing Jade, he turned back to Kay. Kay looked at him and he nodded. "Jade?" then more demurely, "Jade?"

"Yes," he simply stated.

Kay turned and walked back into the house and up to her room. She paced the floor. She couldn't think straight. Is this something that she had known all along and simply refused to acknowledge? Jade was so young. She was so... Indian. She was so beautiful. Her heart ached for the young girl and for herself. She was torn with conflicting emotions. At least the child would be David's. At least they wouldn't have to tell the world that she was barren. She assumed David wouldn't reveal where they got the baby. Would the baby look Indian? She had no other options at this point. What would Jade do when they took her baby? Would they tell her prior to.....she couldn't bear to think of David and Jade making love but she knew now they already had.

She slowly walked to the end of the hall to the last bedroom and opened the door. She stepped inside. This was the room that Jade's parents had shared. David had insisted she not go in this room and they kept it closed up. She looked at the dresser and saw a brush and hand mirror. She picked up the brush and saw the strands of black hair. She put the brush down and looked around again. She went to the armoire and opened the door. There were dresses hanging there. They were nice dresses, although not as fine as her own. Then she saw the blue silk dress hanging in the corner. That was her dress. She had thought it had been ruined when cleaned. That is what David had told her. She pulled it out of the armoire and stared at it. There was a mirror on the inside of the armoire door. She could see the doorway in the reflection and David in the doorway. She quickly turned around, furious.

"This is my dress!"

He walked in and shut the door behind him. "You have two choices," he responded. "You can continue to wallow in your self-pity, or you can put that dress back, walk out of this room and forget you saw it. If you do that, you will have a baby in about seven months. If you don't, you won't. It is up to you."

Her chest was heaving with her deep breaths. Seven months? She couldn't believe the cruelty of this man. This man she married. This man her father asked her to marry. This man that took the Indian's plantation and kept it as is. This man that kept the Indian girl. Oh god, she realized the ugly truth of it all. She threw the dress down and ran out the door and down the stairs. In the foyer stood Theresa, Joseph and Jade. They all looked alarmed at her fast descent. She stopped and stared at Jade. Jade's expression was impossible to read. She just stared at Kay. Kay realized then that Jade had accepted her position in this community but knowing David had forced himself upon her, at least initially, she couldn't understand what Jade felt now for David or Kay. Then Jade's hand went to her stomach. Kay looked at her hand and then back into Jade's eyes. Jade would fight for this child; that Kay was certain of. She took a deep breath and walked out the front door with Jade, Theresa and Joseph following. Joseph helped the women into the carriage and they rode into town.

Chapter 26
July, 1844

They arrived at the Dunwody's to find many people working at cleaning up the debris from the fire. Kay was surprised at how little headway they had made at rebuilding. She was glad she and David had not made it to that Christmas party. Several people had been severely burned and one had died. She saw Jane and waved. Joseph helped her down from the carriage. Kay asked Theresa and Jade to stay in the carriage. The dust and soot was everywhere and she was amazed to see Jane speaking with the workers.

"Jane, hello!" called Kay, waving.

"Good morning, Kay. How are you?" asked Jane. Jane Bulloch Dunwody's parents lived next door at Bulloch Hall. She had married John Dunwody and soon after, the house had burned to the ground. It had not been an easy start to their marriage.

"I am fine, but more importantly, how are you?" Kay touched Jane's arm. "I am so sorry again for your loss. You must be exhausted. What are you doing?"

"My parents have been so kind to allow us to stay with them at Bulloch Hall while we rebuild, but it's been two and a half years. I just can't sit there anymore. I felt the need to get out here and supervise!"

"I hope you are being careful, Dear," responded Kay, worried. "I brought you some things that may help get you through for awhile; just some clothes and small household items. I also made you a shawl. I hope you like it. Should we drop them off at Bulloch Hall?"

"That would be wonderful, if you don't mind. I plan on staying out here a bit longer making sure these men keep working. John has been having meetings at the mill and can't seem to focus on the house right now."

"Alright then, we will take the crates over to Bulloch Hall. We are also going to visit Mrs. Moore and Mrs. Gordon today. I want to introduce Jade to them. I am hoping it will give the girl a sense of belonging. I just feel so odd living in her parent's house and her living with the slaves. It just doesn't seem right, but David is insistent. I know there has been a lot of talk around town about her of late. I just want to do something to help her." Kay and Jane both looked over at the carriage. Jade had been watching them, but looked away.

"Well, you are doing a very charitable thing, Kay. Bless you for all you are doing for us too. I can't thank you enough. I will let you get on with your day then. I see some men slowing down over there, so I better get back to it!" Jane smiled. They kissed cheeks and Kay went back to the carriage. They rode the carriage out the path and down to Bulloch Hall. It was such a grand home, Kay admired. They dropped off the crates and headed toward the mill. Both the Moores and the Gordons lived in townhomes, called The Bricks, near the mill. These were the first townhomes of their kind and they were built to house the management workers of the mill.

Joseph stopped the horses in front of The Bricks and helped the women out of the carriage. Kay pulled two small baskets of biscuits from the carriage and handed one to Jade. Jade looked at Kay as she took the basket and with a slight smile bowed her head.

"Everything will be fine, Jade. Just follow me. Mrs. Moore and Mrs. Gordon are really anxious to see you." Kay noticed that Jade had worn her long straight black hair back in a ponytail and had wrapped a ribbon around it. She really was a lovely young woman. She again tried to keep the thoughts of Jade and David out of her mind. It was clearly not Jade's fault. She knew in her gut David had taken advantage of her or worse, forced himself upon her.

Kay knocked at the Moore's front door. Mrs. Moore quickly opened the door and with a wide grin, rushed past Kay and put her arm around Jade, and walked her into her home. She sat Jade in a rocker near the fireplace and knelt down taking Jade's hands in hers. She spoke softly to her for a few minutes in their Cherokee language and Jade's eyes welled up. She spoke back to her also in her language and Kay realized she probably had not spoken much at all since her parents had left other than to Theresa. And David. She had learned English fairly well so she knew she hadn't spoken in Cherokee in several years. Kay raised her hand to her mouth to keep from sobbing. She looked at Theresa and Joseph and motioned to them to walk back outside.

"Let's give them some time together. We can't possibly know what it means to Jade to see another Indian face."

Just then, Mrs. Gordon came out of her home and walked towards the Moore's front door. Kay nodded and pointed her inside.

Kay, Theresa and Joseph stayed outside for well over an hour and when the door reopened, they could see on Jade's face that she was rejuvenated. Her face was full of emotion, although hard to read. Kay hoped it had been a positive experience for her. She prayed it didn't remind her of the terrible ordeal she had been through in losing her family. Both Mrs. Gordon and Mrs. Moore stood in the doorway waving goodbye and thanking Kay for bringing her by. "Please come again soon," said Mrs. Moore.

Joseph again helped the women back into the carriage and Theresa sat in the back with Jade and put her arm around her. Jade laid her head on Theresa's shoulder and closed her eyes. At one point on the ride home, Kay turned around to look at Jade again and saw her staring at her. Jade smiled at her. Kay smiled and turned back. She had made the right decision. It was time for another right decision. She would insist that Jade move into the house. They would raise her baby as a family. Kay knew it was the right thing to do.

Chapter 27

July 31, 2010

I t was a beautiful Saturday morning. They had been blessed with cooler temperatures than normal. Apparently, one of the tropical storms in the Gulf was pushing cool breezes up into Georgia. The high would only be in the low eighties that day. That would bring people out to Roswell to enjoy the shopping, museums, art galleries and restaurants. That was just what they needed, Carolyn thought as she unlocked the door. She turned on the lights and looked around Charm. Even though it was a small space, it was more dazzling than she could have ever hoped for.

"It's like seeing your first baby born!" Kacey exclaimed as she walked in behind Carolyn.

Carolyn turned around and grabbed some of the bags Kacey was carrying. "Well, I wouldn't know about that, but it sure is beautiful! Didn't the bar turn out nicely? Scott and Mike spent days getting the stain and polyurethane just right. I love the curve. It's gorgeous. And the paintings we did are amazing. The lighting really makes them pop against the dark walls. That was such a good idea to add the silver paint! You would never guess that we painted them ourselves! What's in these bags?"

They put them on one of the tables. "Step away from the bags!" Kacey said. "It's a surprise!" Just then the door opened and Gabby walked in.

"Well hi, Charming Ladies! Say hello to your lucky 'Charm'," she winked. Her arms were full of sunflowers and wild flowers. "For our tables outside," Gabby said. "I need to get busy in the kitchen. If you want to work on setting up the tables we can start rolling out the samples. I also made some lemonade and iced tea last night. The jugs are in the fridge."

"I love your excitement and confidence," Carolyn smirked.

"Before you run off I have something for both of you," Kacey said as she pulled some tee shirts out of one of the bags she brought. She held up the black tee shirts and showed them the design on the front. It said Southern Charm with the emphasis on Charm in a funky bold font, written in silver. The girls laughed and clapped. Then Kacey pulled name tags out of the bag and gave them each one. Next she pulled out 3 x 5 cards with the items they were going to put out to sample with a yes/no and a comment line next to each. They were determined to get feedback on their menu. They wanted to be sure that when they opened, their menu would be the best it could be. Their goal was to attract the people who frequent the area but also pull in folks from outside of the Roswell area as well.

They spent the rest of the morning preparing the food and setting up the tables on the sidewalk to be ready for the early lunch crowd. At eleven o'clock they felt they were ready. Kacey and Gabby stood behind the tables with the samples and Carolyn walked up and down the street saying hello to the passersby asking them to stop for a taste test. She had tried the samples herself and she wasn't sure they could be any better. Of course there were a few things on the menu Scott wouldn't like since he couldn't stand onions and peppers, but there were plenty of different options to appease even his finicky appetite. Gabby was true to her word to incorporate foods men would like and added pork tacos and cheeseburger sliders. They had such a large lunch crowd they were able to accomplish what they had intended to in about two hours. Carolyn made sure that no one got away without filling out the survey card.

When the crowd thinned out, Carolyn and Kacey took a break and went inside. They poured themselves a glass of iced tea and toasted to the morning's success. They went out the back to their new patio and relaxed. They both agreed not only did the food turn out fabulously, but Gabby was the real prize.

"Sold!" cried out Kacey when Carolyn commented on what a great job Gabby had done.

"Agreed!" sang out Carolyn and they toasted again.

"Hey girls! You out here?" Just when they were thinking about heading back out front, Christina and Kevin peeked out the back door. Kevin was carrying a large bag.

"Hi, how are you both?" Carolyn asked. She was so happy to see Christina. She hadn't seen or heard from her since the meeting two weeks earlier. And she was with Kevin. That was a good sign.

They all said hello and gave each other hugs.

"Have a seat! So what's in your bag?" asked Kacey trying to peak in.

Christina and Kevin looked at each other and smiled. "Go ahead," Christina grinned.

"Okay." Kevin smiled and reached into the bag and pulled out a very nice wooden dartboard. "It's kind of like a house warming present for a bar - a bar warming present."

Kacey frowned. "Oh boy, here we go with turning the place into a sports bar."

"One little dart board doesn't a sports bar make," teased Carolyn. "Actually, this is a fantastic idea. Something for the guys to do while their wives shop. Of course while drinking beer and snacking. No worries, no peanut shells to throw on the floor!"

Scott and Mike walked out the back door. "Hey everyone," Scott called out.

"How did the taste test go?" asked Mike. "Whoa, is that what I think it is?" Kevin proudly held up the dartboard and nodded.

Mike grabbed the dartboard to look it over. "Let's get that thing on the wall!"

After telling the guys about their morning and sending Mike, Kevin and Kacey off to find the appropriate wall to hang the dartboard, Carolyn and Scott turned back to Christina.

"Christina, how have you been?" Carolyn asked concerned.

"First of all, I need to apologize for not being in touch with you in the last two weeks. Daniel and I had a lot to think about and discuss; which we did. We decided to keep moving forward with the renovations. We are still mulling over whether we want to give tours of the house. We don't feel that we have enough information at this point to share compelling stories that aren't full of holes. We decided that we would keep trying to learn more about the house and our ancestors and then if we get to the point where we have enough positive things to talk about on a tour, then we can add the tours later. We still want to renovate it though and when we have events if people ask about the house, we'll just tell them what we are comfortable with. But for the time being, we are not going to have it set up like a museum with formal tours. What do you think?"

Carolyn nodded her head in approval. "You have obviously given this a lot of thought and it makes sense to me. Don't you agree, Scott?"

Scott agreed. "That is really great news. The two weeks actually gave me the time I needed to focus on finishing up the bar here, so I am all yours. Can we schedule another meeting so that I can show you the plans?"

"Yes," Christina responded. "I will call Daniel and send out a meeting invite to you all. I have already spoken with Frank and told him for now we aren't planning on doing the tours and he said he would respect our decision and our privacy. I think he was very disappointed though. I know he really wanted to be a tour guide. Hopefully we can pull the history together down the road, but I don't want it to hold us up from opening it as an event facility. Besides, we don't want to delay any events, because we will need the revenue to pay the restoration expense. Scott, do you think we can get it all done in time for the holidays?"

"I will relook at the timeline to make sure. I will do that before our next meeting. I agree the holidays would be the perfect time for a grand opening and should help us start out making a pretty profit. So, Christina, not to change the subject," Scott inquired, raising his eyebrows and looking over at Kevin, "how are things on that front?"

"Wow, you are just like a girl," Carolyn said. "You don't have to answer that Christina, it's none of our business." Scott laughed as Carolyn nudged him.

Christina's beautiful face turned red. "He has been a nice home-coming present. I'll just leave it at that."

"Time for round two!" Gabby called out as she walked in. "Have you seen the comments? What did you think? Is there anything I should change before the evening crowd comes in? Did you notice the cucumber pita sandwiches were scarfed right up? Who would have thought? Even the guys liked those. I need to get busy."

"You did an amazing job today, Gabby. Your idea really panned out. Let's go in the kitchen and go over the survey cards and see if we need to tweak anything," responded Carolyn.

The two walked into the kitchen. Scott walked over to join in on the dart game underway. The place was really going to work out and they were going to be able to move forward with the plantation home as well.

A few hours later, after refreshing the food and setting back up on the sidewalk out front, they started the evening taste test. They not only had the potential future customers stopping by but Mia, Angel, Josie and Daniel all came by to show their support as well. It turned out Gabby had been right. Starting with a taste test before their doors were even open, proved to be an excellent way to advertise their new venture. Southern Charm was a success in the making.

Chapter 28
August 15, 2010

C hristina welcomed her guests to her home and led them all
to the living room where she had cheese, crackers and drinks
waiting. Kevin, Carolyn and Scott had arrived a few minutes early.
Daniel was the last to join, having had to drive from downtown.
They talked about how they were putting the finishing touches on
Charm, how excited they all were for Carolyn and were looking forward to the grand opening on Labor Day.

When Daniel arrived, they got down to business. Scott had
brought an easel so he could show the plans for Greyson Manor
more easily. He had been out to the house several times working on
the renovation designs for the barn and slave quarters.

Daniel and Christina stood and addressed their friends. "Thank
you all for coming this evening," Daniel started.

"And for your patience with us," Christina added.

"Yes, thank you for your understanding. I believe Christina has
mentioned to a few of you that we do want to proceed with the restoration of the house, and determine what needs to be done with the
barn and slave quarters. We do want to have the home available for
special events like parties, weddings, and bar mitzvahs. However, we
decided we really don't have enough information about the original
Greysons to have tours. The story would be incomplete and we do

not wish to share what we read in the journal pages until we understand the rest of the story. We will continue to go through our family records and see what we can find for that period and if we are able to put the pieces together, we will add the tours. Scott, would you like to come up and share with us your designs?" Daniel and Christina sat down and gave the floor to Scott.

Scott went through the design and restoration needed for the main house. "I have a question. Daniel and Christina, now that we are not doing the tours, did you still want to do the upstairs bedrooms?"

They both nodded yes. "Absolutely, we want to proceed with the original plans you proposed, in preparation for doing the tours someday soon," commented Daniel.

Scott hesitated, looking as though he just had an important thought. "Christina, when we had gone upstairs to the bedrooms, you had mentioned that the bedroom at the end of the hall had always given you a weird vibe. Isn't that right?"

"Yes. It was one of the rooms that we kept the door closed and just had the maids clean from time to time, but we never used it. I always felt some kind of presence there. I'm not saying I saw a ghost or anything," she laughed embarrassed. Everyone chuckled. "But now we know what went on in that room."

"Something is telling me that maybe your search for answers is in that room," Scott mentioned. "Not that I am saying it's haunted. Have you had any luck finding any journals or letters from family members versus just legal documents?"

"No, most of what I have found in our files is legal documentation. I do still want to go through each bedroom to see if there are any Bibles where notes may have been made, or journal pages kept, and I want to go up to the attic. Quite frankly, I am afraid to go up there alone. As you know, Roswell is known for its abundance of ghosts, so I am just not comfortable going up there by myself. Any volunteers to help me with that search?" Christina looked straight at Kevin.

Kevin jumped at the chance. He had always been fascinated with history and didn't want to miss this opportunity. It helped that it would also allow him to spend time with Christina; something he couldn't get enough of he noticed. "I'm your man!"

"Well, I see that you are, Kevin. Thank you. Maybe we can head up there after the meeting since you are here anyway."

"That would be fine," Kevin responded. And then maybe he could stay, he thought.

"Well, I'm glad that has been settled. Let me show you the designs for the barn and slave quarters." Scott pulled the house design off the easel and put the barn design up.

There was immediate recognition that this was a piece of art. Scott believed this design was his finest work to date. "Now, you fortunate folks are lucky to have not only a historical renovator on hand, but also a contractor who likes to draw. Obviously, to make the barn a place that could be dressed up and dressed down, depending on the occasion, restoring it back to its original is not the right thing to do. Thus, I have designed a structure that can be used for a wedding reception or a casual barbeque. The wood is completely rotted on the original and the space is actually dangerous as it stands. I will need to tear it down and put in place a rendition of its former self. As you can see, the lines of the building are the same, but the wood is new and the use of stone for a patio in front with a large fireplace will provide ambiance for days and nights when our patrons want to be outside. Inside, there are no more stalls. It has been opened up to allow for a lot of seating and a dance floor. The dance floor is not a permanent structure, so it can be moved around to accommodate any size group. Also, depending on the type of band that is engaged, some will need more room than others. Of course, there will be mood lighting everywhere with the use of sconces, recessed and outdoor lighting." Scott stopped for a moment and looked around at the group. They were all nodding their heads and commenting on the design. So far, so good.

"Next, the slave quarters will be converted to a kitchen. This is a state of the art, commercial grade kitchen to allow for parties up to two hundred people. As you can see, I have doubled up on most of the appliances, everything in stainless, of course. And a very large stainless steel prep area. I have added doors to the back to allow for vendors to bring in supplies. Any questions about the kitchen? Carolyn, do you have a question?"

She looked perplexed. "I'm sorry, honey, it's beautiful, but my mind keeps wondering to what it used to be. Is there anything we can do to honor the slaves that worked this land for so many years? It's just kind of strange to me to just move on and change it to something different. Will people forget? No offense to your family, Daniel and Christina, but do you know what I mean?"

"Yes, I do," said Daniel solemnly. "Slavery was a part of the culture back then. Let me think on that. I understand what you are saying; maybe some kind of plaque thanking those that worked the land. I'll have to think about it but I agree with you. Scott, your plans are really comprehensive and I am so glad we hired you. You are right. Your talents in historical renovation, contracting and design are just what we needed here. Thank you for all the effort you have put into this. I am assuming you are going to tell us how much this is going to cost us all? Emphasis on the all, my investor friends." Daniel smiled and looked around the room.

Scott pulled out what he estimated the budget to be and then told them what his father had always told him. "Take the dollars and double them. Take the time estimate and double that too. That way, there will be no surprises."

Silence. Uh, oh, Scott thought. Overkill? Over budget, certainly. "Is this doable? I know it's higher than what we originally discussed but it is what is necessary to feed large parties. I could probably make a few adjustments to reduce the cost a bit. Should we talk about what we should remove?" Scott was disappointed in the concern he was seeing on their faces.

"Scott, that is significantly more that we had originally discussed. I guess I wasn't thinking that the kitchen would be so expensive. I think the house and the barn sound like they are right in line. Kevin what are your thoughts?" Daniel asked.

"If I do the math to determine each of our share in the expense, you are right Daniel, it is above what I can afford at this point. Obviously, we have to have a kitchen, though."

"At the risk of sounding self-promoting, I do have an idea that may work, at least initially. Would you all like to hear it?" Carolyn inquired.

They all agreed that they were open to any ideas at this point.

"What if we don't do anything with the slave quarters for now, or maybe just renovate the building itself but don't add the kitchen and just outsource the cooking to Charm." Carolyn hesitated and checked their reaction. They all seemed to be considering the idea seriously. She continued. "When we have an event, I could hire some temporary workers to help with the food preparation and to work the event. We would need servers anyway. I wasn't sure if you had thought of that. I think the use of temporary workers is the way to go, at least initially."

"So you believe that Charm will be able to cook for a large event here and also attend to your restaurant patrons out of the same kitchen?" asked Daniel.

"It would be a challenge, but Scott designed the kitchen so well that it is very efficient. I think it is definitely worth a try. There would be a lot of prep work that could be done ahead of time as well. As I said, I think it's worth a try at least to get this project started. Once we have had a number of events and the revenue is coming in, we can put the money back into the business to finish the kitchen here. The added revenue for Charm would also help me get that business off the ground too. We already discussed advertising for both places at each of the facilities. What do you all think?"

Christina began, "I think it makes a lot of sense as long as you think it's workable, I am all for it. Daniel?"

"I agree, it's the best option we have. Kevin?"

"I also agree and it keeps it all in the family. The other benefit to using Charm to provide the food and using temps, is that we don't incur the expense ahead of time. We can use the down payment we would be getting on an event to cover a lot of the expense. If you all like, I will call Kaitlyn in the morning and go over the finances with her to make sure she is okay with it as well. If she is, then we have a quorum. When can we start the work?"

Scott nodded at Carolyn. They had discussed using Charm as a backup plan, if the majority owners in Greyson Manor couldn't make the numbers work. Good thing they had taken the time to talk about it. His wife was a smart businesswoman and he knew she would be successful in both ventures. "As soon as you talk to Kaitlyn and you all sign the contracts, I am ready to get started. I will update the contracts and send a copy to each of you. So if I am understanding, we are all in agreement that we will work on the house restoration and rebuild the barn. Then I will renovate the slave quarters, but inside I will not add appliances. We can still use it as a prep area and for storage. I think that about does it. I will wait to get confirmation back from you Kevin after you speak with Kaitlyn and when you each send me your contracts, I will begin."

The group toasted to their plans and the excitement that Scott had generated and thanked him for all the hard work. They had another drink and then Scott, Carolyn and Daniel went home. They left Kevin to spend time with Christina looking at the closed off bedroom and the attic. None of them believed they would ever get to that tonight. They knew there were other plans in the air.

Kevin stood and walked to the bar. "Do you mind if I have one more drink, Christina?"

"Not at all, in fact, I wouldn't mind another glass of chardonnay," she said as she walked toward him. He took her glass and hesitated for a moment looking into her eyes. Then he poured them both a drink. Christina took her glass and walked back toward the doorway of the living room. "Shall we?" she asked.

Kevin raised one eyebrow and followed her up the stairs. She took his hand and led him down the hall. About half way down the hall, she stopped and turned to look at him. He kissed her deeply and pushed her against the wall. After a few minutes, Christina pulled away and said, "Well we aren't going to get much work done that way, are we?" She gave him her sexiest smile and grabbed his hand again and continued down the hall to the last bedroom. She opened the door.

Chapter 29
August, 1844

She opened the door. Kay stepped inside and turned around to Jade who was standing in the doorway, looking terrified. "Come in, Jade. This is your room from now on."

Jade couldn't believe that Kay was asking her to live in the house with them. She was afraid that once Kay found out that she was pregnant, that her generosity would cease. But how long could she hide it?

Kay walked over to the bed and sat down on the side of it. She patted the bed next to her. "Jade, please come here and sit with me. I want to talk to you."

Jade slowly made her way to the bed and sat on the edge of it. She was clearly uncomfortable.

"Jade, I know you have had a very hard time these last few years. When I first came to live here, I thought your family had left you behind. Now I know that is not true. I believe they died. Is that what you believe as well?"

Jade nodded. "They did die. Greyson had them shot. I saw it happen."

Kay took a deep breath. She put her hand on Jade's. "I am so sorry for what you have been through. I know this was once your home and I want to try to make your life a little easier and have you move back in here. David said this room was once your parents' room. Is that correct?"

"Yes. My room was across the hall."

"We will make this your room now, since it is more fitting for a young woman, and we can turn your room into the nursery."

The surprise on Jade's face made Kay smile. "You didn't think I knew, did you?" Kay asked.

Jade looked down, ashamed and shook her head. Tears began to stream down her cheeks.

"I know the baby is David's, Jade. I also believe he forced himself on you but you seem to now accept his advances. Am I right?"

"What choice did I have? I hate him for what he did to my family. I hate him for taking our house. I hate him for what he did to me. But now that I am having his baby, I have to let the hatred go. So you know I am having his baby and you still want me to live in the house with you both?" Jade was so confused. It didn't make sense. Kay had to hate her for having her husband's baby, especially since she couldn't have one herself. How could she be this generous?

Kay thought about what Jade said, tears filling her eyes. "Jade, I cannot have children of my own. I want a child so badly. I don't always understand David and I am so very sorry for all he has done to you and your family. It's time we atone for what he did. I just think it is fitting we take care of you now and I would like to see your baby grow up in this house, healthy and loved. I promise to help you and to love your child as if it were my own. Will you allow me to do that?"

Again, the tears streamed down Jade's cheeks. This woman with a kind heart and soul was trying to make things right. How could she refuse when her child's life could be fuller just to have Kay in it, just as her life has been enriched to know Kay as well.

"Yes, Ms. Kay. I would like that. Thank you. Does David know what you are offering?"

"Please call me Kay. Yes he does. We spoke about it at length. He wants to raise his child in this house. He cares for you Jade. I will not stand in the way of that. We will all take care of each other, but more importantly, we will all care for your child. Now, I will leave you to think about our conversation and get some rest." Kay put her hand on Jade's cheek. She was just a girl still; a girl who had been through hell. She would need her help and that would give Kay's life purpose. She would not think about David's time with Jade. She would have to share him for the good of the family. Lord, let me be strong, she thought. She got up and walked out the door, closing it quietly. She went downstairs and out to the slave quarters to find Theresa. She found her washing clothes in the shade by the barn.

"Theresa, I need to talk to you. Can you walk with me?"

"Yes, Ma'am," Theresa responded and wiped her hands on her apron. They walked down the path toward the main road. Kay told her about the plans for Jade and her baby. Theresa was surprised Kay was taking Jade in knowing she was going to have David's baby. Kay seemed to be resigned to it. Theresa knew she had been very sad when the doctor told her not to try to have any more children. She is a stronger woman than I, thought Theresa. So going forward, the focus would be on Jade's baby. Theresa was happy Jade was able to return to her home and the child would grow up in the house as well. She wondered what Ben would think of all of this.

When they returned to the slave quarters, Kay hugged Theresa. "Thank you for listening to me. Talking it out with you helped me confirm in my mind this is the right thing to do. We can now look ahead and anxiously await the arrival of the baby. Can you ask Ben to take her things to the last bedroom on the left?"

"Yes, Ms. Kay, I will. I know he will be happy for her as well." That was probably not an accurate statement. Ben will miss their long talks around the fire and doing their chores together. But mostly, Ben will be very unhappy when he finds out Jade is pregnant.

He will finally have to understand that she and Ben never had a chance of being together. Maybe he will finally look at Sally. Theresa knew Sally still cared for Ben but had all but given up hope on him. Theresa went into the barn and found him shoveling hay in one of the horse's stalls. She told him the news. As she suspected, he was clearly despondent and took off running.

Several hours later around dusk, Ben walked into their quarters. He seemed harder, older somehow, Theresa thought. "Are you alright, son?"

"Of course I am. Why wouldn't I be? I never cared about her. She is just a girl that I tried to help from time to time. That's all. I don't care what she does."

Theresa raised one eyebrow. She thought he protested a little too much. But that was his pride talking. It would take time so she didn't respond and just nodded. Let him get it all out.

Joseph walked in then. "How are you all this evening?" He smiled at Theresa and then noticed the concerned look on both of their faces. "Everything all right?"

"Yes, we are just fine, Joseph," Theresa said shortly. She didn't like how he looked at her. He made her nervous. She knew he wanted more from her, but she would never stop loving Sam. She would go to her grave loving Sam. Her eyes started to water, so she walked over to look out the window.

"Ben, how are you son?"

"I am not your son!" Ben stated sharply. "Don't call me that. I am Sam's son and always will be. Just like Sam is my mom's husband and always will be. Just leave us alone."

"Ben, I am sorry. I didn't mean anything by it. I have come to care for you both and I am concerned. You both seem unhappy. What has happened?"

"Jade is gone." Ben glared at Joseph. Theresa turned around to look at them both.

"She is not gone, she has moved into the house, where she belongs. She is going to have a baby and David and Kay are going to take good care of her and the child. Ben is not happy about the whole situation, but he will come to realize some day this is what was meant to be. Hopefully Ben will find another girl to love soon." Theresa walked over and rubbed Ben's arm. Ben pulled his arm away and walked over to his cot and laid down facing the wall.

Theresa and Joseph watched him for a few minutes and then looked back at each other.

"I assume David is the father?"

"Yes. They will raise the baby as a family."

"Well that is one understanding wife! I wonder what Kay's father will have to say about all of this."

Theresa looked perplexed. She hadn't thought of that. She wondered if Kay and David had discussed whether or not they were going to fess up that the baby was Jade's and David's or if they would keep it a secret. She would have to ask Kay in the morning. She knew the other slaves would talk and the word would get out if they didn't control the situation from the beginning. Jade was three months along, and she figured she would start showing soon, so they had six months in which they would have to hide Jade's pregnancy if that was the plan. She wondered why Kay didn't mention that earlier.

The next day, Theresa took some biscuits to the main house and found Kay in the warming kitchen in the basement. She asked her if she had thought about what other people would say, like her father.

"Yes, we have thought about that. I didn't want to worry Jade about it, since I knew the idea of moving back into the house and all of us being a family was already a lot to think about. Now that she is settled into her room and has had a night to sleep on it, I will talk to her about it today. Our plan is to raise the child together, but outside of this plantation, we want our friends and family to believe that we adopted the baby. We can't afford to have David's reputation tarnished. That would destroy everything. He wouldn't be able to continue working with the mill and the other colony members. I am hoping the baby doesn't look too Indian. I know that is a terrible thing to say, but we can't afford for people to figure it out. Hopefully with David's green eyes and blonde hair, the baby will take after him and have light colored hair and skin. We will just have to deal with it then. But I am so excited to have a baby coming soon. Can you help us keep the secret, Theresa?"

Theresa's eyebrows rose. This was not going to be easy, but she would try for all of their sakes. She agreed to keep the secret and to stress to the other slaves how it was in their best interest to not talk about it outside of the plantation. Theresa went back to her quarters to speak with them.

Kay went up the stairs to Jade's room and knocked on the door. Jade called to her to come in. Kay opened the door and saw Jade sitting in front of the dresser brushing her long black hair. She was indeed beautiful. She would have a gorgeous child.

"Jade, did you sleep well? Are you happy to be back here?"

"Yes, Ms. Kay, I mean Kay," she smiled. "I did. It will take some getting used to, being here with you both, but I will for the baby's sake. I feel my parent's presence here and it is so nice to have my own room again, instead of sleeping in one big room with the rest of the slaves. Some of those men are terrible snorers," she giggled.

Kay smiled. It was wonderful to hear Jade laugh. She didn't think she ever had. "There is something else I need to explain."

Jade put the brush down and looked at Kay. She knew it was too good to be true. Here it comes, Jade thought, bad news.

"As you know, the cotton we plant is mostly sold to the mill. We are its biggest provider. That business is what keeps this plantation running and keeps us all with a roof over our head and food in our stomachs."

Where was she going with this, Jade wondered.

"David's reputation is very solid. We have to protect his reputation to ensure we are able to continue as we have been. So what I am saying is, no one can know of the things he has done here. We have to keep that to ourselves. I know that is probably hard for you to accept." A thought occurred to her. "I didn't think to ask, but you didn't tell Mrs. Gordon or Mrs. Moore about any of this, did you?" That would ruin everything, Kay thought. Now she wished she had thought to have this conversation before she took Jade to visit the Indian women.

"No, I didn't tell them," Jade lied.

"Oh, thank goodness. What did you tell them? Do they think your parents left you?"

"Yes," she lied again.

Kay looked intently at Jade. She was surprised to hear that. It seemed Jade would have commiserated with the other Indian women. Maybe she was ashamed. "Well, alright. I need to tell you though, because we need to protect David's reputation, we need to keep you here so no one finds out you are pregnant. Then we will have to tell them we adopted the baby. Can you handle that?"

"How do I know you won't take my baby away from me? Or that David won't?"

"You have no guarantees," came David's voice from the doorway. "I will do everything I can to keep my baby safe, even if that means taking him away."

Jade was furious. She knew she couldn't trust him. Why did she believe Kay could make any of this happen? Jade stood. "Then you will not have my baby." She glared at David and stood firm.

David laughed and then said, "Do you really think you can keep me from my child? We are generously offering you a place in our home and to continue to be a part of my child's life. However, if you do not do exactly as I say, I will send you back to the slave quarters when the baby is born. Do you understand me, Jade?"

"Your house? Your child?" Jade screamed. "Is there no heart in your chest? I want to stay here. I want to stay with my child. I only ask that if you leave Greyson Manor, you take me with you as well. Please, David," she pleaded softly.

David looked at Kay, feeling awkward Jade was calling him by his first name. He had told her she could in their intimate moments. He guessed it would be acceptable while they were all together.

"I don't plan to leave here, but if I ever do have to, I will let you know then what I decide about you going with me. Us, I mean," looking again at Kay. Kay was clearly uncomfortable with the conversation. He cared for his wife but he wasn't going to give up control of this household to anyone. With that, he walked back out of the bedroom.

Kay looked at Jade who was staring out the window. Jade was holding her head high and stiff. "Jade," Kay began, "we have to do what we can to keep David happy. You and I will work together to keep him that way. He won't leave us. This home and you and I and the baby are all he has. He is just being firm to keep control. Let's you and I do what we can to not upset him. Agreed?"

Jade looked at Kay and understood that was her only choice.

Chapter 30
August 15, 2010

C hristina and Kevin walked into the bedroom. It had a slight musty smell and the furniture was covered in sheets. Christina looked at Kevin. "So you see what I mean? Kind of creepy, huh?"

"Yeah. At least the electricity works in here. Let's turn on all of the lamps and pull these sheets off." He took Christina's wine glass and put both of their drinks in the hall on the floor. Then he walked back in and they pulled the sheets off, folded them up and laid them in the hallway as well. Dust filled the air. They both coughed then laughed. The furniture looked very antique.

"Ok, let's start looking through the drawers and see if we find anything," Kevin said as he walked over to the nightstand. He sat down on the side of the bed and opened the top drawer. It was empty. He opened the bottom drawer and found a few old books. "Let's take these down to the living room so we can look through them, alright?"

"Sure," responded Christina. She walked over to the dresser and began to go through the drawers. She found a few items of clothing and some ribbons. She also found a silver brush and mirror. There were no papers or books in the dresser drawers.

Kevin walked over to the armoire and opened the door. "Wow, check these out."

Christina walked over and looked over Kevin's shoulder. Some very old but very beautiful dresses were hanging in the armoire. They seemed to be faded, but otherwise had endured the years they had hung in the armoire. Christina pulled out a lovely blue satin dress. "This must be over a hundred years old! I wonder whose it was." There were also very petite shoes sitting in the floor of the armoire. "Whoever wore these, must have been a very small woman. They are so dainty and detailed."

Kevin pulled all of the dresses out and laid them on the bed. Christina admired them while Kevin went back to look more closely at the armoire. He ran his hand down each side to see if there were any hidden compartments. He just knew there was a story here. He hoped they would find proof of that. Unfortunately, he could not find any shelves or secret compartments in the armoire. He looked back at Christina who was still looking through the dresses. She held the blue one up in front of the full length mirror in the corner.

She noticed Kevin looking at her over her shoulder. She blushed and put the dress back in the armoire.

"You look gorgeous in that color, Christina. I haven't found anything yet though." Kevin looked around the room and noticed there were a few paintings on the walls. He pulled the pictures off the wall and looked at the wall behind them and also turned the pictures around and ran his hand down them to see if he could feel anything hidden behind the backing of the paintings. Nothing. He sat back down on the side of the bed. Then he had a thought. He went down on his hands and knees and looked under the bed. Again, nothing. Kevin noticed that the bed was a rope bed. There were pegs at the headboard, footboard, and on each side rail. Ropes were tightly strung from peg to peg, from headboard to footboard and then crossed from side to side. The straw mattress lay on top of the ropes. He remembered hearing the saying "sleep tight, don't let the bed bugs bite" came from the use of this type of bed. He put his hand between the mattress and the ropes and felt around. He lifted the mattress, "Bulls-eye!"

Christina ran to the other side of the room to see what he was looking at. There were a number of papers spread out under the mattress. While Kevin held up the mattress, Christina reached in and pulled them all out. Kevin lowered the mattress and they looked wide-eyed at each other. Kevin grabbed Christina and kissed her again, crushing the papers between them.

"Hold on Romeo, you are crushing the papers!"

"Oh, sorry. I just got so excited and you look so beautiful," Kevin smiled. "Let's go downstairs and look them over." He picked up the old books and the wine glasses and they went downstairs and back into the living room. Christina went over to the table and put the papers down gently. She began to go through them trying to first see who wrote them. There was no signed name, so she hoped that the writer would reveal themselves within the text. They were dated. The first one was dated September, 1844. She put them in order of the dates and began to read them out loud.

September, 1844 I cannot find my other journal pages. I left them in the slave quarters and when I went back to get them, they were gone. I think Ben took them. Kay has been true to her word. She has made me feel at home in the house, their house, my house again. She seems to sincerely care for me and the baby growing inside of me. David is rarely here and when he is he seems to just tolerate me. I do see him looking at my stomach at times. I can't wait until the baby is born. Only five more months until you come into the world, our world; as it is. I love being in my room, reading, writing and resting with my baby in my stomach. I can feel it move sometimes. David has not come to visit me since I moved back in. I think he doesn't want to hurt the baby or Kay.

Christina raised her eyebrows and looked at Kevin. He had a look of amazement on his face. He put the books down, poured them a glass of wine and said, "Who do you think wrote that? Could it be the Indian girl? It sounds like she is living in the house with them at this point. Do you think that David Greyson is the father?"

Christina nodded. "That's what it sounds like. If this is Jade, then the baby is one of our ancestors, I assume. If so, that would make Daniel and me part Cherokee. Let me read the next page." She read aloud.

December, 1844 Mrs. Gordon and Mrs. Moore came to visit with Christmas presents. Kay told them I was ill and couldn't get out of bed. Kay doesn't know they know I am seven months pregnant. I waved to them out my window. When Kay gave me the presents, I told her I wanted to open them later so I could open them alone. They are Indian gifts for the baby. I hid them so I could save them for the baby. We had a nice quiet Christmas together as a family.

March, 1845 My baby boy was born on February 27th. His name is Frederick Greyson, after David's grandfather. He has my hair but he has David's green eyes. He is so beautiful, we all cried, even David. David is spending less time at the mill so he can be here to be with Frederick. David seems to be changing. I wish my family could see Frederick. Kay loves to hold him and I can see she loves him too. He is a fortunate boy to have so much love all around him.

June, 1845 Frederick is already growing and he is so handsome. He has the most intense eyes. I can't stop looking at him. David and Kay took Frederick into town to see some of their friends and Kay's father. I stayed here. It is hard but I have to let them be his parents for the world to see. It is the best thing to ensure I get to stay here and live with him. I know he is safe with them. Kay said her father cried when he saw him and was so happy for Kay. He also told David that the mill wants to buy more cotton so that is good for the plantation.

Christina motioned Kevin over to the sofa so they could get more comfortable and read more of the pages together.

Chapter 31

June 1847

Jade decided now that Frederick could walk she would take him to the cotton fields to show him what her parents had started here. She knew some day he would be the master of this plantation and she wanted him to know how it all started. She would not be able to tell him her parents were his grandparents, but hopefully he would still feel a deep connection for what they had accomplished and made possible for all of them. She looked out over the fields and felt her father's presence there. She still missed him terribly. She was still a very young woman herself at twenty-two, but she felt that the last nine years had changed her. She had grown to love Kay and felt empathy now toward David. There was too much damage done to ever feel anything more for him, however, he had allowed her to stay a part of her son's life. For that she was grateful.

She watched Frederick waddle along, stopping to pick up rocks and bugs. He was a curious boy and very generous. He would squat down, investigate something, pick it up and then hold it up for Jade. She couldn't help but accept the gift, even if it was a bug. When he would look at her with those deep green eyes, she would melt. She would die for her son if she had to. She took his hand and they continued to walk through the cotton fields. When she came upon a bush that was still full of the white cotton, she would pull some off and put it in Frederick's hand. He would press his hands together and laugh at it, then throw it in the air.

"That's right, Frederick. This is what our plantation is here for. It's called cotton. It's what we use to make our clothes and blankets and towels. Isn't it pretty?"

Frederick laughed again.

"Jade?" called Kay as she walked toward them in the field. "There you two are! I made us some lunch so we could have a picnic under the maple tree. Would you like that, Frederick?"

When Frederick saw Kay, he immediately ran and jumped into her arms. He loved her just as much as she loved him. That was hard sometimes for Jade to see, but she didn't want to be selfish. She was happy her son had so much love in his heart for Kay. The three of them walked back toward the house where Kay had lain out a blanket for them to enjoy their picnic lunch. They ate chicken and peaches as well as the bread Kay had made that morning. Then Frederick curled up in a ball and fell fast asleep. They both watched him with so much love in their eyes. They looked at each other and smiled.

"Jade, I want to talk to you about something," Kay said quietly. "How have you been feeling?"

"I feel fine, why?" Jade asked.

"David and I have been talking about having another baby."

Jade was surprised to hear that considering she knew Kay couldn't conceive. Could she really be asking Jade to sleep with David again?

"Jade, I know this is an unusual arrangement, but I hope you have felt you are a part of this family. I respect your time with Frederick and you have been wonderful to keep our secret. It is the best thing for Frederick long term and for the family as a whole. You have been selfless and generous with your son. I love you Jade for what you have given me - a life with a child. Is it too much to ask for more children? Can you see yourself being a part of our family and bearing our children?"

Jade was speechless for a minute. She hadn't thought of having additional children, she was so happy with Frederick and with their arrangement. She had thought this life was the most she could ever hope for, considering all that had happened. If she had more children for Kay and David, would she eventually also be able to have children she could call her own if she met someone to love? She asked Kay.

Kay smiled at Jade. "Jade, we have no intention of ever turning you out. This is your home and you are welcome to stay with us forever. If you meet someone and he wants to live here with us, we would welcome that as well. If he wants you to move to his home, then you can visit and of course you could begin a family of your own either way. You have made my dream of being a mother come true. I could never repay you. So do you think it would be possible for you to bear more children with David?" Kay looked intently at Jade.

Jade looked back intently at Kay. She was extremely uncomfortable about being with David again. Kay was asking her to choose this. It felt wrong in so many ways. "You must really want more children that you would allow David to come to me again."

"That part doesn't make me happy, Jade. But what choice do I have? Will you do it?"

"I will have to think about that. I don't want anything to come between you and me and especially between Frederick and me. Can you give me a few days to think it through?"

"Yes, of course." Kay looked out over the cotton fields. There was nothing else to say on the topic. Jade would have to decide. She would have to give herself freely to David this time and she was sure that wasn't an easy thing to do. She was sure Jade and David had not been together since before Frederick was born. She looked down at Frederick, her beautiful son. Then she lay down next to him while he slept.

Jade got up to leave the two to nap together. She went to find Theresa to ask her opinion. She really had no one else she could talk to about it. She found Theresa in the slave quarters baking her wonderful biscuits. They talked about Kay's request and what that would mean to them all, especially to Jade. Finally, Theresa looked directly at Jade and asked, "What is your heart telling you, my dear? Your mother would tell you to follow your heart."

"I just don't know. I can't imagine loving someone more than I love Frederick or even the same as Frederick. I trust Kay, but I still don't trust David. What if someday he turns me out?"

"That is always possible, I suppose, but it seems unlikely. Remember, you know his secrets. He is not going to risk you telling the world about the horrible things he has done. I don't think he will ever send you away. As long as you have something he wants, like the ability to give him more children, I think your place here is safe."

Jade nodded. She agreed that made sense. She smiled. She started to think about what it would be like to have another child to raise. What if the next one was a little girl? She started to get excited. "Thank you, Theresa. You have always been like a mother to me. Thank you for helping me think this through." She left and walked back to the house. She saw Kay and Frederick walking hand in hand up the steps. Kay saw her and stopped to look at her. Jade climbed the steps, took Kay's other hand, then looked her in the eyes and nodded, yes. Kay smiled then took Frederick into the house. Jade saw David leaning against the column on the porch. They looked at each other for a few minutes and then Jade went up to her room.

Chapter 32

August 16 – September 6, 2010

"Three weeks from today is the Grand Opening party!" Carolyn said as she unlocked the front door to Charm. "Kacey, do you think we are ready enough to go ahead and do our soft opening this weekend? I think we are!"

"I agree. We just have three more second interviews today, and if those go as we think they will, we will have our full staff. If we can make our offers today and they can start tomorrow like they said they could, then we can start doing some training and practice runs."

"Hi ladies," called out Gabby. "You have to try this," she said and held out a plate with pieces of steak and chicken on it. "I tried a new marinade and I think adding skewers to our menu will top it off. What do you think?"

"Delicious!" said Carolyn.

"Well, you know I am not much of a red meat eater, but the chicken is really good and I think that adding the skewers is a fantastic idea. Can you also add vegetable skewers as well?" Kacey asked.

"What do you think about the idea of listing the vegetables we have available and then folks can decide what they want on the skewers? Because I know Scott hates onions and peppers and he wouldn't touch a skewer if they were on it, so it made me think of the "build your own" kind of set up. It will also let us change up the vegetables depending on the season. You like that idea?"

Carolyn was still eating the samples and nodded her approval. Kacey gave Gabby a-thumbs up and they got busy with preparing for their interviews.

All three candidates accepted the server positions and said they could start the next day. Gabby spent the afternoon working with the kitchen staff, training them on how to prepare the menu they had agreed upon. They prepared everything on the menu and began to bring it out to the bar for Carolyn and Kacey to sample.

"Wow, you guys do good work! We are going to have to get Scott and Mike over here to help us with these samples. I'll call Scott," Carolyn said as she dug into her purse for her phone.

By six o'clock, Scott and Mike had joined Carolyn, Kacey and the kitchen crew. They sampled the food and tried out some of the wines that Gabby suggested they pair with each dish. The excitement was contagious and the evening was a success. All they had to do was get the servers trained over the next couple of days, then open to the public on Friday night. It was a good business practice to do a soft opening so they could work out any kinks before the official grand opening.

The next three weeks came and went with only a few glitches. Carolyn worked with the servers to practice focusing on their section of the restaurant, but she wanted them to also keep an eye on the other sections if another server was busy when a meal came up or a patron's drink was getting close to empty. Since it was a small space, they really had to work together to ensure they didn't bump into each other or all end up either in the front or the back. It was almost like having to choreograph how they moved around the restaurant. They did a much better job of that Saturday night, so at the end of the evening when they closed and locked the doors, they all agreed they were ready for the big event on Monday evening, Labor Day.

Around four o'clock on Labor Day afternoon, Scott and Carolyn walked down Canton Street hand in hand. They had gone home to shower after spending the day preparing the restaurant for the Grand Opening. "Have I told you how proud of you I am?" Scott asked and kissed her on the cheek.

Carolyn squeezed his hand. "Only a hundred times, but tell me again after tonight!"

"Are you nervous?"

"Not really. I am more excited than anything. I really don't think there is anything more we can do to prepare. And thanks again for spending so much time on the bar. It looks gorgeous. I know the men and women will love sitting at it."

"Hey you two!" It was Josie, crossing the street to meet them in front of Charm carrying a very large bouquet of Gerber daisies. They hugged and Carolyn thanked her for coming, accepting the flowers. "Congratulations, Carolyn. Did you think today would ever come?"

"It wouldn't have without you. You really helped me open my eyes to the possibilities and this place turned out more hip, chic and fun than I could have imagined. Thank you for your guidance. Come on in and let me get you a drink." Carolyn waved at Kacey who was standing behind the bar talking with Andrew, the new bartender. Kacey grabbed a tray of champagne and brought it around the bar, greeting her friends and partner.

"We have to start with a toast! This was such a group effort to get us where we are today. I couldn't thank you all enough!" Kacey beamed. They all lifted their glasses and drank a sip.

"Wait for me," said Mike.

"I'm sorry, honey," Kacey said handing him a glass. They clinked and sipped.

"I have to say, this is the best restaurant in town! And with my experience in the restaurant business, I would know!" Mike kissed Kacey and then they all raised their glasses again.

The two female servers, Jamie and Liz, were dressed in the funky t-shirts that Kacey had gotten and black skirts with a small black apron. Lou, the male server, was wearing the tee shirt with black slacks. Kacey, Carolyn and the rest of the staff all had on their funky black tee shirts as well.

"This is incredible!" called out Mia as she walked in with Angel.

"It's gorgeous," said Angel. "We are so proud of you both."

Mia grabbed Carolyn's arm and said, "Isn't it great news about Lucy's baby girl? She is tiny, but just precious! Five pounds, one ounce!"

"I have not had a chance to get by to see her, but she is home from the hospital, right?"

"Yes," replied Angel, "they got home yesterday. They named her Taylor! Isn't that cute?"

"It sure is. I am so happy for them! I will have to take some food over there tomorrow and see Taylor for myself!" Kacey handed them champagne and they all toasted, yet again. Kacey decided she and Carolyn should switch to water if they wanted to make it through the night. They could have a late night cocktail when it was all over. She didn't want to miss a minute of this night. She brought the iced water over to Carolyn. "Here's to us, partner. And to the best partner, anyone could have." They hugged and turned just in time to see Kevin and Christina walk in. Carolyn left the bar to walk over to greet them.

"Hey you two, welcome to Charm, Southern Charm that is," Carolyn put on her best southern drawl. She handed them champagne, showed them around and then found them the most romantic seat in the place. She was very pleased to see them together. They seemed like a really good fit. "So did you two discover anything in the bedroom?" she asked.

"What?" Christina blushed. "Oh," she looked embarrassed at Kevin, "you mean the closed off bedroom at the end of the hall."

They all laughed at her embarrassment. She clearly thought Carolyn had meant between Kevin and herself. She hadn't been ready to go there yet. But soon, she thought. "Actually, we found a gold mine. We found journal papers from Jade that spanned years. You won't believe some of the things that happened back then. We are still reading, in fact, we were planning on going through some more tonight after your party."

"Yes, it's an amazing story and I am hoping when it's all said and done, there will be a story worth repeating. One that Christina and Daniel will not have to be ashamed of," responded Kevin as he draped an arm on the back of Christina's chair.

"Really? That is good news. I can't wait to hear all about it, assuming you will share?" she asked Christina.

"Yes, I would be happy to share the stories with you and Scott; still deciding about the rest of the world though." She looked past Carolyn then and waved. Daniel had just walked in. She waved him over to their table.

Kevin stood up from their very romantic table that had suddenly gotten very crowded and said, "It's good to see you Daniel. Would you like to join us?"

"Actually, I was going to head over to the bar to have one drink then I need to head out. I have a lot of work to do," Daniel said not wanting to intrude.

"Oh, Daniel," Christina teased him, "you work too much already. Stay and have some fun."

Carolyn realized tonight was the perfect night to introduce Mia and Daniel. Mia wanted it to be a casual introduction in a party environment. "I'll walk with you to the bar. I have some friends I would like you to meet." She looked over her shoulder at Christina and winked.

Kevin's eyebrows rose, then he understood. "Nice seeing you Daniel."

Daniel walked to the bar and ordered a drink.

Carolyn waved Mia and Angel over and introduced them to Daniel. It only took them a few minutes to engage in a conversation about how they had all met, where they were from and what they did for a living. Knowing they could each hold their own, Carolyn got back to greeting the guests that were coming through the door.

"So where were we?" Christina asked Kevin.

"I think we were about here," he leaned over and kissed her neck, "or maybe here," he kissed her cheek. "No, I think we were here," he kissed her on the lips. Then he held her hand and said, "I have really enjoyed getting to know you, Christina and I am honored that you are allowing me to read the journals with you. I know they are very personal and precious to you."

"I like you Kevin and besides, if you told anyone what you read, well I would just have to tar and feather you and run you out of town. Isn't that what a southern belle would do?"

"Uh, I don't think southern belles are known for their tar and feathering, but I get the point. You have nothing to worry about. I won't even tell our partners, I will leave that up to you - what and when you want to tell them. I am looking forward to reading some more though. It is so interesting to be reading an actual journal about real events that happened over one hundred and fifty years ago. And you know the Indian aspect to the story has really captured my attention. I just hope we find a happy ending."

Christina wasn't sure if he meant he hoped that Jade would find a happy ending or he and Christina, but she hoped for the same thing, either way. "Let's order. I'm starved and I can't wait to try all the fabulous recipes that Carolyn was talking about. It will be a good test to see how we feel about using Charm as the food provider for Greyson Manor Events."

"Congratulations!" called out Carolyn's parents.

"You all did a great job putting this place together. Are you happy with how it turned out?" asked her dad.

"Yes, I can't think of anything we would change," answered Carolyn.

"I'm so glad you two could make the trip up from Pensacola for our Grand Opening!" said Kacey hugging them both.

"Thanks for inviting us! We wouldn't miss it for anything," said Carolyn's mom.

"Well, we are going to have to get busy, but I saved the best table in the house for you, so let me show you the way." Carolyn took her parents to one of the bay window tables, handed them menus and kissed them both on the cheek. She waved over Liz. "Have a great time! I'll come back and check on you in a little while."

Carolyn and Kacey worked the room, welcoming their guests, pouring champagne and making sure everyone enjoyed themselves. The place was packed. They couldn't have hoped for a better turnout.

Scott and Mike walked over to them. "We were going to play darts," Scott said motioning over his shoulder, "but the place is too crowded to be throwing dangerous weapons across the room. We'd probably poke someone's eye out!"

"Yeah, did I tell you how beautiful you look tonight, Kacey?" Mike kissed her on the cheek.

"Stop that," said Scott. "These two are so love dovey, what's up with that?"

"Oh, you are just jealous because you didn't say it first!" laughed Carolyn.

After the last guest had left and they had locked up the place, they all sat down with heavy sighs. "Could we have asked for a better night?" asked Kacey.

"I don't think so," responded Carolyn as she rubbed her lower back. "I hope it's a sign of things to come. I saw Christina and Kevin slip out as well, but she gave me a-thumbs up right before she walked out the door. I think she was talking about Charm, but who knows, maybe she was talking about Kevin?" They all laughed.

"They did seem awful cozy," said Scott.

"Oh, before I forget Scott, they did find more journal pages and were going to go back to Greyson Manor tonight to read some more."

"Yeah, right. I am sure that is what they are planning on doing tonight."

"Oh stop," Carolyn said. "One track mind, my husband, one track mind."

Chapter 33
Labor Day, September 6, 2010

Christina unlocked the door, let Kevin into the house and flipped on the lights. He flipped them back off and grabbed her at the same time pulling her close. He kissed her deeply. After a few minutes, Christina took him by the hand and led him up the stairs. This time instead of going to the last room at the end of the hall, she took him to her room.

The next morning Kevin woke to sun in his eyes.

"Wake up, sleepy head!" Christina said as she tied the curtain back letting the sunshine in the bedroom. "I brought you breakfast in bed."

"Ugh," replied Kevin. "What time is it? I was really enjoying the dream I was having." He lifted his head to look at her. "Oh, it wasn't a dream," he smiled. "Wow, look at this. I don't think anyone has ever brought me breakfast in bed. Isn't that just something they do in the movies?" he teased.

"I have to get your energy back up," she winked at him. "We have a lot more journal pages to go through. You want to stay and read them, right? Since we didn't get to them last night? I mean that was your fault, not mine." She leaned over and kissed his cheek. She crawled back under the covers and they shared the tray of delicious fluffy, scrambled eggs with cheddar cheese, crisp bacon, toast and fresh squeezed orange juice.

"How about let's finish this fine breakfast, then you give me a few minutes to get my clothes back on, you can make me coffee while I do that, by the way," he winked, "then I will meet you downstairs and we can go through the rest of the pages." He kissed her on the nose. "Will that work?" She nodded, mouth full. "And by the way, last night was really something. I hope you know how special you are to me, Christina," he said more seriously.

She looked him straight in the eye. "I know I am. I could tell." She smiled.

They finished their breakfast, got dressed and went downstairs to read the pages over coffee. Christina had put them in chronological order and for the most part, the pages over the next two years focused on Frederick, how precious he was and how he was growing. Jade told him stories about her family and how the house was built and the cotton was planted. It didn't get really interesting until June, 1847 when Kay asked Jade to have another child. Christina and Kevin looked at each other amazed.

"If you think about it, it wasn't like Kay could go through invitro and since Jade had already given them one son, it made sense to keep going; it's just not something that would happen in this day and time. The only way they could accomplish having another baby was to have Jade and David consummate. I just couldn't imagine how hard all of this had to be for Kay."

"I know. It's pretty selfless on all of their parts, except David's of course. I can't wait to see how it all turned out."

They read several more pages and discovered Jade had her second child, a girl, on September 15, 1848. They named her Rose Ann. Rose Ann had red hair and her mother's dark brown eyes. A few years later, she had another boy. She named him after her brother Michael. David didn't object. Michael was born on April 3, 1852. He also had red hair and his father's green eyes. That same year, Jade mentioned that the town, now called Roswell, had built their second mill. The Roswell Manufacturing Company referred to the mills as the Roswell Mills. David had become extremely wealthy by maintaining his standing as the number one cotton provider for the mills. Kay had also begun to do some work for the mills. Apparently, she was a very good seamstress, so they hired her to make samples for them. About once a month, Jade would take the children to the mills to see their parents' place of work. David wanted them acclimated to their lifestyle from a very early age. The workers and town folk thought Jade was the nanny.

"Listen to this," exclaimed Christina.

June 1852 Kay asked me to go with her to see her father and to help her with the children. David never seems to have time to see Kay's father and David's parents passed away years ago. David only has us. David is always busy with the plantation and the mills. This was the first time I had met Kay's father. Usually, when he comes to visit Kay and the children, Kay asks me to go to the slave quarters. She didn't want her father to meet me, which is why I was surprised when she asked me to go with her today. She said her father, Mr. Temple, asked to meet me. He is a nice man. He asked me how I was. He seemed concerned for me. He said he had heard my parents had left me. I started to correct him, but Kay shook her head at me. That was difficult. He thanked me for caring for the children while Kay worked at the mills. He said it is the biggest mill company in Georgia now and they need more women seamstresses, but the women can't leave their children at home. He said they just finished building a nursery at the mills. He asked me if I would like to work in the nursery taking care of the children so the mothers could work. At first I was so surprised by his offer, I wasn't sure what to say. Then Kay said she thought it was a great idea so she could see the children while she was at the mills as well. She then told Mr. Temple I have done quite well with my studies and could help the children learn to read and write. I told Mr. Temple as long as Mr. Greyson and Kay approved, I would like to be able to go to work at the mills. It feels shameful to have to lie to Mr. Temple. I know Kay doesn't like lying to him about the children, but I understand why she does it. She is afraid her father won't love the children if he knew they were not of Kay's blood. After we visited Mr. Temple, Kay took us to the mill to show us her office, her samples and the new nursery. The mill she works in is a very large place with over one hundred and fifty people working there. I have never seen anything like it. I also got to see Mrs. Moore and Mrs. Gordon, who are working there now too. I was able to pull them aside and ask them to continue to keep my secret. They know about the children. They said they would keep my secret as long as I was still happy with the situation. I told them at least for now, I didn't have a choice. I wouldn't leave my children. I saw a very handsome man at the mill. He looked like he might have some Cherokee blood in him. He had beautiful thick dark hair and dark brown eyes. I hope I will see him again. He noticed me and smiled, but his boss told him to get back to work. He went back to work, but he kept smiling at me. I hope David agrees to allow me to work in the nursery. The children will really like being there. Only Frederick goes to school, which is right across the street. I could bring him to the nursery when he is finished and we could all be together.

Kevin looked at Christina, she seemed moved by reading the journal pages. Christina put the pages down and got up, refilled her coffee then went to look out the back door. Kevin got up and went to stand behind her. He put his hands on her shoulders. "What are you thinking?"

Christina put her hand over his. "I am just thinking this is the most amazing story and I wish my parents had known about it. I can't believe this is about my ancestors and I have never heard this before. I am glad I have finally learned the truth." Then she turned, stood on her toes, and kissed him. "Want to continue?"

"Yes, let's read the rest of the pages." They spent the day reading the remainder of the pages that covered the years until the Civil War began. Christina wondered, would they find more pages?

Chapter 34
September 8, 2010

O n Wednesday, Scott's crew showed up at Greyson Manor to begin the renovation work. He had two crews going at the same time, one working on the house and the other starting on the barn. The guys working on the house were historical specialists. Scott only had to go over the plan with them and then let them get on with doing what they did best. The barn was another story. The historical specialists were not needed to work on the barn, since the goal was to replace it completely and just build it to replicate the basic shape of the barn. Scott was ecstatic to finally be getting started. He pulled the demolition guys together out front of the barn for a quick meeting.

"Welcome to the project, guys. This is a very important project to a lot of people, in addition to me. If you think I have been anal about the other projects we have worked together, get ready for dealing with me on this one." The guys grumbled. "My wife and I, as well as several of our friends, have invested a large portion of our savings in this place. We need it to be quality work and we need it to be an exact replica of the original. So I have set up this easel to show you the plan. Let's go over the details." Scott went through the information and then asked if there were any questions.

One of the men raised his hand. "Scott, can I take you home to go over this with my wife? That way she will see that my job isn't just manual labor, it's more like I have to be an engineering genius and maybe she'll get off my case to get a 'real' job!" The guys laughed and the one standing next to him punched him lightly in the arm. "No really, Scott, I think we got it."

"Okay, then let's get started. Ask me if you have any questions. I will be here the entire time, other than when I am up at the house checking on their work."

The crew worked through the morning taking down the old barn. Carolyn pulled up with sandwiches for everyone and was surprised to see how far they had already gotten. It always amazed her how long it took to put up a building but how fast one could be taken down. "Hey honey!" she waved as she walked over to Scott who was reviewing the plan, again. "Wow, your guys are fast. I hope they know to save anything they find that could be reused, especially things like old tools, horseshoes, reins. Those would be great to decorate the new barn."

Scott smiled and pointed to a pile of things next to a large oak tree.

"Oh my gosh! Look at that! What great finds!" As she was going through the pile, Christina came out of the house and walked over toward Carolyn.

"Can you believe the barn is already down?" she asked. "What is all of this?"

"Look at this stuff. There is an old wagon, some reins, and old buckets. Check out this really cool wooden bench. I wonder what kind of wood that is. We can definitely use that. Oh, and look at the horseshoes!" Carolyn said as she pointed at the pile and looked at Christina. "How are you, by the way?"

Christina blushed, put her hands in her pockets, kicked dirt and looked around the grounds.

Carolyn raised an eyebrow and grinned. "Care to share?"

"Well, Kevin and I have been spending some quality time together," Christina smiled, embarrassed.

"That's wonderful, Christina. I am very happy for you both. I knew you would hit it off." Carolyn rubbed her hand down Christina's arm. "Don't be embarrassed!"

Christina took a deep breath. She wasn't ready to talk about the details or to jinx it for that matter. She felt they had something very special and wanted to take her time with the relationship, hoping it would last this time. Kevin was a great guy and they had so much in common. If the relationship didn't work out, she wanted to make sure they stayed friends so she felt it was important to move forward slowly. Ok, so it had only been a few weeks and they had already spent the night together, but maybe they could slow down now. She looked at Carolyn who was watching her.

"Is everything alright, Christina?"

"Yes, it's fine. Sorry, I just have a lot on my mind. Kevin and I have been reading the journal pages and we have learned a lot about my family. The journal stops right when the Civil War was starting so we are hoping we can find more pages but we searched the bedroom Jade stayed in and only found what we have so far. Can you tell Scott to tell his guys to keep an eye out for any books or papers they find?"

"I think they would have already found them in the barn if there were any there. As you can see, they have demolished it already," said Carolyn as she looked over to the pile of rubble.

"I understand. I think I will go look around the slave quarters since they haven't done anything in there yet and see if I find anything." Christina left Carolyn to look through her pile of treasure and walked over to the slave quarters. She used to play there as a kid but never really understood the significance of it until she was in high school. She learned the hard way. There was a gang of African American kids at her high school, who once they found out she lived at Greyson Manor would rib her and Daniel relentlessly about their ancestors having had slaves. One Sunday morning her family awoke to find graffiti all over the slave quarters.

She had tried to talk to them about the fact that she couldn't change the past, but they didn't want to listen. She and Daniel both had their lockers painted with graffiti as well, multiple times. The consistent message was "racist", which broke Christina's heart because it was far from the truth. But the fact that they lived in a historical plantation, gave the impression of wealthy, snobby white folks, at least to that gang of kids. She couldn't talk them out of feeling that way about her and Daniel. The kids were finally caught in the act of bullying Christina and were put in detention, which only made the situation worse.

One Saturday evening after a football game as Christina walked to her car, one of the kids threw a bottle that hit her in the forehead. Christina had to go to the hospital to get six stitches and she still had a small scar. Someone's father had seen the incident happen and got a policeman who was patrolling the area to arrest the kid. That kid was expelled from school. He happened to be the gang leader, so the rest of the gang backed off once he was gone.

Christina never got over the feeling that the kid had a right to be upset about his slave ancestors, but really didn't know how to address the issue. She began to summer intern at the local Roswell paper and would write about community affairs and events. She made sure she included any African American focused events she would hear about to try to show she wasn't racist at all. She felt it was very little, if any, reparation but throughout her life she had always tried to compensate for her ancestors. She had no idea until recently, her ancestor David Greyson had done so much damage. Killing several members of a Cherokee family and keeping and raping a young Indian girl, was something Christina could not comprehend. She would have to find a way to compensate for that as well. But how?

She walked around the slave quarters, mostly empty other than some wheelbarrows, a few old chairs and one cot in the corner. It smelled terribly and she made a note to ask Scott to have the men clean out the rest of the debris. There were some built in cabinets in several rooms with old cans, rags, broken plates and cups. She pulled out a pot that was missing the handle and looked at it. It seemed very old. What stories could you tell? She thought. She held onto that pot as she continued to look around. She didn't see where there could be any journals hidden unless they were put in the wall somehow, like a secret compartment. Okay, now you are going overboard, she mumbled. Thinking she was wasting her time, she walked back out of the old rundown building. She was disappointed that she hadn't been able to find any more journals. She had to find a way to learn the rest of the story. What happened to Jade? What happened to Kay and the children? Which of the children was her great, great grandparent? She had a thought. She may be able to figure that out by going back to the files her parents had on the family tree. She went back to the house and into the den. She pulled out the file where she had first seen the family tree. The names hadn't stuck in her head because there were so many and several generations back. There were her parents, Henry and Theresa, and her father's parents, Grandpa Ralph and Grandma Frances. Then Ralph's parents were Albert and Roberta. Albert's parents were Michael and Victoria…. Michael. There he was. Michael's parents were listed as David and Jade. Did anyone ever learn the whole truth before now? If they had, no one documented anything about the Cherokee heritage or discussed it. And what happened to Kay? Christina put the folder down and looked out the window. Shame.

Chapter 35
July 1852

K ay and Jade dropped Frederick, now seven, off at the school then took the carriage across the street to the mill. Kay kissed Rose Ann and Michael, told Rose Ann to be good and to mind Jade, then waved at Jade and they went their separate ways; Kay to the sewing room and Jade to the nursery. They were both grateful David had agreed to allow Jade to work at the mill and to bring the children. Jade had grown into a lovely young woman and felt that her life finally had purpose. Being at the mill also gave her the opportunity to see her friends, Mrs. Gordon and Mrs. Moore. They were always making Cherokee toys for the children. Frederick loved the stick and ball they made him and proudly showed his friends. They played stickball often. They also gave Michael a set, but since he was still an infant, Jade hung it high in his room so he could dream of the days when he could go out with the other boys and play the famous Cherokee game of stickball. Rose Ann, now four, was given a Cherokee doll. David was not happy they were given these Indian toys, but was afraid to draw too much attention by disallowing them, so he relented.

Jade took the children to the nursery, put Michael in a crib and then asked Rose Ann to take a seat with the rest of the children. There were seventeen children that came to the nursery ranging from one month (Michael) up to five years-old. She separated the four babies by putting the cribs in the back corner and hanging a sheet around them, hoping they would be able to sleep. She gave the older children paper and pencils and then asked them to draw for the first hour to get some of their creative juices flowing. It also gave them the opportunity to expend some of their pent up energy but remain quiet so that the babies could nap. She found that starting with drawing helped the children focus on their studies. About an hour later, she asked them to hang their new drawings on the wall, and then to describe what they drew. When she got to the third child, the nursery door opened and in walked the man she had seen several times now from afar; the one with the great smile. There was that smile again.

"Ms. Jade, may I have a word with you?" the man asked politely.

Jade looked at the children who all began to giggle. They covered their mouths and tried to stop; to no avail.

"Children, please stay in your seats and be quiet for a few min-utes. I will be right back." Jade walked out the door and right before she closed it behind her, she heard the children burst out laughing.

Embarrassed, she asked, "May I help you, sir?"

Big smile. "I am hoping you can but first let me introduce myself. My name is Oscar Hicks."

"My name is…"

"Jade Hawkins. I know," smiled Oscar. "I asked. I hope you don't mind."

Jade blushed and looked down. Then she held her chin up. "What can I do for you, Mr. Hicks? I really need to get back to the children. I am not supposed to leave them alone."

"I understand. I won't keep you. I wrote you a letter." Oscar handed Jade a letter. "It will explain everything." He nodded once, smiled and walked down the hall.

Jade stood staring after him for a few seconds. He turned and looked at her and of course, smiled. Humiliated that he caught her watching him, she put the letter in her pocket and went back into the nursery. She was tempted to read it right away, but knew she had to tend to the children. Once her day got going, she forgot it was there.

At the end of the day as she and the children met up with Kay to get back in the carriage for the ride home, she saw Oscar off in a distance. He saw her and tipped his hat. And smiled.

She couldn't get into the carriage fast enough. She quickly pulled out the letter, tried to turn her back to the children, hoping they wouldn't see it and started to read.

"Ms. Hawkins, I hope someday you will allow me to call you Jade. Jade is one of the most beautiful, precious stones there is and is perfectly appropriate for the woman named for it. Did you know that jade was considered the "imperial gem"? From about the earliest Chinese Dynasties until present, jade has had a special significance, comparable with that of gold here. How do I know this? I read every chance I get. I have applied for a position as a teacher at the Academy and hope to obtain that position within a few months. I believe, as others do, Roswell will grow substantially over the next few years due to the success of the mills. Teaching will be an improvement over what I earn today in the mill and will give my life the purpose it currently lacks. My sincere hope is you will give me the opportunity to court you once I have secured a position more worthy of you. From the first moment I saw you, I knew you would be an important part of my life. I hope to someday make you my wife, if you will have me. I believe it is important to be forthright, so I am making my wishes clear to you. Please consider what I have declared here as my truest desire for our happiness together. When next I see you, a simple smile will tell me you are interested in pursuing a

special friendship with the hopes to become something more one day. Always, Oscar Hicks."

Jade folded the letter and put it back in her pocket. She looked out the window. Then she pulled the letter out and read it again. She shook her head. She had never read anything more beautiful nor more meaningful, nor more bold. No one had ever said anything like that to her. She wondered if her parents named her after jade because they thought she was precious. She could only hope. They would never have the opportunity to tell her so she chose to believe that was the reason for her name. She didn't realize it but tears were streaming down her cheeks.

"Ms. Jade?" asked Rose Ann. "Ms. Jade, why are you crying?"

Jade turned to look at Rose Ann, Michael, and Frederick, the children she loved more than life itself - if they only knew how much. She hoped they could sense her love for them. She glanced at Kay.

Kay looked worried. "Jade, what is the matter?" She feared Jade would not keep their secret, although she had never given Kay any reason to doubt her loyalty. She knew Jade understood that if she revealed the shameful truth, it would devastate all of their lives and Jade would be sent away. Away from the children she cherished.

Jade smiled. "Nothing is wrong," she said as she looked at each of them. She took Rose Ann's hand. "I was just thinking about my parents. I miss them."

"Do you think they will ever come back?" asked Frederick.

Jade took a sharp breath then looked at Kay and back to Frederick. "No, they won't be coming back."

Kay looked at the letter in Jade's hands. Jade was folding it, unfolding it and folding it again. "Is that something I should know about, Jade?"

Jade looked down at the letter. "No, it is a letter from a possible suitor. Of course, I don't have the time to be courted. It was just nice to read the words."

Kay's eyebrows went up. "Really? Can I ask who it is from?"

Jade looked again at Kay. "Do you mind if I keep that to myself for now? I promise if anything comes of it, I will tell you. For now, I would just like to keep it private."

"Of course, I didn't mean to pry. I understand," said Kay. "Well, Frederick, tell me how school was today?"

For the rest of the ride home, Kay asked the children questions about how their day went and asked Jade about her day as well. Everything seemed to be falling into place. She no longer had to hide Jade from her father or the community. She had three beautiful, healthy children. Everyone seemed to accept the fact that Jade was the nanny and now the nursery attendant, so no one was asking questions. She did wonder who this mystery man was. Would he come between them? What if he wanted to take Jade away? Would she go quietly and not try to take the children? She wouldn't do that. Would she?

Chapter 36
October 11, 2010

Charm had become the hotspot of Roswell in a very short period of time. The atmosphere that Carolyn and Kacey developed along with their incredible, outgoing and attentive staff, made it comfortable and welcoming with enough pizzazz to help the patrons put their bad economy woes away, even for a little while.

"Watch out! Coming through!" Gabby called out as she backed out of the kitchen through the swinging stainless doors. "Oh good, you're here," she noted as she eyed Kacey and Carolyn over her reading glasses.

"Since when did you start wearing readers?" Carolyn asked. Then she giggled and both she and Kacey pulled theirs out of their purses. "Guess it's the age! So what do you have there?"

"Whatever it is, it looks really yummy and smells delish!" exclaimed Kacey. "No... it's not what I think it is, is it?"

"Well, if you think it's Lobster Spring Rolls, then it is what you think it is, or something like that," Gabby smiled proudly. "Try them!"

They both reached for the gorgeous morsels that looked like something you would get in a five star restaurant and carefully took a bite. Eyes rolled back in their heads and Carolyn made an "A-OK" gesture. Kacey put her hand on her chest and rolled her eyes appreciating the delicacy. They started to reach for another and Gabby pulled the tray away.

"Enough internal testing. Time to get these out to our patrons and start making some money." She proceeded to walk throughout the restaurant with her tray asking the diners to take a sample and tell her what they thought. When she finished she strolled past Carolyn and Kacey, "It's unanimous. New menu item. Got three orders." With that, she walked back into the kitchen.

"She is a genius," Kacey said. "Hey, look who is here!"

Carolyn looked toward the front door. Frank walked in, hands in his pockets, looking around. "Hi Frank! It's good to see you! Can I get you a table?"

Frank smiled. "Your place is fabulous. Actually, I think I will sit at the bar. Can I get dinner at the bar?" Carolyn nodded, showing him the way. "Wanda had her first dance, the Sadie Hawkins tonight. I dropped her and her date off at Naylor Hall and thought I would stop by here. If I go home, I would just sit and pout about my girl growing up. Now I am really glad I came," he said, looking at the menu. Carolyn and Frank made small talk for a few minutes, and then Kacey tapped Carolyn on the shoulder.

"Look who else decided to stop in tonight."

Christina and Kevin gave Carolyn a big hug and said hello to Frank. "We haven't seen you since the meeting," said Christina. "I am so sorry for getting all emotional and running out the way I did."

Kevin rubbed her back, which didn't go unnoticed by Kacey and Carolyn who made a knowing face at each other.

"No need to apologize, I should have discussed the content of the journal with you privately, I see that now," offered Frank. "I am sorry to have brought out the information the way I did."

"Well, Kevin and I found some additional pages and have read them. In fact we are meeting Daniel tonight to tell him more about them. His business is picking up so he hasn't had much time to read them for himself. We thought we would catch up over dinner and tell him the rest of the story. Or at least the rest of what we know. Frank, we have uncovered that Jade was indeed the mother of one of our direct ancestors and had a couple more children with David Greyson. She is also listed on our family tree as being our great, great, great grandmother, but no reference to her being Cherokee and no reference to Kay that I could find. Part of what I want to talk to Daniel tonight about is, are we comfortable revealing that information. I'll see what Daniel says."

Frank looked surprised. "So you found more journals? What I read said Jade thought she was with child, but didn't go any further."

"We found additional pages in one of the rooms upstairs. We are hoping to find more, but so far have not had any luck with that," said Christina.

"If Daniel agrees with revealing the story, do you think you would consider allowing me to be one of the tour guides like we originally discussed? I would only tell the story as you want me to, but I think I can make the stories come alive. I would really like to do it, if you would allow me," Frank anxiously inquired.

"We'll see, Frank. I have no problem with that and since I love your deep voice, I think you are perfect!" she squeezed his arm and smiled.

Frank smiled back, "Well that is a compliment. Just let me know what you decide. By the way, it looks like they have made some great progress over the last couple of weeks. The barn is erected. Is it finished on the inside?"

Scott walked up just then. They all looked at him and Christina held out her hand for Scott to do the honors.

"Hey all! We are putting the finishing touches on the inside of the barn this week. Then we will start on cleaning up the slave quarters. The house will be done by the beginning of December; just in time to decorate for the holidays! It's looking real good. Feel free to stop by Frank to check it out," said Scott. "But right now, I have something very important I need to do." With that, he grabbed Carolyn and dipped her, then kissed her longingly.

"Wow! What was that for sexy husband?" asked Carolyn.

"You didn't really forget our anniversary, did you? Or did you just think that I forgot it?" asked Scott.

"You have had so much on your plate, I wouldn't have blamed you this year if you forgot our anniversary. But it's so sweet that you remembered." She looked at the rest of the gang standing around. "We usually surprise each other with a short romantic trip for our anniversary. This is Scott's year, but honey," looking at Scott, "like I said, I am just happy you remembered it at all with everything going on!"

Mike walked in carrying a dozen red roses and handed them to Scott who handed them to Carolyn. Carolyn's jaw dropped and her hands flew to her mouth. "They are beautiful!"

Gabby then walked out of the kitchen with a bottle of champagne and lots of champagne flutes. She popped the cork, everyone cheered, and then she poured. They toasted Carolyn and Scott and congratulated them on their tenth wedding anniversary. Scott whispered something into Carolyn's ear.

"No way, really?" Carolyn exclaimed. "Carmel? I love Carmel and have wanted to go back. When do we leave?"

"First thing in the morning," Scott said, clinking their glasses together.

"Kacey, can you handle the rest of the evening? I need to pack!"

"No problem, go, have a great time!"

"Oh my gosh, I just realized, this will be the first time I am leaving you with the restaurant for a whole weekend. Are you okay with that?"

"Yes. Even though Scott is surprising you, he talked to me about it a couple of weeks ago. I've got it covered."

"Wow!" exclaimed Carolyn, squinting her eyes at Kacey. "I'll have to remember how good you are at keeping secrets!"

"Mike said he would help too, didn't you Mike?" Kacey ribbed him.

"Uh, sure, whatever you need Honey Buns," Mike leaned over and kissed Kacey. The crowd laughed.

"Well congratulations," said Christina. "Daniel just got here so we are going to take a seat and have some dinner. Have a great time in Carmel."

"Thanks," said Scott, hugging Christina and then shaking Kevin's hand. "By the way, one of my guys, Chuck, is going to be the fore-man on the project while I am gone. He drives the blue Ranger, if you have any questions or need anything at Greyson Manor. They should be wrapping up a few things after this weekend. Oh, and don't forget about the article in Saturday's paper about the restora-tion. Can you save me a copy? I hope they spell my name right!" Scott winked.

Kevin said, "No problem, I will be sure to get you a copy and I'll probably hang around this weekend, make sure the guys stay in line."

"Oh yeah, that's why you're hanging around," chided Mike.

They all said their goodbyes. Carolyn and Scott went home.

Christina and Kevin greeted Daniel who went over to say hello to Frank before they sat down for dinner. They enjoyed a wonderful meal and Christina and Kevin told Daniel all about the journal and what they had learned.

"So Michael grew up during the Civil War. Can you imagine all of the things he saw? That must have been terrible. In fact, he was only nine years old when it started. That means his brother, Frederick, was the age to fight in the war. I wonder if he did. You know, I bet that I could find more information at the Roswell Historical Center." Christina looked at Kevin, hopefully. He nodded in agree-ment. The three looked at each other recognizing this was about to get very real.

Chapter 37
June, 1857

The ceremony for the opening of the newly constructed covered bridge was one of the social events of the decade. It signified the growth of the town of Roswell. It also instilled the importance of the mills to the region. The Roswell Manufacturing Company built the bridge from Roswell across the Chattahoochee River to gain faster access to the railroad hub in Atlanta. Atlanta was clearly one of the largest growing metropolitan areas in the South.

Jade looked around the crowd of bystanders. She couldn't help but notice Oscar in the crowd. He was tall and broad and so handsome. It broke her heart to see him. It had been five years since he had written her his first letter, professing his love for her. He wrote her several letters since. But when she returned none of them and didn't provide him with the smile he asked for each time he wrote, he had only to assume her feelings were not the same as his own. After a few years, he stopped pursuing her, although he never stopped looking at her the way that he did.

Jade believed she could never marry. By doing so, she would have to leave the plantation and begin a new family, thus leaving her children behind. She just could not do that. It was better for Oscar to realize their life together was not a reality and he should find someone who could make him happy. It broke Jade's heart to even think of Oscar with another woman. She was surprised he had still not moved on. Many of the young women in town were clearly interested, but he would just ignore them.

Jade left the family to walk down to the Chattahoochee. The children, David and Kay were so engrossed in the festivities of the bridge opening, they didn't even notice when she wandered off. She walked down to the river's edge. She looked up the river and saw how quickly it moved downstream. She marveled at its beauty. She knew the current was strong in this area, which is why the mill was built here. She knelt down to run her hand through the rushing water. The way it felt against her palm was so calming. She rubbed the water across her face and sighed and then she put her hand back into the river. She liked how it rushed around the rocks and made small waterfalls. The sound was magical.

Suddenly, a hand came from behind hers in the water and held onto hers. Jade, surprised, quickly looked behind her. His face was so close to hers it took a moment for her to recognize him but in her heart she knew it was him before she had even turned around. Oscar. He no longer smiled like he once did. His gaze into her eyes was so heartbroken that she had to turn away. Jade pulled her hand from his and walked into the woods. She was out of breath and grabbed a hold of a large tree. She had never felt such sorrow. Here was a living, breathing person who loved her, and she had to turn him away. She couldn't fathom she had it in her to do that. Just thinking about the loss of her family crippled her so much, yet here she was hurting someone else. How could she? How could she not?

Oscar grabbed Jade by both arms turning her to face him so he could look her squarely in the eyes. "How can I convince you of my love? You torture me with your defiance. I had hoped by now we would be a family, but you have yet to even look lovingly into my eyes or even bestow me with a simple smile."

"Oscar, please let me go. You are hurting me," Jade pleaded, looking away.

"I'm sorry." He loosened his grip. "But look at me and tell me you have no feelings for me and I will leave you be."

Jade looked at Oscar. She couldn't say the words. Tears filled her eyes. Then she closed them as the tears ran down her cheeks. "I cannot leave my family."

"Your family? You are employed by the Greysons. Don't you want to start your own family? I know that your parents went west and you were left behind. I respect your strong commitment and allegiance to the Greysons, and I would not keep you from visiting them."

"You don't understand and I can't explain it. Just know that I do care for you. I don't want to hurt you but you need to find someone else. I cannot, will not, leave Greyson Manor," cried Jade. "I cannot leave....the children." She looked away. She could not reveal their secret. They would all be disgraced and she would lose everything.

Frustrated Oscar dropped his hands. He turned to look at the river and ran his hand through his beautiful, thick black hair. He kicked a rock into the river and then bent down, picked up a stone and threw it into the river. He spoke more softly this time. "I don't understand. I really don't understand. I have poured my heart and soul out to you. I have told you my intentions are pure and honorable. I love..." he turned to Jade but she was gone. He looked up the river bank and saw her disappear into the crowd. He was furious. She didn't respect him, much less love him. This conversation was not over, he thought. He ran up the bank to where he saw her and found her standing near the Greysons. She was running her hand down Rose Ann's hair. Kay was looking at her curiously and David saw Oscar coming toward them. He put his hand out to greet him. "Good afternoon, Mr. Hicks. How are Frederick and Rose Ann doing in your classes?"

"Good afternoon," Oscar said not taking his eyes off Jade. "They are doing very well. You should be proud of your children. They study and work hard."

Jade was looking at Oscar, concerned. Kay saw the recognition in Jade's eyes and knew there was something between them.

"Jade, we were not finished with our conversation," Oscar stated firmly.

David looked at Jade. "Conversation?"

"Yes, Jade and I were talking and I had not finished what I was trying to explain to her."

"Oscar, please," Jade begged.

Rose Ann looked up at Oscar then at Jade. She put her arm around Jade, tugged on Jade's dress and said, "Ms. Jade, Mr. Hicks is a very nice man. He wants to talk to you. Don't you want to talk to him?"

Jade stared at Rose Ann, incredulously. This child was too smart for her own good. She then looked at Kay and David.

Kay put her hand out. "Mr. Hicks, I appreciate all that you do in the classroom for my children. They have really matured and their reading, writing and arithmetic skills are very strong. I am impressed with your ability to get through to them. Is this something about the children? Can I help you?"

Oscar took Kay's hand, bowed his head slightly, took a deep breath then said, "I am in love with Jade and I intend to make her my wife, if she will have me." He looked at Jade whose eyes were as big as saucers. "I seem to be struggling with the 'if she will have me' part. I just want to speak with her. Will you allow me to speak with her in private?"

"Well, I don't know," grumbled David.

"Of course you may," said Kay. "Will you give me a moment with Jade first?" She grabbed Jade's arm and walked away out of earshot. "My dear, what are you doing? He is a lovely man, a teacher like yourself, and he clearly loves you. I had heard that his family was killed in a fire when he was a young man, so he probably yearns for the love of a family. You have that in common. Why are you holding back? You are thirty-two years old. These opportunities don't come along very often, especially at your age. Trust me, I know."

Jade looked at Kay horrified. "How can you ask me that? I can't leave my, uh, the children!"

Kay's face dropped. "Jade, I know this is hard for you, but you do realize these children are David's and mine." She put her hand on Jade's arm when she saw the pained look in Jade's eyes. "We took you in and have cared for you in return for giving birth to our children, but that's just it. They are our children. We would never deny you the ability to visit with them, but it's time. It's time that you begin your own life and your own family before it's too late. You'll see Michael in the nursery for one more year and you can visit all three of them at the school or at Greyson Manor anytime you like. No one would deny you that. It would be cruel if we did and it would hurt all of our reputations as well. You have my word, Jade. Go be with your man. Hear him out. Give him a chance."

Jade's eyes filled with tears. She was afraid but for the first time, she thought it might be possible. She looked over at the children who were watching her and Kay. She always wondered if they sensed the truth. Couldn't they tell she was their mother, not Kay? Then she looked at Oscar who was speaking with David. What were they talking about? That worried her.

"Are you sure?" Jade asked Kay. "Do you promise me I can see them anytime I want?"

Kay smiled. "Well, within reason, of course. Really, anytime, I promise. I will always be grateful to you Jade; and grateful you kept our secret as well." Kay hugged Jade.

Kay took Jade's hand and walked back to the rest of the group. "I believe Jade would like to have that conversation now, Oscar."

Jade looked at each of the children again, then at David, who didn't look pleased, and then at Oscar and smiled. "Would you like to go for a walk?"

Chapter 38

October 16, 2010

Frank had fallen asleep in his recliner but awoke with a start. Had he heard something? He looked at the clock. It was one a.m. His heart racing, he quickly went upstairs to Wanda's room to see if she had gotten home from her date. She was supposed to wake him. He opened the door and peeked inside. She was sound asleep. I guess she forgot to wake me, he thought. Relieved, he went back downstairs.

So what was it that woke me up? He looked out the front window, all looked quiet and still, nothing out of the ordinary. He went to the side window and pulled the curtains open. His breath caught. He thought he could see shadows moving by the newly finished barn. He squinted to try to see more clearly. Then he saw it, fire.

He ran for the phone and called 9-1-1. He put his shoes on and grabbed his cell phone. He dialed Christina's number. She didn't answer. He tried it again. No answer. He was able to reach Daniel. He grabbed his jacket and walked out on his front porch. He went back into his hall closet and pulled out the baseball bat he kept there. He went back outside and around the house toward the barn. He was worried whoever had started the fire was still there, or maybe they were hurt and didn't get out in time. He was tip toeing around a tree when a teenager ran into him, full force, knocking him down.

The kid knocked the breath right out of him then hesitated not sure what to do. He grabbed Frank's bat.

"Come on! Let's get out of here," someone called out from the driveway.

"He saw me!" The kid looked back at Frank. He looked like he wasn't sure what to do. Frank held up his hand. The kid made a bad decision but made his move.

About ten minutes later the fire truck came up the drive and several firemen jumped down off the truck. "Get the hose to the fire, I'll take care of him," yelled one young man. Wanda was leaning over her father. "What happened?" asked the fireman.

"I don't know, I just got here and saw my dad on the ground. Help him! Daddy, are you okay?" Wanda cried.

Frank didn't answer.

"We need a stretcher over here," the fireman yelled out as the ambulance pulled into the driveway behind the fire truck.

The paramedics put Frank into the ambulance. Wanda jumped in with him and they took off for the hospital.

The firemen worked through the night putting out the fire but luckily the barn was the only building impacted. It was, however, destroyed.

In the morning, Christina drove her car into the drive as quickly as she could. She jumped out and ran over to Daniel who was standing, hands on his hips, shaking his head.

"Well, I am glad you weren't here, but where were you and why didn't you return my calls?" Daniel yelled at Christina.

"Oh no," Christina cried when she saw the barn. She looked at Daniel. "I was with Kevin at his place. It was the first time I had stayed with him there. I had turned off my phone. I didn't think…"

"No, you didn't think. Don't ever turn off your cell phone!"

Christina started to cry. Daniel held her for a minute and patted her back. "Okay, don't cry. It is what it is at this point."

"No one was hurt, right?" asked Christina.

"Didn't you listen to my message?" yelled Daniel. Shaking his head, furious, he said, "Frank is in the hospital! Apparently he came out to see what was happening and he was hit in the head with a bat by the arsonist. They found the bloody bat on the ground next to Frank. The fireman that called me told me about it. He was unconscious when they took him to the hospital. I have to get over there. I have been here since about two a.m. Can you stay here to answer any questions for the firemen while I go check on Frank? Wanda is with him and she is probably beside herself." Without waiting for Christina to answer, Daniel jumped in his car and headed to the hospital.

Christina stood looking at the burned out barn, hands over her mouth. She couldn't believe it was destroyed. Who would do this? She said a silent prayer for Frank.

Kevin pulled into the drive and jumped out. "I'm sorry I was in the shower when you got the call. Are you alright? Was anyone hurt?"

Christina went into Kevin's arms and then told him about Frank.

"Oh no, I hope he's okay. Is Daniel going to call you?"

Realizing she left her cell phone in the car, she ran to retrieve it. She checked the messages. There were several from Daniel throughout the night she hadn't bothered to listen to once she had heard the first one. There were no new messages from Daniel since he had gone to the hospital. There were two missed calls from Frank. There was also a message from the fire department letting her know about the fire around one-thirty a.m. She shook her head and looked down at the ground. "I shouldn't have turned my phone off." She looked at Kevin. "I didn't want us to be disturbed last night. But I never should have shut my phone off. I can't believe I did that." She kicked the ground.

"Christina, there is nothing you could have done about the fire, or Frank, even if you had gotten the message earlier."

"Well at least I got laid, is that what you are saying Kevin?" Christina spat at him.

"Uh no, that is not what I am saying. I just don't want you to beat yourself up. You could have been hurt if you were here, so I am glad you were at my place. Have you thought about how this might have happened?"

"No, I hadn't thought about that," Christina said. "I'm sorry I said that. I am just frazzled."

"I know. It's all right. Let's look around." Kevin took her hand and they walked around the side of the barn closest to the slave quarters.

"Oh no!" yelled Christina.

Kevin saw it too.

Painted on the side of the slave quarters was, "RACIST!"

"I can't believe it. It must be those kids from high school. I can't believe they still think that and would do something like this! Damn it! And they hit Frank too. What were they thinking! They have to know I will report them. Unless they think I am too afraid. I am kind of afraid to report them…" she mumbled, looking meekly at Kevin.

"Those irresponsible brats! I'm not afraid to report them," Kevin yelled. "And neither are you. Come on, let's get to the police station then we will head over to the hospital. We have to at least give them the information so the police can follow up."

After telling the police about the incident in high school and giving them the name of the gang leader that had been arrested back then, they left the police station feeling nervous but at least they felt they had done what needed to be done. They headed to the hospital.

When they got to the hospital, Daniel was on the phone with the insurance company. "Wanda, has your dad woken up yet?" Christina asked the teenager.

CINDI CRANE

"No, he hasn't. I am so scared. He's going to be alright, isn't he?" Wanda cried.

"I'm sure he will be. Your dad is very strong and he'll come out of this," Kevin assured her. "Do you know what happened, Wanda?"

"No, I just heard the sirens and looked out the window and saw the fire. When I realized my dad wasn't in our house I went outside. I saw someone driving away and when I went over to your house Christina, I saw him lying on the ground. He was bleeding!" Wanda started to cry.

"Well, you stay by his side. Can I get you anything?" Christina asked.

"A Coke would be good."

"Ok, I'll get you one. And just so you know, Kevin and I just stopped by the police station to tell them about Greg Jones."

"Greg Jones? What about Greg Jones?" Wanda asked eyes wide.

"Greg was arrested back when I was in high school because he threw a bottle at me, see the scar? And he wrote graffiti, "racist", actually on our buildings. You probably didn't notice, but it was there again today. I just let the police know so they could investigate him. I'm sure he has been out of jail for several years now. He didn't get much of a sentence when he threw that bottle at me, and I hadn't heard anything from him since then. If he did do it, I wonder what set him off now." Christina looked at Kevin then back at Wanda. Wanda looked ill. "Are you okay, Wanda?"

"The guy I have been seeing is Greg Jones' little brother, Alan. I told Alan about your plans." Wanda put her hand over her mouth, then removed it and said, "I shouldn't have done that."

"Wanda, how could you have known? Don't worry, if it was Greg, he will be serving a very long sentence this time." Christina walked over and hugged Wanda. "It's not your fault, honey. There was also an article in the paper yesterday, talking about our plans. He could have gotten the information then."

Chapter 39
April, 1858 - 1861

I t was a beautiful spring morning for a wedding in Roswell. Jade stood staring at herself in the mirror in the bride's room at the Roswell Presbyterian Church. She could hardly believe her eyes. Kay had made an exquisite wedding gown, very delicate and it fit her beautifully. Kay had also helped her with her hair. It was very long but Kay pulled it back for her and made ringlets that hung to her waist. Small flowers were inserted throughout her hair.

"Ms. Jade? Are you ready for your bouquet?" asked Rose Ann.

Jade turned to her daughter. Her shiny red curls and deep brown eyes took Jade's breath away. Rose Ann was her flower girl. She was so grateful to Kay for allowing the children to be in the wedding. They knew no one would question it since Jade had been their nanny their entire lives. Jade leaned over and took the flowers and smelled them. "Oh Rose Ann, thank you. They are beautiful. You remember what I told you, right?"

"Yes. Mommy and Daddy named me after the rose because the rose is so pretty and then you chose roses for your bouquet because of me! You look really pretty, Ms. Jade. So do you, Mommy," she said as she looked over at Kay. Kay was Jade's Matron of Honor. The three of them did a quick hug and then headed toward the door.

David knocked then peeked in. He started to say something,

then seeing both women, stopped. "You both look amazing. I am the luckiest man in the world." The ladies didn't appreciate his implication.

"Yes, you are a very lucky man, my dear, but Mr. Hicks is also a very lucky man and let's not keep him waiting, shall we?" Kay pulled the door open the rest of the way and asked David to hold it. She picked up the train of Jade's gown and they walked toward the sanctuary. The music started, the doors opened and she saw Oscar near the altar. And Oscar saw Jade. As she walked down the aisle toward Oscar, her heart beating fast, she just kept her eyes on him and that smile. She smiled back.

The wedding was very touching. The guests couldn't remember when there had been a more beautiful couple, their love shining through their eyes. It was the happiest day of Jade's life. She now had someone that loved her unconditionally, she could still take part in her children's lives and she could have children with her new husband. Life couldn't be more rich or fulfilling. A tear escaped her eyes as she thought about her dear parents and her brothers. If only, she thought. But she knew her parents and her brother, Michael, watched her from heaven and they would continue to protect her and show her the way.

She was grateful to Mrs. Gordon and Mrs. Moore, for they had told her of the Cherokee wedding traditions. She had asked Oscar if he would allow a few of the ceremonial rites and Oscar was more than happy to comply. It turned out that Oscar was not of Cherokee descent, as Jade had thought. He was part English and Scottish and having lost his family, he understood Jade's wish to incorporate the Cherokee customs in their wedding and their life. One of the customs was to bless the ceremonial site for seven consecutive days. The preacher explained to Jade that the Church was already blessed but he was happy to perform a daily blessing anyway. He had also married the Gordons and the Moores, the other two mixed marriages in town, so he was familiar with the customs. Oscar, as well as the preacher felt that it was the least they could do for Jade. She was but one of the few Cherokee left in the area and they were grateful for her and her loving, devoted spirit. She seemed to hold no grudge for all that had been done to her and her family and she lived her life in a servant manner caring for others.

Another tradition was to bless not only the bride and groom but all participants of the wedding and the guests. Both the bride and groom were then each covered in a blue blanket, and Mrs. Gordon and Mrs. Moore sang a Cherokee song. Jade was moved by everyone's acceptance of her request to have the Cherokee rites and traditions as a part of her wedding. She loved Oscar even more for loving her so completely. He obviously respected her wishes and strived to help her maintain some semblance of her Cherokee heritage. The preacher then removed each blue blanket, and covered the couple together with one white blanket, indicating the beginning of their new life together.

After the ceremony, they had a small reception at their new home Oscar had built. It was much smaller than Greyson Manor but it was quaint, cozy and efficient. And it was theirs. They couldn't wait to begin their lives together in their new cottage. The cottage was less than a mile from Greyson Manor. Jade was very pleased because the children could walk to visit.

Once the guests had all gone, they went to their bedroom and made love all night. Jade never knew it could be this way. She wondered if Oscar knew she wasn't a virgin, but she had not told him about the children. She had promised Kay and David and that was the condition to be able to continue to see them. She hated keeping such a huge secret from her husband, but what choice did she have? She would have to take that secret to her grave. She also could not tell him that her parents and Michael had been killed by Greyson's men, or the whole story would come out. She let Oscar believe that her family had been forced to leave her behind and told him the story was too painful to discuss. He never pressed her for the details.

Within the first year of their marriage, Jade conceived. Their baby girl, Ruby was born on July 7, 1859. Ruby had a full head of dark brown hair and brown eyes. Oscar had named her and referred to Jade and Ruby as his "gems". Eleven months later, June 6, 1860, a son was born. Oscar named him Charles, after Jade's father.

Jade continued to manage the nursery and teach the younger children art, reading and writing. She was pleased that by the time Roswell's children got to the Academy, and to her husband's classes, they were very prepared for a more in-depth curriculum. Oscar and Jade prided themselves with developing the most intelligent children in Georgia. They were sure of it.

Jade would take her children with her to the nursery and she was able to spend time with Michael each day as well for that first year. In 1860, he enrolled in the Academy. Now all of her first born children were at the Academy together. She would take Ruby and Charles to see them all at the end of each day. Although they didn't know that they were kin, they did love each other, she could tell. The older children were very protective of the babies and always took time to play with them. Jade wondered if people noticed how much they looked alike, but she couldn't allow herself to worry about it.

They were all very happy and content with their lives. Both families were very involved in the community and enjoyed watching and participating in the growth of the town of Roswell, the mills and the school. They had picnics in the town square and enjoyed every day of their lives together. Jade's love for Oscar grew as did her trust. She knew he loved her and would do anything for his family. He was a wonderful man and she was grateful to Kay for convincing her to give him a chance.

Then in 1861, everything changed. They called it the Civil War, The War Between the States.

Chapter 40
October 17, 2010

C arolyn and Scott drove right to the hospital from the airport. They had gotten a call from Kacey telling them what had happened. Frank had woken up the night before after being unconscious for about eighteen hours. At first he wasn't sure where he was, and then he remembered everything.

Wanda had not left his side. The adults tried to get her to eat and brought her magazines, but she couldn't take her eyes off her father. She was still feeling guilty since they believed the offender was the brother of the boy she was dating. The police still had not found Greg Jones.

"Frank, are you up for more visitors?" Carolyn asked.

"Please come in." Frank said in a very low voice. His throat was still dry from being unconscious for so many hours. He was holding Wanda's hand.

Carolyn could tell she had been crying. She walked over next to Wanda and gave her a squeeze. "You doing okay kiddo?" she asked.

"I am fine, but my dad has a huge gash in his head and it's all my fault!" She lowered her head. Frank looked at Wanda and shook his head.

"Your fault?" Scott asked. "How could it be your fault?"

"I've been trying to tell her it is not her fault. In fact, this one time she did not wake me when she got home from her date, probably because she was late," he chided her. "But if she had woken me in my recliner, I would have gone to bed."

"And you wouldn't have been hit over the head with your own bat, Daddy!" Wanda exclaimed.

"But I also wouldn't have called 9-1-1 and who knows what else could have burned down or how many people could have been hurt if I hadn't looked outside when I did. It's okay, honey. I am going to be fine. Stop blaming yourself."

"Why are you blaming yourself, Wanda?" Carolyn looked confused and concerned.

"We think that the guy who burned down the barn and probably the same guy that hit my dad, is the brother of a boy I've been dating. The police haven't found either one of them yet. Now I am worried that my boyfriend," she looked at her dad, who was scrunching his brow at the word "boyfriend", "might have been involved too. I sure hope not. I would have to kill him."

"Wanda, don't say that. We will see what the police find out." Frank looked at Scott. "You probably want to talk to Daniel. He has talked to the insurance company but I don't know the details."

"Yes, if you don't mind, I'll just step out in the hall and give him a call." Scott excused himself and went to call Daniel. As he was starting to make the call, he saw Christina walking toward him. He asked how everything was going.

"Well, did you see Frank?" she asked. Scott nodded. "I am so glad he woke up. I don't know what I would have done if he hadn't. This is all my fault."

"Your fault? Wanda thinks it's her fault. I have a feeling the only person or people at fault are the perpetrators, not you girls."

"I wasn't home. I was at Kevin's and I missed several phone calls because I had turned my cell phone off."

"Christina, don't worry. Frank is going to be fine and I am sure the insurance company will pay to have the barn replaced. It has put our plans back a bit, but at this point let's just hope they find the guys that did it. We can start with the clean up, but I wouldn't start the rebuild until they catch these guys, don't you agree? What do you think was their motivation?" Scott asked.

"If it is who I think it is, they are part of a gang; some African-American boys who think that anyone that lives in a historical home and has slave quarters still standing is racist. I had several run-ins with them in high school. I just don't know how to get through to them. I just had a thought. Maybe I should go see their parents. Actually, when Frank is better, maybe we should go see them together so I can explain what we are doing and how we plan to try to give homage to the slaves and the Indians. I am more convinced than ever we have to tell the stories. We have to make it right. Maybe it will help reduce the tension around the topic. I just don't know. I do think talking to those boys' parents could help though. What do you think?"

Scott shrugged. "It couldn't hurt. Maybe they can shed some light on why the boys feel so strongly about your house and your family."

"Alright, as soon as Frank is able, we will go see them."

Scott called Daniel and said he would meet him at the house to look over the damage and discuss the rebuilding plans. Scott left Carolyn with the girls and headed over to the house. He and Daniel spent about an hour looking through the ashes and debris. What a waste. It was disturbing to see all that hard work gone up in flames, literally.

They stood looking at the slave house and the word "racist" painted in large, red letters. Scott rubbed his chin. "Have you thought about tearing this building down and not rebuilding it? You could just add a kitchen onto the barn when we rebuild again."

Daniel looked at Scott. "No, I hadn't really thought about that.

Mainly because I guess I assumed you needed to keep all the out buildings in tact to be considered historical. That not the case?"

"No, not the case. Obviously, the more you have the more interesting a place can be, but in this case, I don't know if it's worth it. Especially since we had already decided that we weren't going to bother trying to renovate the slave quarters, we were just going to restore the house and rebuild the barn."

"I'll talk to Christina about it. If we get rid of the slave quarters, I think we should also get rid of the carriage house - that's where Jade's brother, Michael was killed. It gives us the creeps and it's an eyesore."

Back at the hospital, Christina and Carolyn sat with Frank until he began to tire.

"Wanda, you look exhausted and since your dad is going to be in here another night, would you like to stay with us tonight?" Carolyn asked.

"Thanks, but I don't want to leave my dad."

"That is a very generous offer," Frank said. "Wanda, why don't you go with them? You can come back and see me in the morning and you can drive me home."

"You would let me drive?" Wanda inquired.

"You have your permit. You know as long as I am in the car with you, you can drive; and it's not that far. Yes, I would let you drive me home. But go on. Go with Carolyn for tonight and get a good night's sleep." Wanda leaned over and kissed his bandage, then said she would.

"I'll take her by your house in the morning to get your car and we'll come back first thing. Get some rest tonight, Frank." They left the room. "You know Wanda, sometimes people need to be left alone just so they can sleep. A lot of times, they don't sleep when they know you are there because they feel guilty. It's really best for him to get a good night's sleep since he's going home tomorrow."

"Okay, I appreciate you letting me stay at your house. Do you mind if we run by my house so I can get some clothes and my toothbrush?"

"Sure, let's go," smiled Carolyn.

"Well, it sounds like you girls have a plan. I am going to go by the Roswell Historical Society. I have an idea about how I might be able to find more information about the family I didn't know I had. See you later!" Christina waved and went to her car, then drove to the Roswell Historical Society office. She knew they closed in thirty minutes but she was dying to look up Frederick Greyson and see if she could find anything about him in the Civil War files.

"Hi, I'm Christina Greyson. My family owns Greyson Manor."

"Hello, I am Ellen Coleman. I'm one of the Certified Archivists. How can I help you?"

"Well, I am not sure if you had heard, but we are restoring our home. We have actually hired a historical renovator, Scott Kane. Are you familiar with him?"

"Yes, Scott came by here when he was doing some research on the house and told us of your plans. We are so happy to see you restoring your home. As soon as it is completed and certified, we will provide you with the Historical property designation sign. We close in about twenty minutes. Did you want to see information on historical properties?"

"No, actually, I would like to see the Civil War files. I am just trying to find information about a few family members and one of them was the right age to be in the Civil War. Can you point me to those records?"

"Certainly. I will help you. What is the name?" Ellen asked.

"Frederick Greyson. While you are looking him up, can you also tell me if David Greyson, his father fought in the Civil War?"

"Well, let me see. Yes, here is Frederick Greyson. Oh, I'm sorry, he was so young. Apparently, he fought and died in the War, right here in Roswell. He was born February 27, 1845 and died on July 18, 1864. He is buried at the Presbyterian Church Cemetery. I don't see a David Greyson though listed as a soldier. Here let me make a copy of an article that talks about when the Union invaded Roswell. It was July, 1864." She handed the article to Christina and a copy of Frederick's death records. "Since Frederick was buried at Presbyterian Church Cemetery, his father may have also been buried there. Let me search those records for you real quick." She went to a different archive and pulled out the list of people that are buried at the Roswell Presbyterian Church Cemetery. "Ah, there he is. Yes, David Greyson is buried there - looks like he is in Plot 27 and Frederick is in Plot 32."

"When did David die?" Christina asked.

"He died before Frederick in February, 1861."

"Does it say how he died?"

"No. I'm sorry. There is no detail in this record. I'm sorry, I have to close, but you are welcome to come back and search through some other files that may have more information. We do have some pretty detailed records about the owners of the large plantation homes. You know we call them the Founding Fathers. Some of the families in the past have donated letters and journals, for example."

Christina lowered her head. She did not feel that David was worthy of that title considering he had destroyed the Indian family and taken their home. She wasn't ready to get into that story though with Ellen. She was encouraged by what Ellen had said about the journals. Maybe someone in her family had found the rest of Jade's journals and had given them to the Historical Society. She just wasn't ready to believe that Jade had stopped writing them, or that they had been destroyed. "Thank you, I will come back tomorrow." Christina took the copies of Frederick's information and went back out to her car. She read the article:

"*Georgia seceded from the Union in January, 1861 and many Roswell residents, especially the wealthiest, left town for safe shelter. The Civil War came to Roswell in July, 1864. The Union deployed 36,000 troops to Roswell. The soldiers used the plantation homes for sleeping quarters and the church for a hospital. The mills along Vickery Creek were destroyed. It is said that some of the plantation homes were not destroyed because they displayed Mason symbols and because General William Sherman was a known Mason. Many of these homes still stand today.*

The Union was moving south from Chattanooga to capture Atlanta and when they got to Roswell, discovered that the covered bridge that would take them from Roswell to Atlanta was burned. This bridge crossed the Chattahoochee River. The Union soldiers crossed at Shallow Ford by foot. There were very few Confederate soldiers in the area but they fought to keep the Union Soldiers from crossing. Apparently, the battle that took place in the river proved that rifles could be shot underwater.

The majority of the mill workers did not have the means to flee. The mill employed a French man who desperately flew a French flag over the mill claiming neutrality. Sherman's men discovered the letters "CSA" on the cloth that was being made at the mill for the Confederate soldiers' uniforms. Sherman charged all the mill workers, approximately four hundred mostly women and children with treason and burned the mills. He sent the prisoners to Marietta where they boarded a train for Louisville, Kentucky. They were never tried for treason but most were never able to return to Roswell due to the distance and expense. Many of the soldiers returned to find their wives and children gone and assumed dead."

Of course being a Roswell native, Christina knew all about the story of the four hundred mill workers and had been on several of the historical tours, including visiting the monument that was erected in their honor in July, 2000. She was starting to realize that it was very possible that she had relatives that had not only fought in the war but also that could have fought so close to home. She wondered if any of her relatives had been part of the four hundred that were sent to Kentucky. She had to know more.

Chapter 41
February, 1861

Georgia seceded from the Union on January 18, 1861 and kept the name, "State of Georgia". In February, Georgia joined the newly-formed Confederacy. Robert Temple called a meeting of The Colony. They called themselves that to distinguish themselves as an elite group of leaders in the town of Roswell. They met at his home to discuss what if anything they should do about the war that was just beginning.

"It's our way of life. Those damn Yankees can't tell us how to lead it. They don't understand how critical it is to have slaves helping us on our farmland. Where would the slaves be without us? We give them homes and feed them, they wouldn't want it any other way!" declared Henry.

David snickered over his drink.

Robert gave David a quick glance. "Regardless of the reasons we are in this war, we need to determine what we are going to do about it. Will we send our sons to fight in Virginia? I know our friends in Savannah have already sent troops. We definitely don't want the Union to come down to Georgia, so do we head them off by sending troops now? Joseph, what do you think?" Robert took a long pull on his cigar.

Joseph sipped his drink. "My opinion is we start by seeing if there are volunteers that will go. The war has not reached Georgia at this point, but you never know when it will make its way here, so I don't think we want to send all of our young men to Virginia. My son says he and his friends want to go, to protect us. They believe if they go now, they may be able to keep the Union from ever coming here. I just don't know how realistic that is."

"David? What are your thoughts?"

"Frederick feels the same way. He is chomping at the bit to get on the road. I told him I need him here. We need to keep cotton flowing to supply the mills. This town would not continue to grow without the mills, as you all know. We also need to ensure that we have protection for the mills."

"I have an idea," said Donald, the mill Manager. Someone needs to provide the Confederate soldiers with uniforms. I was told that grey wool is the preference. We can make that. Obtaining the funds from the State should not be a problem. So yes, David, we would need to continue to get your cotton. In fact, I would like to see you add more crops. In addition, we are going to need more food in case of an influx of men in this area as they come through heading north. Jones, can you increase your vegetable production this season? Since the building of the bridge over the Chattahoochee, our direct access to the Atlanta railways will help us move both the uniforms and the food production. This could be a strong time for our local economy."

"Then let's all agree for now, with no battles in Georgia, we will keep most of our young men close to home. Let's add more shifts to the mill and David, any extra hands or slaves you can afford to keep that cotton coming would be smart."

The men finished their drinks, their cigars, talked about the recent snowfall and the next social event and said their goodbyes.

Back at the plantation, David sat down with Frederick. "Son, it was unanimous. We all agreed that for now, we need you here. We have got to increase the cotton production because the mill will be making Confederate uniforms. I am going to put you in charge of the field hands. Think you can handle that? I am going to be talking to the State, the bank and our neighbors about pooling resources. What do you think?"

"Father, I will stay for now. If this is our place at this time to help our cause, then here is where I will stay," Frederick said with conviction. "But if the war comes to Georgia, I want to fight."

"Agreed, son. I am proud of you. Now let's get to bed so we can get an early start tomorrow. I want you to ingrain the same conviction you have into the minds of our workers and slaves. They have to know we are fighting for our way of life, and in our case, growing cotton. Let me know if any of the slaves start pushing back. I am hearing some of them around the region are making a break for it and heading north. I don't think we have any flight risks, but you never know. Keep your eye on Ben, son. He has always had a temper."

The next morning, Frederick gathered the workers and slaves around and told them of the plans. He said expediting the cotton would help keep the war out of Georgia and it was up to them to make it happen. They all seemed in agreement, only Ben stood with arms crossed.

Coming up the drive in her carriage was Jade with Ruby and Charles, still infants.

"Hello, Frederick! How are you today?" She came to pick up Kay, Rose Ann and Michael on her way to the mill.

Frederick told her about the plans and Jade was pleased this news meant he would not be going north. She had heard many mothers speaking about the young men wanting to fight.

When Jade arrived at the Mill, she was told they were calling a meeting. She, of course, had to stay and care for the children. She asked Kay to come see her after the meeting to tell her what it was about. Kay obliged.

About an hour later, Kay returned to the nursery to fill Jade in on the details. The mill Manager, Donald, explained the State had awarded the Roswell Mills the contract to supply the army with uniforms. They were going to be working longer hours and they were encouraging everyone to invite anyone they knew that needed employment, to come to work at the mill.

It was an exciting, tumultuous time for the town, especially the mill workers. They felt they were making a difference and to date the war still had not made its way to Georgia. They felt safe and secure.

Frederick was walking the fields trying to assess the mood of the slaves. Most seemed to be working hard, and he had always known they were hard workers. They seemed to appreciate their way of life, their home and their work. Frederick wasn't concerned about them running away.

He walked down each row and saw how easily they worked with each other. Their small children would bring the workers water and empty sacks in which to put the cotton. The older children would then take the full sacks back to the barn. Frederick walked back to the barn to see how the day's supply was coming along. The mill wagon would be here shortly to take the cotton. As he rounded the side of the barn, he saw Ben slip inside. When Frederick got to the barn door he looked for Ben but did not see him. He was sure he saw him go inside.

He called out. "Ben, are you in here?" No response. "Ben? Where are you?" Nothing. The hair went up on Frederick's neck. His father had told him to keep an eye on Ben. Ben had always been aggressive. He was also very strong. Frederick went back to the house to get his shotgun, just in case there was an altercation. He was sure he saw Ben enter the barn. Why was he hiding? He had to find him. As the Field Manager, he had to maintain the slaves' respect in order to manage them successfully. Frederick grabbed his shotgun and then headed back to the barn. David saw Frederick leave with the gun. He went to the window to see what Frederick was doing. They typically did not need a gun to control the slaves, but what was going on that made Frederick feel the need to wield his shotgun? David also didn't want to question his son on his first day as the manager so he watched Frederick approach the barn from behind the curtain in the parlor.

David watched as Frederick cocked the shotgun then entered the barn. That worried David, so he grabbed his own and quickly followed.

Frederick slipped inside the barn and quietly began to search the stalls for Ben. When he got to the large pile of cotton, Frederick slowly walked around it. Crouched in the corner, was Ben. Ben jumped up and grabbed the shotgun. They struggled, but Ben was too strong for Frederick. He easily pulled the shotgun from Frederick's hands. Frederick was initially surprised then he became furious. He had his father's temper. He lunged at Ben. Ben held the shotgun to Frederick's forehead.

"Don't make me shoot you," whispered Ben. "This is not what I wanted to happen. Why couldn't you look the other way?" Ben's eyes were wide. He was terrified because even though he held the shotgun, he felt cornered. He didn't want to shoot Frederick. He just wanted out of here. He had planned on slipping under the cotton once it was loaded onto the mill wagon and quietly slip away. He wanted to head north and be free like so many others he had heard about.

Suddenly from behind Ben, came the sound of another shotgun being cocked. Ben's eyebrows flew up when he saw the smile on Frederick's face. David had come up behind Ben.

"Put that shotgun down, boy," David demanded through gritted teeth. Ben didn't move. "I said put it down, now!"

Ben, still holding the shotgun, turned toward David. David assumed he was going to shoot. Two very loud shots rang out. Frederick dove into a stall. He heard the bodies fall. He didn't want to look. He had seen the blood splatter on the wall. The barn became very still. Then he heard footsteps. He was crouched down, his face in his hands, shaking his head. He was afraid to look. Then he felt a large hand pull him up. It was Joseph.

Joseph was carrying a shotgun. He pulled Frederick out of the stall to force him to see what had happened. Both Ben and his father were on the ground. His father was dead from a shotgun wound to the back. Ben was close to death. Frederick looked at them both and then looked at Joseph. Joseph didn't say a word. It had been Joseph that had shot his father, he was sure of it, to protect Ben. He slowly took the shotgun from Joseph; it was still warm. Joseph looked at Frederick sure that Frederick would turn the gun on him. He did not. Frederick stood staring at his father. His father's eyes were still open, but lifeless.

Joseph kneeled down to Ben. Ben whispered to him. "Tell her I always loved her." Then he was gone. Joseph lowered his head. He knew who Ben was referring to. Ben had always been protective of her and since her marriage Ben had seemed a lost soul. Joseph had had the feeling that Ben was going to make a run for it. He secretly prayed that he would get away safely. Now he was on a different journey.

The funeral for David Greyson was well attended. The town folk attributed much of the success and growth of Roswell to him and his cotton plantation. Kay and the children dressed in black, stood closest to his grave as the preacher said his final rites. He was buried at the Presbyterian Church Cemetery. "Ashes to ashes, dust to dust…" Rose Ann cried loudly and Kay tried to comfort her, to no avail. Frederick stood tall and sure, trying to be the man of the family, while inside grieving for his father, the anger building.

Jade, Oscar and their children stood off to the side. Oscar thought it odd that Jade did not shed a tear for the man that had taken her in and cared for her as a young girl and the man for which she later became the nanny for his children. She was stiff and almost serene.

He asked her about it later, but she shook her head and told him that she didn't want to talk about the funeral.

Ben was buried in the Pleasant Hill Cemetery, which was a part of the Lebanon Baptist Church the slaves had established. Theresa and Sally were allowed to attend. Kay attended out of respect for Theresa. She was accompanied by two of David's workers who attended to ensure that the slaves didn't escape. The tension between the slaves and the Greyson Manor workers had increased significantly. The relationship between Kay and Theresa was now strained. They didn't hold each other accountable for what had happened, but knowing David had shot Ben was a fact they would never get past. Joseph was being held in the stockade awaiting hanging for David's death. Theresa's life had ended as far as she was concerned. When the short ceremony concluded, they returned to Greyson Manor in silence.

Jade had not attended Ben's funeral. She and Ben had not spoken much over the last ten years and she didn't feel it was her place. She said a silent prayer for him.

Joseph was hung in the town square. Frederick stood by with Theresa, as they watched him hang. Theresa cried for the loss of her son and now the loss of the man she had grown to love, although she had never told him. Joseph knew and loved her too. He never took his eyes off of her as they put the bag over his head. They hung Joseph at noon.

Frederick took Theresa back to Greyson Manor and they all began to try to put the pieces of their lives back together.

One day shortly after the funerals and the hanging, Jade came to see Theresa. She brought her flowers and sat with her while Theresa cried. Jade held this woman, whom she had known as her mother for much of her young life. Theresa had been there for her the day David's men had destroyed her family and she had taken her in like a daughter. Words could not heal the pain that Theresa must now be going through.

Theresa looked at Jade. "Right before Ben died, he asked Joseph to tell us both he loved us." Jade was surprised by this revelation. Jade and Theresa held each other and cried.

"Theresa." They turned to see Sally standing in the doorway. "I am going to have his child." Tears streamed down her face. She had known that Ben had always loved Jade but Sally was willing to give herself freely to him, hoping that some day he would love her in return. She would love him for the rest of her days through his child, but she would never have the chance to hear Ben say, "I love you".

Chapter 42
October 18, 2010

Frank was released from the hospital and as promised, allowed Wanda to drive him home. She was so happy her father was out of the hospital and felt very grown up driving. "I'm so glad you are all right, Dad. Does your head hurt?"

"It's pounding, but nothing that a good nap won't cure. I just need to take it easy for the next couple of days. You don't mind if I watch golf on TV when we get home, do you?" Wanda enjoyed reading while her father watched golf.

"No, that sounds like a good idea."

When they arrived home, they noticed there were quite a few cars at Greyson Manor, including a police car.

"I'm going to go see what's going on," Wanda said. She helped her father into the house then she ran next door. She approached Christina and Daniel, who were speaking to the policeman.

"We want to take down the slave quarters. I know it's got evidence on it, but has your team finished their investigation so we can take it down? I just feel the sooner we get rid of it, the sooner these acts of violence will stop," said Christina, who saw Wanda approaching. She held her finger up to say, "give me a minute."

"I don't see why not," the policeman said. "We've taken the pictures of the graffiti and we have dusted for finger prints and we took the shoe prints as well. Maybe taking it down will prevent more vandalism here. Let's hope. In the meantime, we are still looking for the suspects."

Wanda was disappointed to hear that Greg Jones was not caught yet. She was glad to hear that Christina and Daniel were planning on taking down the slave quarters. She had to admit she never liked looking at that building either.

The policeman left. Daniel said he was going to give Scott a call to let him know they could begin demolition of the slave quarters and the carriage house as soon as possible. The insurance company sent an email letting them know their claim had been approved and they would be receiving a check soon for the rebuilding of the barn.

Christina walked over to Wanda. "So you got your Dad home safely I see," she said smiling.

"Yes, I did. He is resting; looks like he will be okay. I just wanted to say again how sorry I am about all of this. If Alan was involved in anyway, I will be so shocked. But Greg is his big brother. He is several years older and could probably talk him into some things. If he was a part of this, he probably went along for the ride, not realizing what Greg was doing. I just can't believe he would do something so destructive." Wanda shook her head.

"Let's don't worry about that right now. I am sure the police will find Greg and Alan soon and then hopefully we will know the real story. We are going to go ahead and take down the slave quarters and the carriage house right away," responded Christina.

"Why the carriage house?" asked Wanda.

Christina took a deep breath. "Well, apparently, someone was killed there a long time ago. I'll tell you the rest of the story as soon as I figure it all out. In fact, I need to head over to the Roswell Historical Society to do some more research. Let me know if you or your Dad need anything."

They waved and Christina got in her car to head back to the

Historical Society office. As she was leaving Greyson Manor, Carolyn passed by her and pulled into Frank's driveway. Christina saw her get out with a bag marked "Charm", obviously with some food for Frank and Wanda.

"Hi Ellen, I'm back. I thought about this a lot last night and I had a few ideas, where we might find information about my ancestors."

"I'm glad you are back, Christina. I have something that I think you will really want to see. After you left last night, I remembered that your Mother was here several years ago and she gave me a box of things that came from Greyson Manor. We were asking for any historical artifacts from the plantation homes and she brought in this box." Ellen handed Christina a box that had the words, "Greyson Manor, 1861 – 1896".

Christina, eyes big and full of excitement, took the box over to a table and removed the top. She pulled out several journals and some pictures. She looked at the pictures first. She saw several pictures, mostly of women. She turned them over to see names and dates printed on the back. One was a picture of a young woman. She was stunning. The name on the back said "Ruby Hicks, 1879". Another was a picture of young man. The picture said "Charles Hicks, 1879". Then there were two photos of two different families. The first photo said, "Greyson family, 1858". Then it listed, "David, Kay, Frederick, Rose Ann and Michael". Christina quickly turned the picture back over to study their faces. She felt that she was starting to know them. She looked over at Ellen who had gone back to her desk. They smiled at each other. Christina was so happy to have found such a prize. The other family picture made her pause. She saw her. This had to be Jade. She had very long black hair and was one of the most beautiful women she had ever seen. She was clearly Indian. The man was extremely handsome, Christina thought. Oscar. The last journal pages she and Kevin had read covered right up until the Civil War. Oscar and Jade had married and had Ruby and Charles. This was their picture. On the back were their names and the date October, 1860.

What a find, Christina thought. She went to the copier and made copies of the pictures. "Do you mind if I check out these journals? I would like to read them front to back and I know my brother will want to as well."

"Yes, of course. As far as I am concerned, you own them, they were just on loan here for safekeeping."

"I will bring them back when I finish reading them. I like the idea of them being here. In fact, I will bring other journals back with me that I have recently discovered. I am so excited, as I am sure these journals will fill in the blanks for me. Thank you."

Christina stopped by Charm to get take-out and took the food and the journals home. She called both Daniel and Kevin and told them of her luck. "I plan to stay home tonight and read them. You can read them as soon as I am done."

When she got home she noticed the crew was working on taking down the slave quarters and when she looked out back, she noticed that the carriage house was already gone. She also noticed how beautiful the fall leaves were and that the view out back of the woods was no longer obstructed by the carriage house. "Jade, we are getting rid of the bad memories. Tell me the rest of your story and give me a sign that will tell me what I should do with it. I will never forget you, what my family did to you and the sacrifices you made for my family."

Christina took her dinner into the keeping room and lit a fire in the fireplace. She grabbed the precious quilt that Carolyn's mother had made her and laid it over her feet. She ate the delicious stew she had gotten at Charm, picked up one of the journals and started reading.

Chapter 43
March 1861

J ade closed the journal and turned the lamp off. She went into the bedroom where Oscar was already asleep, slid the journal under the mattress on her side of the bed and crawled in next to her husband. She lay awake, staring at the ceiling for awhile thinking about the last month. She was at odds with herself, not sure how to feel about Ben and David's deaths. She had had strange relationships with both men. They had been both good and bad to her. They had been both irritating and alluring at the same time. She had known both men had feelings for her, but her own feelings for them had been mixed. She had thought of Ben like a brother and David, well he was David. He was both the man responsible for her parents' and brother's deaths and for sending away George and Joe, but he was also the father of her children; the children she loved dearly but had never wanted to bring into the world the way they came.

Oscar sensed that she was still awake.

"Are you alright Jade? You've been very quiet lately. I know these last few weeks have been extremely hard for you."

Jade rolled toward her husband and curled into his arms. She felt instantly calmer. She was so grateful to Kay for convincing her that she could be married and still see her children. That was another strange relationship. She loved Kay, but had at times been jealous of her. The children thought Kay was their mother. She could never tell them the truth, so she had to continue to play the nanny role in their lives. At least she could openly be Ruby and Charles' mother.

"I'm fine, my love. It's just been hard on the children and Kay with David being gone and I am just trying to figure out if there is anything else I can do to make things easier on them."

Oscar rolled up on his elbow to look at Jade in the moonlight. "Darling, you couldn't possibly do more than you already do for them. They all know that you love them. And I hope you know that if there is anything I can do to help them, I am here for them as well."

"I know, Oscar. Kay and I both appreciate it."

There it was again, Oscar thought. She couldn't seem to separate herself. She was their nanny, not their mother. I guess that's what makes her such a wonderful nanny, he surmised. He kissed her lightly at first and then more deeply. They made love and then slowly drifted off to sleep.

The next day, Robert Temple came for a visit at Greyson Manor. He was worried about his daughter. It had been several weeks since David's funeral and he had not seen her. He wanted to be sure she was alright. He also needed to talk to her about mill business and the cotton. The volume had slowed down since the deaths of David and their slaves. He had to reiterate to her and to Frederick how critical it was now more than ever, to keep the volume up. Their soldiers depended on them. The demand was there, the supply needed to follow.

"Kay, when do you think you will be coming back to the mill? The girl that Donald put in charge while you have been out just doesn't have the supervisory skills or expertise you have. We get new girls in all the time and someone needs to train them. That someone is you." Robert smiled, hoping he had convinced her. "Of course, I understand you are still grieving. Take it from me; you will grieve for a long time. I still grieve for your mother, but you must go on with your life for your sake, your children's sake and now also for the sake of this town. Not that I am trying to make you feel guilty, you understand."

Kay leaned in to kiss her father on the cheek. "I understand, Father. Things are slowly starting to get back to normal around here. Frederick has been quite angry. He feels responsible for his father's death. He thinks if he had not taken the shotgun to the barn, his father would not have followed him to help and would not have been shot. He also thinks because we lost both Ben and Joseph, it is his fault the cotton production is down. I have been spending as much time with him as I can to be sure he puts this behind him. I am afraid he will take his anger out on the other slaves. That would not help our situation at all. Michael seems to be handling it the best of the three, although he seems very quiet. Rose Ann cries for her father every night. She hasn't wanted to go to school and even though I have convinced her to go, she comes home crying every day."

"Has Jade been here? Is she helping?"

"Yes, she comes by every morning and takes Rose Ann and Michael to school. She has taken a walk with Frederick several times. He seems calmer after those walks." Kay looked out the window. She knew no one knew Jade was their mother, but it always surprised her that the bond between Jade and the children was so strong.

"Will you agree to return to the mill on Monday?" It was Friday and he thought with having a few days to prepare herself, she should be able to accommodate his wishes.

"Alright Father, I will. Can you go speak with Frederick? Let me know what you think about his frame of mind. I need to know he is capable of managing the workers before I leave him here with them. Of course, the men will still be here to protect him."

Robert joined her at the window and saw Frederick coming back from the fields. He picked up his coat. "I'll go talk to him now."

Kay watched as her father approached her son. Maybe that's

exactly what he needs right now. If anyone could help Frederick, it would be her father. They talked for about twenty minutes and when her father came back into the house, he seemed pleased.

"That's a good boy you have there, my dear," Robert said removing his coat again. "He will be fine. He understands the urgency of the improvements we need to make here in the cotton production. He knows his town and our great state of Georgia are at risk. When I put it that way, his eyes lit up. He wants to help. I believe he will be able to handle the responsibility. I will have a talk with the men as well before I leave. I'll make sure they watch his back and keep an eye on the slaves. We can't afford to lose any others. Now let's talk about your money situation. I can help manage the books for you too, Kay."

Kay was grateful to her father and she knew he would ensure they were profitable and cared for. Greyson Manor was quite a responsibility for anyone, much less a widow.

Kay went back to work at the Roswell Mills and managed the seamstresses. Their main focus now was the Confederate soldiers' uniforms. They didn't like to think about the fact that the need for the volume of uniforms was directly related to the number of young men being killed and the new men joining the war. Kay was grateful she could keep Frederick close to home. With the State funds the mill was receiving, he felt he was directly helping the cause and with his father's death, he felt more than ever he should stay in Roswell to protect his family, Greyson Manor, and the town if needed. So far the war was still several states away. He would see the Confederate soldiers marching down the road and he would wave to his friends as they headed north to keep the Union soldiers at bay.

The next couple of years were more of the same. The war however, was moving closer to Roswell and those who could afford to leave town and go to safer ground were beginning to do so. Robert Temple stayed to help manage the mill with Donald. They no longer had their Colony meetings because most of the founding fathers had left Roswell by this time. Most of their sons had gone off to war. Some had already died. Frederick had married a young woman named Samantha. She was a seamstress who worked with Kay. She moved into Greyson Manor and became part of the family. At times Kay felt she had another daughter under foot but she enjoyed her bubbly personality and her son was happy again.

Jade and Oscar continued to care for and teach the town's children. They taught them as much about the war as they could. They kept up on the news and the parents appreciated what they knew about what was happening. Their community had grown closer during these hard times. News of the young men that had gone off to war arrived daily. There were successes and defeats but more so, defeats. There were many injured soldiers returning as well and the hospital became overburdened with the injured and sick.

The mill was still running strong and the owners kept the money coming in to ensure the workers stayed. They had nowhere else to go, so they continued to produce. Greyson Manor also continued to grow and Frederick was doing an extraordinary job keeping the slaves and the men working hard and producing the bulk of the cotton for the mill.

By the time the Union invaded Roswell, the town was nearly vacated. All but the mill workers, a few doctors and preachers, and the field workers had left their beautiful town. Kay and her family, Jade and Oscar and their family stayed the course. They didn't know what to expect, but they prayed for each other, their lives and their futures in Roswell.

Chapter 44
October 19, 2010

Around midday, Scott walked into Charm to see Carolyn. He said hello to the staff and kissed his wife. He said to the bartender, "Andrew, do you mind turning on the television? There is some news I want Carolyn to see." Andrew skipped through the channels until he came to a breaking news update.

The newscaster began her report. "The missing suspects in the arson case at Greyson Manor have been apprehended. Greg Jones, along with several other young African-American men, including Jones' younger brother, allegedly burned the barn at Greyson Manor to the ground. What is more disturbing is the graffiti they allegedly wrote on the historical slave quarters. "Racist" was written in bold red letters. Their crimes tell an unsettling story about current day reactions to historical slave quarters. There have also been reports of graffiti painted on other historical sites around the town of Roswell. It's a sad day in the history of the South. This is Joanne Lagrange, WTPT coming to you live from Greyson Manor."

"Thanks, Andrew. Carolyn, do you have time to have a late lunch with me? I'm starving and I want to head over to Greyson Manor to make sure all of the land was cleared around the slave quarters and the carriage house. I've been working on the new design all morning. The investors approved adding the kitchen onto the new barn. It was tough though to keep the design within the budget."

"Shoot, I know I gave my approval as well, but I was hoping Christina would want to lean more heavily on Charm for the events," replied Carolyn.

"The kitchen is really just to give you the space to store, prepare and clean up. She still plans on using your restaurant to provide the food and servers."

"Oh, good. So any idea on how long it will take to rebuild the barn this time? I can't wait to have the first event there. If there is any way to get it done before Christmas and New Year's, that would be fabulous!"

"I think New Year's is probably a safe bet. You know I will do everything I can to get it done in time. This place is rocking!" Scott said looking around at the crowded restaurant. He was enjoying his steak skewers and lobster spring rolls, his two favorite items. "Anyway, I am really glad they have caught those kids. I feel bad for Wanda. It sounds like her boyfriend Alan was also apprehended with his brother."

"I know. I'll give her a call to see how she is doing. I have to get back to work, thanks for being such a steady customer!" She kissed him then waved and went back to the kitchen to give Kacey the news about Greyson Manor.

Scott drove over to Greyson Manor and was pleased to see the debris had been hauled away and there were just a few men smoothing out the ground where the slave quarters had been. He saw Kevin's car in the driveway and didn't want to intrude so he stayed outside. He rolled out his new design on the hood of his car and was reviewing it when he heard Christina say hello.

"Hey," Scott said. He kissed her on the cheek and shook Kevin's hand. "Are you ready to start this project over?"

"Yes, I am," said Christina. "I am reenergized. I found some more of Jade's journals. I was just telling Kevin about them. Apparently, my mother had taken them to the Roswell Historical Society several years back. I am so glad I stopped by there! I still have two more to read, but I am pretty sure they will take me through the rest of Jade's life. I plan to finish them this week. Oh, and inside the first one I read, there was a letter from Oscar to Jade. He was her husband. I can't wait to fill you all in on the details. Now that the arsonists have been captured, assuming those kids are convicted, I think I will be able to sleep better."

"I can help you with that!" laughed Kevin.

Christina gave him a funny look. "I'll bet! No seriously, all of this," she motioned to the empty space where the barn and slave quarters had stood, "has convinced me we need to say more about the history of Roswell than just what the Founding Fathers did for our town. When we have our first event, I would like it to be a grand opening party, open to the town of Roswell, but dedicated to the Cherokee Indians who came before us in what they called the "Enchanted Land" and the African-Americans who worked side-by-side with us through the years to build our wonderful town and help make the mills the successes they were. Roswell wouldn't have grown the way it did without the success of the mills. I am learning more about that through Jade's journals."

The guys could see she truly was energized and they were proud of what they were doing here. This was a project none of them would ever forget.

"Let's have a planning dinner at Charm on Saturday night. Kaitlyn is coming to town, so we can get all of the investors together and ensure we are in agreement with the new plans. I can also fill everyone in on what I have learned and by then I will be able to tell you all what I want to tell the world about Greyson Manor and my ancestors. I'll get a hold of everyone about Saturday night."

Canton Street was decorated for Halloween and people were out in droves enjoying the shops and restaurants. It was a crisp, cool fall evening and magic was in the air. The Greyson Manor investors met at Charm at seven p.m.

"Wow, your place looks wonderful, Carolyn! And business looks good. Has it been steady?" asked Kaitlyn.

"Yes, I have been pleased with the lunch crowd and dinner is typically full each night, especially on the weekends. I have a great team, what can I say," Carolyn smiled.

"To Southern Charm!" said Daniel. He held up his glass to toast. They all toasted to Charm's success. "Now let's talk about Greyson Manor and how we guarantee success there as well. Scott, you want to tell us about the new plans?"

Scott proceeded to tell the investors about taking down the slave quarters and the carriage house and that the plan was to add a kitchen onto the new barn. "Of course, the plan is to utilize Charm for the catering. The new kitchen will give the Charm cooks and servers a place to work. This way, we won't have to put them on our payroll, we'll just share in the profits of our events. Are we all still in agreement with that plan?"

They all agreed. Phew, Carolyn thought. Then, wow, I'm going to be busy!

Scott filled them in on some of the details of how the barn and the patio would look and then talked through the timeline. "It will be cutting it close, but I am confident we can complete it before New Year's. I wouldn't recommend trying to push for any Christmas parties, but I feel it's safe to plan on New Year's Eve. And since the house restoration is complete, you can add tours to the party as well."

"So what do ya'll think?" asked Christina. "I think New Year's Eve would be the perfect grand opening! Do ya'll agree?"

They approved the plan and Kaitlyn decided to come up from Florida with her husband, Ken, for the party as well.

"Here is the other part of what I wanted to share with you all this evening," Christina said. She proceeded to tell them about the journals and gave them the highlights of what she had read.

Chapter 45
July 1864

On the morning of July 6, 1864, Jade was starting her nursery classes with the typical art project. She had just asked the children to draw something and then hang it on the wall so they could discuss it. She noticed they were unusually quiet today. As the children finished their drawings and posted them on the wall, Jade began to see a trend. Most of the drawings were of battles, or at least of what young children would think battles looked like. Some of the pictures where actually disturbing. There were soldiers with missing limbs, blood splatters, and weapons of all shapes and sizes. Jade looked at a few of them closely and then turned around to look at the children. They were looking out the window.

Jade looked to the window and saw something she would never forget. Coming down Roswell Road were hundreds, maybe thousands, of Union soldiers. Their dark blue uniforms were in sharp contrast to the Confederate gray uniforms that they were making at the mill. As they got closer, she could hear the rumble of their advance. Jade looked back at the children, some were crying, some ran to the window, some hid under their desks.

"Children, remember our drill? Please get into a single file line and follow me. Now, children!" She saw Ruby and Charles immediately jump in line and were encouraging the other children to follow suit. Thank you God, she thought. She opened the nursery room door and peered out. There were people running up and down the hallways. She turned to the children, she had to keep control and keep them calm. "Put your right hand on the right shoulder of the person in front of you and don't let go. Follow me." She walked them down the hall to the stairwell that led to the basement. On her way, she ran into Samantha, Frederick's wife. "Samantha, please come with me and the children. I need you to stay with them so I can talk to the manager. Will you do that?"

Samantha was visibly shaken but agreed to take the children to the hiding room in the basement. It was the safest place in the mill. Jade went with them to help them get settled in the room. She told them to stay calm and quiet and to say their prayers, and then she quickly ran back up to the main floor of the mill.

As she passed a window she could still see the Union soldiers marching down the street. She ran to Donald's office. Kay was already there. The two women embraced and Jade explained that Samantha was with the children in the basement. A French mill-worker came running into the office. He explained to them that he could tell the Union the mill was run by a French company and since France was neutral, the Union would probably leave them in peace. Donald thought it was worth a try. The French man grabbed a French flag he had been keeping at his station and slowly walked toward the main door. He turned and looked at the three and put his hand out to them as to say, "stay". He went outside and raised the flag.

Frederick had learned the news of the arriving Union soldiers. He grabbed his horse and his rifle, told his men to follow him and headed out. Theresa and the other slaves watched him ride out of the plantation heading toward town. That was the last time Theresa would see Frederick.

The slaves stopped picking cotton and walked slowly to their quarters. They had mixed feelings about the war. If the Union wins, they would be free. Freedom was something they could barely imagine. Theresa wondered if Kay and the children were safe at the mill. Some of the slaves huddled in their quarters and prayed, including Theresa; the others ran for their freedom.

Frederick and his men arrived at the river and hid on horseback in some woods near the mill. Frederick dismounted and motioned to his men to follow him. They were heading toward the mill. When they got closer, they could see a French flag flying and a lot of chaos. They snuck up the backside of the mill. There were a few Union soldiers patrolling the riverbank. Frederick and his men grabbed them, killed them and hid them in the bushes.

They quietly went inside the mill to find Kay, Jade and Samantha. They heard a Union officer speaking with Donald, the mill manager. He was asking about the French flag. Donald was telling the man, General Kenner Garrard, the mill was owned by a French company. The General told Donald not to allow anyone to leave then he went back out the front to send a note to General Sherman to get his direction. Once he sent his messenger off, he told the soldiers to find rest in any of the homes. Most of the larger homes were vacant.

Frederick could hear gunshots going off all over town. The Union was either killing the remaining Southern men who had stayed to protect the town or capturing them. Frederick wasn't sure which would be worse, but he knew they were all in serious danger. He said a silent prayer that the women and children would be spared. He would do all he could to protect them. He went to talk with Kay and Samantha.

"We can't stay here and wait. My men and I are going to go out tonight and see if we can learn what their plan is and if needed, take action."

"No, Frederick, please! Stay here!" cried Samantha. "Please don't leave! You'll be killed!"

"Sweetheart, it is my duty to protect you, the rest of my family and this town. I need to go out and make sure they don't come back and harm you. These Union soldiers will not think twice about killing women and children. I have to go. I love you." Frederick held Samantha as she cried in his embrace. Then he looked at his mother. Tears were streaming down Kay's face.

"I am proud of you. Your father was too. Always know that. Please be careful, my son," cried Kay. As Frederick held his mother, he saw Jade over Kay's shoulder, watching them. He knew Jade loved him like a son. He knew she loved them all. He went to Jade and hugged her. They looked into each other's eyes, then he turned and he was gone.

For the next two days, the Union soldiers rested in the Roswell mansions and other homes and used the churches for a hospital. The mill workers kept working hoping to assure the Union they had no interest in this war. They slept in shifts in the basement and ate the little food rations that were available.

Oscar had also made it safely to the mill with the children from the Academy and they all hid out waiting for the soldiers to either leave or make their move. They prayed for the former.

Then their worst nightmare happened.

General Garrard came back to meet with Donald. He had several soldiers with him. He was holding a piece of gray fabric. On the back were the initials, CSA (Confederate States of America). He ordered his troops to gather up everyone that was in the mill. He explained to Donald they were all under arrest for treason.

Kay, Jade, Samantha, Oscar, and the children did their best to stay together. They had not seen Frederick or his men since the night before. The soldiers came into the mill and forced everyone out. They told them they would walk to Marietta, a twelve mile walk, where they would be transported to the North because they were prisoners of war and had committed treason.

They learned that two days earlier, on July 5th, a battle ensued on the road to Roswell. The remaining Confederate Calvary that had stayed to protect Roswell had been in a major battle against the Union soldiers. Their goal was to protect the covered bridge to keep the Union from crossing the river to Atlanta. The Union soldiers far outnumbered the Confederate soldiers. So upon orders from James R. King, the grandson of Roswell King, the founding father of Roswell, the bridge was burned.

Apparently, the Confederate soldiers tried to fight off the Northern army and keep them from crossing the river but the Union men backed the Confederate soldiers into the river and followed them in. It was fairly shallow at this point in the river. Many of the Union soldiers were able to get to the other side and they had already begun to make their way toward Atlanta. Others stayed and fought the remaining Confederate Calvary. The Union soldiers that were accompanying the four-hundred to Marietta, told them there were no survivors. Jade and Kay said a prayer for Frederick.

Once all four-hundred mostly women and children were out of Roswell, General Garrard ordered his troops to burn down the mills and all of the outlying buildings. They also burned many of the Roswell homes and other buildings. They did not burn down the beautiful plantation homes because they were still being used for shelter and hospital space but also because they displayed Mason symbols. General Sherman was a Mason and ordered those buildings to be spared.

It was the heat of the summer and the walk from Roswell had been a very difficult trip. Oscar and Jade did their best to carry the small children, who were very dehydrated and hungry. Jade could not help but imagine this was what her brothers, George and Joe, had endured when they were forced out west. Kay was struggling, but Jade helped her as much as she could. She was grateful Oscar had brought the older children from the Academy. At least they were all together. Michael and Rose Ann also did their best to help Ruby and Charles. They would huddle together at night when they were permitted to stop and rest.

"I thank God every day for you, my love," Jade said to Oscar one evening while they rested. He had his arm around her and she rested her head on his chest. "I pray we all make it to where they are sending us. They said trains will be waiting for us."

"At least we will all be together and we can begin our lives again. Let's not think about that now. Rest, for we have a long walk ahead of us still."

Twelve days after they were charged with treason, the four-hundred arrived in Marietta to be transported by train to the North.

Chapter 46
October 31, 2010

T he night air was chilly. The atmosphere was exactly how it should be; eerie yet alluring. They sat on the porch at Greyson Manor to provide the goodies for the trick-or-treaters of Roswell.

"Thank you for inviting us to spend Halloween here," Carolyn said to Christina and Daniel. "What a perfect night. It's cool, and breezy, but not too much. The wind in the trees really makes you think that there are ghosts in the air," Carolyn exclaimed. The porch was lined with Jack-o-lanterns.

"You better watch out. You never know when one is going to get ya!" laughed Daniel. "Can I get you another Irish coffee?"

"Yes, get her one and I'll take one too!" laughed Scott. "Seriously, you guys, we are almost there. Isn't it exciting?"

Carolyn, Scott, Christina, Kevin, Kacey and Mike, were all sitting in rockers, each with their pumpkins filled with candy. Of course, they were in costume. Carolyn and Scott came as a Charm employee and a construction worker, because they had just come from work. Christina and Kevin came in Civil War garb; totally decked out. Christina was wearing the light blue gown she had found in .the room at the end of the hall and Kevin rented his costume. They said they were trying to get into the spirit of the upcoming events. Kacey and Mike came as Hippies. No one could decide if they were really in costume, or just pulled out some of their coolest clothes.

Daniel had invited Mia and they had come in black tee-shirts and jeans; one shirt said "I" and the other said "Pod" and when they were asked, they said "we make sweet music together". This was their second date and they did make a cute couple. Mia and Daniel went inside to get the Irish coffees. Coming up the driveway were a few unexpected visitors – Frank and Wanda. "Don't ask," said Frank. Everyone was trying to figure out what they were dressed as. Wanda had clearly chosen the costumes. They matched really well, but the group couldn't decide if they were supposed to be workers from Willy Wonka's Chocolate Factory or creatures from Alice in Wonderland or Avatar. Everyone laughed, and no one asked.

"I guess you are feeling better if you are out trick-or-treating, Frank!" laughed Daniel. He gave him a high-five on the costume. Frank wasn't sure if that was good or not.

"Yes, I have been a party pooper lately, so I thought I would spend time with my daughter," Frank put his arm around Wanda's shoulders and squeezed.

"Stop squeezing, you'll push out the stuffing!" Wanda yelled, pulling back.

Everyone laughed.

Christina walked down off the porch to fill their pumpkins with goodies, figuring they deserved a treat or two after what they had been through.

"You look fantastic, Christina," Frank said admiring her dress. "You should definitely wear that at your New Year's party!"

"So you already heard, huh?"

"Word gets around fast in these here parts, Ma'am." Frank said, trying on a cowboy accent that definitely did not go with the outfit. He couldn't help it. The costume made him goofy.

Christina raised an eyebrow. "Yes, Scott assures us the new barn will be complete so we can have our grand opening on New Year's

Eve. Of course you are invited. I would also like to meet with you to tell you what I have learned about our family history and discuss your offer of being one of the tour guides. Are you up for working on a script with me?"

"Absolutely! This is really exciting. I am honored to be a part of it."

"Wanda, I am so sorry to hear Alan was indicted today," said Carolyn.

"I know. It's so sad. Greg really pulled his brother into this mess. Well, since Alan is only sixteen, he will go to Juvi, not jail. I hope he gets it together and realizes he doesn't have to do what his brother does or says to do. He really is a nice guy." Wanda looked at her dad then down at the ground shaking her head. Her father knew it was a tough spot for Wanda to be in, trying to figure out how much to support someone in this situation.

"Well," Daniel interjected, "we can all put this behind us and move on. Hopefully, now that we took down the slave quarters, there will be no more harassment about it."

A car pulled up at the end of the drive and an elderly African-American couple got out and slowly made their way to the front porch. They definitely were not trick-or-treaters.

"Hello, can we help you?" asked Christina.

"Yes, we are looking for Christina and Daniel Greyson."

"That's us," Christina motioned to Daniel and herself.

"We are Ted and Helen Jones. Greg and Alan are our sons. We got your messages Christina and I'm sorry we haven't called you back. We have been very involved with the court system trying to help our boys. I am sure you heard they were indicted this morning," said Helen looking over at Wanda and Frank. Wanda had not met Alan's parents.

"Yes, we did hear."

Wanda walked over to Helen and said, "Alan and I.....well we have been dating. I don't believe he would have done this. I am so sorry he was involved."

"I agree," said Helen as she touched the girl's arm. "Thank you for saying that."

Ted stepped forward a few more steps. "We wanted to apologize in person for our sons' behaviors. They are good boys. Greg has just been caught up in Civil War history and can't seem to get past the slavery issue. We tried to talk to him about it, but he wouldn't listen. We are very sorry for what he did to your property and we are grateful to the Lord no one was killed." They looked at Wanda. "Alan apparently just went along for the ride, but that didn't matter to the judge."

Looking at Frank, Helen said, "Are you the man that Greg beat up?" Frank nodded. "We are truly sorry," Helen said looking at each of them.

"Thank you for coming here and saying that," said Daniel. He put his arm around Christina's shoulders.

The Joneses turned to leave. "We had the slave quarters demolished and we won't be rebuilding them," Christina said. "We are hoping that will send a message that we don't want to keep the reminder of slavery so visible. It's a small way for us to try to repair the damage done in the past. We will be having a grand opening for our plantation home on New Year's Eve. We hope you will join us. We plan to say some words about trying to show reparation for the slaves and also the Indians who owned this land before us. I think you will appreciate what we are trying to do here. Please come."

The Jones' smiled. "Thank you," Ted said. "We will do our best to be here. That is a very nice thing that you are doing, and not necessary, but it's a really good thing. Thank you again." They turned and walked back to their car and left.

The friends returned to their Halloween celebration and enjoyed the rest of the evening.

When they were leaving, Carolyn said to Christina, "I know your parents are smiling down on you. The Jones' were right. You don't have to redeem what your ancestors did, but it's a really noble thing you are doing. Happy Halloween!"

Over the next two months, everyone was busy with the holidays and the grand opening planning. The barn was finished and it looked better than the last one. The Greysons spent a great deal of time and care decorating the house and property for the holidays. It looked magnificent. Christina was sure her ancestors would be proud of what they had accomplished.

On Christmas evening, Christina pulled out Jade's journals and read them again. She wanted to be sure she captured the details and the spirit of her great, great, great grandmother, when she told the world about her.

Chapter 47
July 1864

The boxcars were unbearably hot. Most of the children were sleeping, exhausted from the walk from Roswell. What was ahead of them, Jade wondered? There was a little sunlight coming through the wooden slats. She got out her journal and began to write. She described what had happened in Roswell and that they were on their way to parts unknown to begin a new life. She put the journal down. She would not accept that. If they were not hung for treason, she was determined they would somehow, someday get back to Roswell when the war ended. Roswell was their home. And Greyson Manor would always be a special part of her life.

She thought of Frederick, sure he had passed; she could feel his spirit. The pain of the loss of her first born was unbearable. She looked over at Samantha. The girl was not handling any of this well. She was extremely depressed. The loss of Frederick had almost paralyzed her and she was actually tougher to help along than the children. Jade thought about what she could do to help her move forward. She would definitely make sure she knew she was always welcome to stay with her and Oscar, although she was sure Kay would want her with her. What was she thinking? She was assuming they would all have homes to live in. She was so unsure of what the future held. They had no money and only the clothes they were wearing.

She touched Oscar's arm. "Oscar," she began, "have you been thinking about what we will do when we get to where we are going? That's assuming they won't put us in jail or hang us. I guess they would have done that in Roswell, if that was their plan. But what do you think they will do? Just let us off the train and send us out to fend for ourselves?" she was starting to panic.

"Darling, please don't worry so much. I know this is a terrible predicament, but think about this. We have skills they will need and want where we are going. I can teach school, you can run a nursery and Kay and Samantha can work as seamstresses. I just don't know where we will stay when we get there. We will have to figure that out when we get off the train and see where we are and what the options are. The difficult part is there are so many of us. I believe I heard them say there are over four hundred of us. That is a lot of jobs that will be needed, mouths to feed and roofs to cover. But we have to stay positive. This too shall pass." Oscar kissed her on her forehead.

"I know. I will try. You want to go back though, right? As soon as we can? As soon as we can save up enough money to get back? After the war of course."

"Yes. We will make it back to Roswell. When the soldiers come back, I wonder if they will know what happened to their wives and children. I will try to get word back to them and to Kay's father. Thank goodness he and some of the others had joined the Kings at their home in Savannah."

"I know, that's where the Gordons and Moores went too. I am so glad they weren't in town when the Union came marching in." Jade laid her head on Oscar's shoulder.

They dozed fitfully over the next few hours and the next morning the train pulled into a station. When the train stopped, a soldier came down the aisle telling them all they were being released. When someone asked where they were, the soldier responded, "Louisville, Kentucky." They gathered their few belongings and exited the train.

There was mass confusion and the women and children were both sick and upset. Oscar did his best to keep the families together, while helping some of the other women and children off the train.

Jade ran to Oscar, "I just spoke with a nurse from a local hospital. She said they will accommodate as many of us as they can. It's not far from here. Hopefully, they will have food for us as well."

Oscar agreed and once all of the women and children had departed the train, he led them to the hospital. It was only a few blocks from the train station. When they arrived, the nurses and doctors immediately went about getting them settled into rooms and helping the sick. The families stayed together, grateful to have a roof over their head, a place to rest and food to eat.

The next morning, Oscar woke Jade. "I am going to walk around the town and see if I can find work." He left the hospital and stopped at the first store he came across. He asked the owner if he knew of any work. The owner wanted to know where Oscar had come from. Oscar hesitated. Then the owner of the store glared at him. "You are one of those southerners that just arrived, aren't you? Now why would you think I, or anyone for that matter, would give a traitor a job? Now go on! Get out of my store." Oscar was stunned. He had hoped the town people would take pity on them, but it didn't look like that was going to be the case. This was going to be more difficult than he thought.

After a couple of weeks, Oscar finally met someone who thought what the Union had done by shipping the mill workers north was disgraceful and unnecessary. On one of his daily walks, Oscar came across the newspaper office. Hank Harper, the paper's owner, was working the desk when Oscar walked in. Oscar introduced himself then asked Hank if he knew of any work. He explained that he was a teacher, but he was willing to do anything and he needed to find a place for his family. He explained that in addition to him, there were three women and four children.

"You look really tired Oscar. We could use some help here if you are interested. I am assuming as a teacher you can write well enough to put a story together?"

"Yes! Yes, I would say I could definitely write articles for your paper! I would be grateful and excited to do that. What would you want me to write about?"

"Well, where are you from, Oscar?" Hank asked.

Oscar looked dismayed. He hesitated, afraid to tell the truth.

Hank peered at Oscar. "You know, if you happened to be from the South, you could bring a unique perspective to our paper. That wouldn't be the case, would it?"

Oscar was hopeful Hank meant what he was saying. "Yes, I am one of a group of four hundred or so just recently transported from Georgia. Most were working in a mill that was making Confederate uniforms." He paused, waiting for Hank's reaction.

"I have heard the story. There are many of us here that are outraged. Oscar, are you aware of what has been occurring here in Kentucky over the last couple of years?"

"Somewhat. I have tried to stay informed about the war activities. My plan is to write a book about it someday. I know Kentucky has been divided somewhat and you have had both a Union and Confederate governor. However, I know that the Confederate Governor Johnson, fled Kentucky when Grant moved through in '62. He was killed in the Battle of Shiloh and since the Union mostly now dominates the state, the Confederate government here really only exists on paper. Or at least that is what I have read."

"You have kept up, Oscar, I am impressed. There are only a few representatives in the Confederate government here and they have become very discreet. I, however, refuse to stay quiet. I print stories that tell the facts, whether it's in favor of the Union or the Confederacy and so far, I have not been given too much trouble for it. I guess the army has too much to do to worry about a small paper like mine. I have talked to several of my friends, both Union and Confederate about what happened in Roswell. We all feel the burning of the Mills should have been enough damage done."

Oscar had not heard the mills were burned. He wondered what was left of Roswell and if they would ever be able to return to find out. He shook his head in dismay. "I appreciate all that you are saying. You are the first person I have spoken with since arriving that feels the way you do. I must tell you my goal is to save enough money so when the war is over, we can go back to Roswell."

"I understand, Oscar. I think that may be some time off, so for now, you are welcome to join my paper and tell your stories." He discussed what he could pay and told him about a small house he owned that was currently vacant. "It needs a lot of work. If you and your family can fix it up, I will trade the repairs for your rent. That way you can save your earnings from the paper. What do you say?"

Oscar was ecstatic. "I say you are a kind and generous man and you have yourself a new writer! We will fix up your home and I can't wait to start working. When can I start?"

"Why don't you go get your family? I'll have my son move out some of the things we were storing at the house and you can move in this afternoon. Can you start work tomorrow?"

"Yes, thank you, Mr. Harper! I cannot thank you enough!" Oscar said as he enthusiastically shook Hank's hand.

"You can call me Hank."

Chapter 48

September 1864

Atlanta was captured by Sherman on September 2, 1864. Oscar and Hank quickly wrote their articles. Both were dismayed at the turn of events. It seemed clear to them what the outcome of the war would be, but they continued to write articles about the battles and would be truthful whether the news was good or bad for the South. Oscar was grateful for the writing job and Hank paid him a fair wage. He was able to save much of his salary because Hank was true to his word and was not charging him rent for the house.

Kay picked up work as a seamstress at a local clothing store. Jade stayed with Ruby and Charles and did the cooking for everyone. Michael and Rose Ann attended the school within walking distance of the house. Samantha didn't do much of anything, still very depressed over losing Frederick. Her depression was difficult for everyone to deal with because they were all sad about Frederick. They just couldn't afford to sit around and sulk. But Samantha's depression was crippling her. It had only been two months since they lost Frederick, so they tried to care for her and give her the time she needed to mourn.

When Jade would ask Kay how she was doing, she would just say she was fine and end the conversation. Jade worried about Kay as well. She was holding her grief inside for the sake of the rest of them, but that couldn't be good for her. Kay would leave early in the morning before the children were awake to walk to the store and wouldn't return until dinnertime. She would eat very little in silence and then adjourn to her bed. She had lost a lot of weight.

Jade spoke to Oscar about it, who had noticed as well. "What should I do? She won't talk to me and I'm not sure I could say anything to make things better."

"Keep trying. You have such a way with people. I know if she would open up to you, it will help her," said Oscar. "Maybe you should take her back to the hospital to see if something is wrong. Maybe you should take Samantha too. I don't know if it would help, but it would be worth a try and they would know you are trying to help."

That night when Kay came home, Jade suggested they go to the hospital. Kay refused. When Jade tried to talk to Samantha about it, Samantha just ignored her. So they continued as they had been, depressed, not eating and keeping to themselves.

A few weeks later, Jade noticed Kay was still in bed much later than usual. When Jade went to check on her, she noticed she was very cold but had a high fever. She was sweating and trembling. Jade asked Michael and Rose Ann to stop at the store on their way to school to let them know Kay was ill. Oscar borrowed Hank's carriage and took Kay to the hospital.

Kay stayed in the hospital for several days. Jade stopped by to check on her one evening and left the children with Oscar. She couldn't trust that Samantha would pay attention to the children, so she didn't feel comfortable leaving her alone with them.

"Kay, are you feeling any better?" Jade asked and took a cold cloth and pressed it to Kay's forehead. Kay's eyes were closed. She didn't look any better and she had a gray tint to her skin. The doctors were concerned she was not improving.

Kay took Jade's hand in hers and opened her eyes. "I think I may not be long for this world, Sweetheart."

"Please don't say that. You will be fine. But you have to believe that. You have to get better so we can go back to Roswell as soon as the war is over."

"Jade... I want you to know how grateful I am to you for the sacrifices you made for David and me. I can't stop thinking about the fact that Frederick passed without knowing you were his real mother."

Jade looked down at Kay's hand. She had thought the same thing but never voiced it. Tears escaped her eyes, but she didn't say anything.

Kay said, "I want to tell Michael and Rose Ann."

"Why? There is no need to do that. I promised you I would keep the secret and you are going to get well."

"But you promised so we would allow you to share their lives. That was so unfair to ask of you but I am still so indebted to you. And now, it may be my time to go and I want the children to know. I need to be the one to tell them. Will you go get them and bring them to me?"

Jade was shocked. "Are you sure you want to do that? They will be so confused. What if they are angry at both of us?"

"It's something they will eventually get over and I want them to know how thankful I am you were able to give them to me and I had the time with them that I did. Please, bring them to me."

Jade went home and told everyone she thought Kay may not make it through the night. She wanted them all to go back to the hospital with her to see Kay. They quickly went back to the hospital. When they arrived, she asked a doctor to see Samantha hoping he would be able to help her in some way. The doctor took Samantha into his office to talk to her.

Jade took the rest of the family to see Kay. They all went into Kay's room. She looked worse than when Jade had left her. Jade was very concerned now and worried she may be too late. Kay slowly opened her eyes. The illness had taken its toll on her. She looked very weak. Oscar put his hand on Kay's forehead then bent down to kiss her cheek. She smiled up at him and squeezed his hand. Ruby and Charles were hiding behind Jade's skirt, not wanting to get close to Kay. They could sense something was very wrong. Jade asked Oscar to take Ruby and Charles out into the hall. Oscar knew Jade wanted to stay with Michael and Rose Ann while they said their goodbyes to their mother. He still did not know the secret between Kay and Jade and Jade wanted to tell him herself later.

Jade put her hand on both Michael and Rose Ann's shoulders and walked them closer to Kay. They were both in tears and Kay began to cry as well. Jade tried to stay strong but had to look away. She stepped back to let them have their space.

"There is something I have to tell you," Kay began. "I hope you will understand why we did what we did. We love you very much." At that she looked over at Jade and smiled. The children looked confused. This seemed like more than a goodbye speech.

"Your father and I loved each other very much. God rest his soul."

Jade looked away. She was sure David was not with God. He had committed too many horrible acts to be in heaven. She supposed he had changed somewhat before he passed away and she hoped he had begged the Lord for forgiveness. Maybe God had forgiven him. She had not, but she had gotten to a point in her own life where she had put the painful memories aside, for the sake of the children.

"I don't know how to tell you this so I am just going to say it. I had hoped I would never have to tell you, but now I realize it is the right thing to do." She hesitated then looked at Jade again. The children turned and looked at Jade. She walked closer and put her arms around them both. "Jade is your real mother."

"No, that's not true!" cried out Rose Ann. "You are our mother!"

She looked desperately at Jade who took a deep breath. Rose Ann tried to pull her hand from Kay's and pushed Jade away from her. "You are our mother," she said again to Kay, this time with less force. "How could Jade be our mother, you are our mother?"

Michael just stood not moving, shocked. Then he pushed Jade away and ran out the door.

"Please, Michael, come back!" called Jade. She looked at Kay then went after Michael. Oscar had caught Michael, who was crying intensely, just saying "no" over and over.

Oscar looked at Jade and mouthed the words, "Is she gone?"

Jade shook her head and looked at Michael. She knew she would have to tell Oscar now. She looked back at Oscar then walked over to them both.

Ruby and Charles ran up and hugged her, holding onto her skirts. They looked up at her wanting to understand everything that was going on. "Is Aunt Kay all right?" asked Charles.

"No, not really. Aunt Kay is very sick." Jade rubbed his head and then held both of her youngest close. Oscar and Michael both just stared at Jade and waited for her to say more.

"Michael, it is true what your mother said."

"You are not my mother! She is!" Michael yelled.

Oscar's face dropped. He looked from Michael to Jade, confused. "What is he talking about?"

"My darling, I am so sorry. I should have told you. It's true."

"No, it can't be true!" Michael yelled. He pulled out of Oscar's grip and ran back into Kay's room.

Oscar just stared at Jade in disbelief.

"Please let me explain," Jade said.

Charles and Ruby were still holding onto Jade's skirt, confused and afraid with all of the commotion.

"Let's sit over here and…"

"No, just tell me now." Oscar was fuming. He didn't know how this was possible, but he knew she had never told him and that was the biggest betrayal of all.

"I told you my parents left me behind when they were forced to go west. That was not true."

Oscar looked at her with even more confusion.

Jade turned away, the children still holding onto her skirt. Realizing they weren't going to let go, she walked over to a seating area and made them sit down. She turned to look at Oscar and walked back to him. "David Greyson killed them," she whispered so as not to scare Ruby and Charles. "Then he raped me, many times." Her voice cracked. She tried to ignore the outrage on Oscar's face. "It was over many years and finally he married Kay. Kay couldn't conceive. She discovered David was taking me to bed and assumed it was an affair at first. She later realized the truth and then she and I became close. It was always a strange and strained relationship, but I didn't have anywhere to go and I was still very young and I became with child. She felt sorry for me and didn't want to send me out of my own home so she said I could stay if I would allow David and her to raise Frederick as their own. Eventually, she asked me to have more children, and I did." She stopped to see if Oscar wanted to say anything.

"I always thought there was something more to your relationship with the Greysons. You wouldn't leave them to be with me. You treated them as more than an employer. I should have known. I should have noticed the resemblance. How could I be so blind? Why did you lie to me? How could you not tell me?" he said angry at her and at himself.

"They made me swear not to reveal the truth to anyone. They would have taken my children away. I wanted to tell you. I am so sorry I couldn't. I promised. And I was afraid you would stop loving me if you knew the whole truth. I thought on our wedding night you would have figured it out, but you never said anything."

His face went pale. "I, I did wonder, but I couldn't ask you if you were a virgin on our wedding night. I figured it was probably just my imagination. It wasn't worth the risk to discuss it. I loved you so much."

"Do you no longer love me, now that you know?" Tears streamed down her face.

Oscar turned his back on her not wanting her to see his own tears. He cried for Jade, the young girl who lost her parents and was put through a living hell by that monster David, whom he had respected. How could he have done that? Any of that! All of that....he turned back around to her and grabbed her arm and pulled her close. They cried together. Ruby and Charles jumped out of their seats, ran to them and hugged them both, still not understanding.

Michael came back out of Kay's room. He looked at Jade and said, "She's gone."

Jade ran into the room and to Kay's side. Rose Ann was draped across her crying. Jade did the same thing. After awhile, she got up and went to the other side of the bed and pulled Rose Ann slowly off of Kay, held her by both arms and looked her in the eye. "Did you believe her? Did you make your peace with her?"

"Yes," was all Rose Ann said. She walked out of the room.

Samantha came down the hall then and saw all the tears and knew Kay had passed. Rose Ann and Michael ran to her. Then Michael whispered something in her ear. She looked at Jade in amazement. Then she realized that meant Jade was also Frederick's real mother as well.

"You will have to tell me the whole story," she said to Jade.

Oscar went to find the doctor to tell them about Kay and make the final arrangements.

Chapter 49

May 1865

Although their lives had been strained by the news about Jade, they all seemed to be getting used to the idea she was the mother of all of the children. Over the last seven months, Jade had tried to ease into the role without taking anything away from their memories of Kay.

Samantha had improved in spirit and had even met a young man. Ross Jackson was a Union officer who had been injured and sent home to Louisville. She had met him at the hospital where she had begun to volunteer a few months before. They enjoyed talking to each other and she slowly began to show signs of the old Samantha.

Oscar stayed busy at the local paper and seemed to be extremely engrossed in the news of the war. He didn't spend much time with the family, working late to get the articles completed. When he did come home he seemed distant. Jade wasn't sure if it was because he was upset about the war and what was happening to the South or if he was still angry with her for not telling him the truth. She didn't ask. She knew it would take time to regain his trust. She went about caring for the children and trying to help them through the loss of Kay. She missed Kay terribly.

Several weeks earlier, on April 15th, Oscar had come home from work and told them that President Lincoln had been shot the night before and passed away that morning. He had been shot in the head at Ford's Theater in Washington. Oscar had spent the day writing with Hank. They made sure their article was respectful and reverent towards the late president. They had mixed feelings about Abraham Lincoln but knew he would go down in history as a great president.

In May, the remaining Confederate soldiers surrendered and the Civil War ended.

Oscar and Jade began to make their plans to go back to Roswell. They were indebted to Hank for all he had done for them. Not only had Hank given Oscar a job, but he had allowed them to stay in the little house while only asking them to fix it up as payment. Hank had also taught Oscar how to write for a newspaper which gave Oscar the satisfaction of knowing he had poured his heart and soul into his written words. The public came to know Oscar as the "Rebel Howler", and he believed he had helped the Southern cause in a small way. They would never forget Hank and how he had helped their family.

Samantha decided to stay in Louisville and continue to work at the hospital. She was going to become a nurse and Ross hoped someday she would marry him.

Oscar, Jade and the children boarded the train back to Georgia. They saw horrible sites along the way; wounded men making their way home and property that had been destroyed; land that had been burned. They were not sure what they would find when they got back to Roswell, but they knew they wanted to help rebuild the town they loved.

Over time, Oscar forgave Jade for keeping her secrets from him and grew to understand and respect her even more.

When Jade and Oscar returned to Roswell, they repaired Greyson Manor and Jade and the children worked the cotton fields until they could afford to hire workers. The slaves were all gone by that point except Theresa and Sally who had stayed in Roswell. Sally had a baby boy, who she named after Sam. Once Oscar and Jade could afford to hire them, they came back to work for the family; this time as employees.

The mills were destroyed in the war but Barrington King and the original owners came back to Roswell and rebuilt one of the mills. Greyson Manor began supplying the mill with their cotton and again became the largest cotton producer in the area.

Their friends returned to Roswell, grieved for their lost sons and slowly began to rebuild their homes, the school, the town and their lives. Roswell flourished. Oscar worked at the Roswell newspaper until he died of natural causes in 1892. He was well-known for his stories about the Civil War.

Jade became a teacher in 1875 and was able to share the stories of her Cherokee heritage with her children and her students. She sent letters to Oklahoma in 1878 to her brothers and was thrilled to receive a return letter from Joe. However, it was then that she learned that her brother George had not made it to Oklahoma. Joe explained that he had a family and the tribe had built homes and schools on their new land. He said the land resembled the hills of the original Cherokee Nation. Jade was saddened they had lived the majority of their lives apart but she was pleased to learn that her tribe and her brother had gone on to live full and productive lives in their new land. In 1896, on a beautiful, sunny afternoon, as Jade napped on her porch with her children and many grandchildren playing in the yard, Jade peacefully passed away; undoubtedly dreaming of re-joining her Cherokee family.

Chapter 50
New Year's Eve, 2011

"C heers!" Scott said, holding his champagne glass high.
"Cheers!" rang out the crowd. They were surrounded by their friends, new and old. They were dressed in formal attire and were dancing to the soft music from the four piece band. It was a beautiful night. The stars were out and Greyson Manor had never looked more magnificent. There were candles everywhere and the house was lit up so everyone could enjoy the view of it from the barn where the party was going strong.

Christina, Daniel and Frank had been giving tours through the house all evening and Carolyn thought they seemed pleased with how it was going. There were over two hundred people in attendance and she was proud of the work Scott had done to finish the barn and the restoration of the house in time for the grand opening. She was also glad Kacey and Gabby had agreed to manage the catering for the party so Carolyn could celebrate since she was one of the investors.

"Are you as happy as I am with how everything turned out?" she asked Scott.

"Absolutely. I am very glad we took on this project. And you finally have your restaurant, which is really successful. You have done a tremendous job with Charm, Carolyn. But this was your original dream," Scott said looking around the plantation, "to turn a historical home into an event facility. If you hadn't kept looking for the right place, this place, we never would have met all of these wonderful people, and I wouldn't have had this fantastic place for my first historical renovation. I have to admit, it looks fantastic." Scott beamed. Then he kissed her.

Carolyn looked over at Christina and Daniel who were talking with the Mayor. "I am happy Christina and Daniel were finally able to learn what they didn't know about their family. They can finally let their parents rest in peace, knowing they were meant to learn the truth. This has turned into so much more than I had ever imagined. Oh, here comes Christina to say her speech." Carolyn and Scott joined her parents and friends at their table.

"Ladies and Gentlemen, if I could please have your attention," Christina began. She was wearing the beautiful blue dress that had once belonged to Jade; given to her by Kay. "Thank you for spending your New Year's Eve with us here at Greyson Manor. Before the clock strikes midnight, I wanted to share with you a little history of how Greyson Manor came to be and to give honor to those who came before us; the *real* original owners of Greyson Manor." Daniel pulled a large drape off a marble monument and the crowd gave a standing ovation.

Once they settled back into their seats, Christina began again. She looked around at all the beautiful faces, smiling. "This land was once called the "Enchanted Land" by my ancestors, the Cherokee Indians…"

The End

Discussion Questions

1. In the opening chapter, Jade experiences several devastating events. Describe how you think her state of mind was when she wakes at the beginning of chapter two. As she fully remembers the details of the day before, how does she cope?
2. As you start to learn about the Cherokee tribe, how would you describe their nature? Their way of life?
3. How did you feel about the relationships between Kay and Jade and David? Could you relate to why they hid the secret about Jade and the children? What are your thoughts about how the secret molded all of their lives?
4. What did you think about Oscar as a suitor and then later as a husband? What were his strengths? Weaknesses? When Oscar learns Jade's secret, did you think he was harsh and unforgiving? How did you feel when he stayed with Jade?
5. Could you picture life in Roswell, Georgia during the 1800's? What were some of the events or descriptions that surprised you to learn? How did the racism aspect make you feel?
6. Discuss how you think the last twenty years of Jade's life went? How had she grown as a woman; a Cherokee woman living in a white southern culture?
7. How would you describe the town of Roswell in the current day?
8. Were you able to picture Greyson Manor in its splendor and demise? How did the plantation home impact the lives of the characters in the current day?
9. Christina and Daniel were important characters in the story.

Describe the relationship between them and the other investors.

10. The journal was critical to helping Christina and Daniel understand their ancestors. How did they react when they learned the secret of their family's past? Did learning the secret change them in any way? If so, how?

11. How would you describe Carolyn's relationships with her husband, her friends, her family, her fellow investors?

12. Did you believe that the current day characters were able to provide some redemption for those that came before them?

CPSIA information can be obtained
at www.ICGtesting.com
Printed in the USA
FSOW01n1327260217
31292FS